A Jack Griffin Detective Adventure

LET'S SAY JACK KENNEDY KILLED THE GIRL

The Jack Griffin Detective Series

WILLIAM F. CRANDELL

HAWKSHAW/DPP

Published by Hawkshaw Press,
an imprint of Devil's Party Press, LLC.

Library of Congress Control Number: 2021950342

ISBN:

978-1-7340918-8-5 (hardcover)
978-1-7340918-6-1 (paperback)
978-1-7340918-9-2 (eBook)

hawkshawpress.com

DEDICATION

Let's Say Jack Kennedy Killed the Girl is dedicated to the tarnished ideals of political democracy, that coat of chainmail in which every citizen's disparate link forms our protection against two-bit crooks and hungry politicians.

This book is also dedicated to the two most important people in my life: my wife, Judith Speizer Crandell, author of *The Woman Puzzle*, and our daughter, Anna Elisabeth Speizer Crandell, who makes me laugh.

WFC

ACKNOWLEDGMENTS

I'll admit it: I wrote *Let's Say Jack Kennedy Killed the Girl*, and I get much of the credit or blame. Okay, all the blame. But I owe copious thanks to a legion of people who contributed, knowingly or not. Leading that parade is my wonderful wife, Judith Speizer Crandell, author of *The Woman Puzzle* and several other marvelous novels and short stories. Judith has been my muse for a third of a century, inspiring me, encouraging me, and editing my work. More than that, she keeps me going and fills my life with love and fire.

My colleagues and friends in The Milton Workshop – a remarkably gifted handful of novelists, memoirists, poets, and short story writers – have demonstrated that a critique group needn't be mean to be tough. They've helped me sharpen images, push my own work forward – despite being a reticent Midwesterner – and spot the problem areas I didn't see. Dianne Pearce and David Yurkovich of Devil's Party Press are also skilled editors and publishers, moving mountains to turn *Kennedy* and the other novels of the series into books, remarkable in an age when all the time-honored publishing traditions have vanished.

But writing historical novels requires history as well as writing. I owe special thanks to historians Douglas Brinkley and Gary W. Reichard for their support, inspiration and advice on the Jack Griffin novels. Gratitude also to my other professors and *confreres* in the Ohio State University's Department of History, where we read, wrote, and made history. Over the decades I've also received sustaining friendship from my remarkable brother, Terry E. Crandell, and his gem of a wife, Cindy, as well as Allan D. Goldfarb, Linda Gillooly Perriello, Ed Murphy, Rick Weidman, and Jac Conaway. And there's nobody like my readers. Thanks, gang!

William F. Crandell
November 2021

LET'S SAY JACK KENNEDY KILLED THE GIRL

ONE

Jack Kennedy and I had nothing in common when we met but our first names, the Purple Heart, and the hots for Betty Dyson. Kennedy was Navy, and I'd been Army. He was thirty but looked a scrawny twenty, while I was thirty-four and felt older. He was Harvard, I was Ohio State. He was so rich he didn't carry a wallet, and I was so broke I hardly needed one. He was a freshman congressman, and I was a private detective. Neither of us knew Betty would drag us into murder.

Except that her hair was heavy and strawberry blonde—luxuriously heavy, at that—Betty Dyson looked to me for all the world like the *Life* magazine picture of Rita Hayworth in a nightgown I'd kept folded in my helmet in lieu of a girl back home. Betty's snug-waisted navy-blue dress showed off her full breasts decorously. The string of pearls encircling her delicate neck and her white cotton gloves reinforced her glow of propriety. A guy could fall in love with her Midwestern laugh. I guessed she was in her late twenties.

"It was so sweet of you boys to come." Her smile freshened Washington's sticky summer air. "All the times I served coffee and doughnuts to the soldiers and sailors at the U.S.O. canteen during the war, every guy I met was either on his way *to* the war or had made darn sure he wouldn't go *anywhere.* It's nice to meet some men who've actually *been* in the war."

Kennedy and I grinned. We liked each other right away, and we both liked the lady between us even faster. Always nice to be appreciated by a really magnificent woman. Clearly, the prospect that the evening might not end with just coffee and *Goodnight* occurred to all three of us.

The dismay in Kennedy's face was real. "Betty, if only I'd seen you at the U.S.O. the time I visited *after* I came back from the Pacific!" His "Bah-ston" accent crackled with charm.

I blinked my eyes. "What exactly was the U.S.O.?"

Betty giggled at my pretense that I'd never been so far from the fighting to have heard of it. Even Kennedy chuckled. "Good one, Griffin."

We three met attending an invitation-only Friday evening dinner the Army and Navy Club hosted at the Hotel Washington to recruit a few young former officers with combat ribbons. They'd asked Kennedy to come because the secretary of the Navy wanted him introduced to some *Important People.* I probably received my embossed invitation because my last battalion commander thought they deserved a wise guy in the audience. I felt like a hobo at a cotillion.

The other knights seated at our particular round table were colonels and generals and admirals wearing attendance ribbons, whose greatest wartime adventures had been scrambles for office space and staff cars. The July air in the Sky Room, eleven stories up, was clammy—even though the tall, boxy windows were open, no more breeze blew than you'd feel in a bank vault. All the dangly glass in the chandelier stood as still as the stones at Arlington.

The empty salad plates with their gilded rims disappeared without a sound into white-gloved hands. Steaks or salmon fillets the size of hubcaps replaced them. All of us sitting at the tables were white, the waiters mahogany brown. Washington in 1947 clung tight to its Southern customs and climate.

Our table stood near enough to the swag-curtained windows to watch the rainclouds begin to clear in the west behind the Washington Monument. I preferred the view of Betty Dyson. My eyes caught hers and Kennedy's. "*Somebody* has to serve in the far rear in wartime. Not everybody can lounge around with a bunch of grimy old paratroops."

"Or sun themselves cruising around the South Pacific on an eighty-foot torpedo boat." Kennedy smiled. "There but for the grace of God, Griffin."

The tomato-faced general next to me sneered. "I remember a time when they barred the communists, the papists, and the Jews from the officer corps. Better world then."

My smile faded. "Probably always let horses' asses become generals, though."

His cheeks turned a raw-liver hue as it dawned on him that he couldn't order civilians shot. He turned back to the commanding class on the far side of the table.

*****

We drank daiquiris, the Army-Navy Club drink. Kennedy's pale-gray suit of tropical worsted looked much better, even on his skinny frame than my tan wool and rayon gabardine that had set me back twenty-five bucks when it was new.

The Dyson woman chuckled into a white glove. "Oh, stop! You boys are terrible. *Poor General Cruickshank!* They're not all like him, y'know. I work at the War Department—I'm going to have to get used to saying 'Defense Department' soon—and we do get some mid-twentieth century minds there."

With traces of Iowa in her voice, Betty told us a joke about an old maid and a cat as her pale-blue eyes shyly swept our lapels. Clearly, she knew the little enameled lapel pins Kennedy and I both wore representing Purple Heart ribbons—purple with white edges—had been issued for war wounds. "Do you mind if I ask what you did in the service? My—My husband flew fighter planes."

We both gathered from her softened voice and her downcast eyes that she'd lost him. Kennedy rested a hand on top of hers for a moment. "I'm so sorry. Actually, nothing much happened to me. I was quite lucky." He turned to me with a level gaze and gave me just the slightest nod. Whatever action he'd seen didn't belong with banter.

My turn. How do you tell a beauty who's never seen a battlefield about the fear and exhilaration of parachuting into Normandy or being surrounded at Bastogne? How do you discuss over a rare steak what artillery does to human flesh or the memories that haunt your nights? "I've probably had my fill of camping."

Betty looked at us with the slightest grin. "Men really *are* impossible. The ones who've actually faced danger, like you two, keep quiet about it. As for the rest, the less they've done, the more strutting and crowing they do to advertise it. Just today, a very important man I work for did something disgusting and despicable." She relaxed the creases in her brow. "But I don't want to talk about that tonight. Why spoil a nice dinner?"

With her grin, they could have sold the fancy lighting. I was starting to like her—a lot. That surprised me. Much as I enjoyed women, much as I liked sex, I'd learned to be wary with my heart. What had begun with wanting to get this lady into bed was mushrooming into more than that.

Betty turned to the Navy guy. "Jack, what's being a congressman like?"

"What's the opposite of a babysitter? I'm young and look younger, but the leaders on both sides of the aisle are old men somewhere from sixty to eighty-five. Sitting in Congress is the biggest thing they've ever done in their lives. Their greatest achievement. All they can think about is holding on to it."

She nodded. "How is it for *you*, though?"

"I'm serving an apprenticeship."

"In Congress? *You're* ambitious!"

Kennedy shook his head. "Not the way you mean it. I came back from the war with bigger fish to fry. The significant issues demand vision nobody has. Politics is the only way to affect them. That's what I want to do, not just get a bigger job. The House provides a place to learn what I need to learn."

Her dazzle turned my way. "What do *you* do, Jack?" I told her I was a private detective. She giggled. "You're not here on a case, are you? Which of us are you investigating?"

"I've had my eye on *you* all evening, lady."

She snickered. "How do you like being a private eye?"

"The good part is nobody tells me what to do, and I never know what the next day will bring. The bad part is about the same as the good part." Leave the tedium and the tenuous income out of it. "It doesn't involve nearly as many desperate, gorgeous women as I'd been led to believe."

She smiled. "What a shame!"

*****

We retreated to witty conversation, laughing the way they did in the *Thin Man* movies. That felt safer to me than blabbing about how much I liked Betty Dyson. Kennedy and I flirted with her, he more outrageously than I. The congressman pressed on, said he'd die if she didn't at least give him her telephone number. Did she want to go find some swing music they could dance to or listen to jazz at Skip Nichols's club? Before Rome fell, hadn't she been a goddess? Where had she found a dress so perfect for her figure? Did she need a ride home? God, the guy was good at it!

Washington in July. The ceiling fans swished the air around like wet laundry. They'd built the dining room on the rooftop, but you couldn't get above the heat. Tiny beads of dew clung to the snow-white valley between Betty's breasts and to our grinning faces.

Betty sparkled, her looks fashioned to outshine chandeliers and diamonds. Her jokes were clever, and she liked toying with words. She arched an eyebrow. "Since you're a politician, do you enjoy lying with women?"

Kennedy grinned. "I could do that tonight."

She turned to me. "He says he wants to *lie* with a woman, and yet I believe him. He must be *very* good, don't you think?"

"Never judge a sailor's credibility entirely by his willingness to lie with a beautiful girl," I suggested. The absurdity struck me that my rival was doing better by making it plain that she was just another flop in the hay to him, while I was holding back because I was falling hard for her. Maybe she didn't want complications.

Kennedy's grin evaporated. "Actually, I came back from the war with a serious condition." He stared out toward the darkening skyline.

Betty's face turned ashen, and she touched the back of his hand. "Oh, Jack, I'm so sorry if I said anything that—anything *painful* to you."

With great control, he shook his head. "A lot of fellows came home hurt quite badly. My—you could simply call it a condition, I suppose—is that I can't sleep unless I've had sex with a beautiful woman." He kept a straight face.

"*You men!*" She laughed, glittering.

It didn't occur to me then that Kennedy was rich. All I saw was this skinny, unassuming guy with a New England accent. His suit hung on his bones as though he were still recovering from the South Pacific, but his grin was a Steinway piano. Kennedy had the kind of charm that made you like him even when he was winning the girl you wanted. How do you outmaneuver a romancer like that?

He touched his thick, wavy hair. "Admiral Hazen's going to start his speech soon. I'd better get you out of here." The sailor wasn't talking to me.

Betty laughed and floated up out of her chair, Kennedy at her elbow. He looked back at me as I jumped to my feet. "Griffin, let's get together soon. Do you have a business card?"

"All the engraved ones are in a small silver tray on my desk." Black letters on the pasteboard job I gave him said

JACK GRIFFIN, MANAGING PARTNER

Aadlund and Griffin Investigations
330 Pennsylvania Avenue
Washington 7, D.C.
LIncoln-1366.

Kennedy slid it into his pocket. "I'll telephone you."

Betty beamed, writing a phone number inside a Hotel Washington matchbook and passing it to me with white-gloved fingers. "Jack, I really hope you'll give me a call sometime."

I said I would. Maybe I'd gone too slowly, quit trying too early. I never guessed that any chance I'd had died when he left with her.

TWO

I also bailed out just before the oratory, a bit sore the boy congressman had out-charmed me. How does a gumshoe compete with a guy like that? As soon as their elevator spirited Kennedy and Betty Dyson down to ground level, I hopped the next one. By the time I stepped out onto Fifteenth Street, the last sprinkles of rain had stopped, and I wished I still smoked.

Washington in July was a steam bath in a sewer, especially after it rained. The thunderstorm hadn't cooled the hot pavements. Daylight was pretty much shot, and a couple of stars stood out against the haze and the streetlights' glare. The tall double windows atop the hotel gleamed in the colorless sky, making me replay the dinner I'd just eaten behind them and wonder if there'd been any chance I'd missed to out-charm the boy congressman. Yet I didn't think Clark Gable could have done better against him than I had.

But she'd asked me to call her. Maybe I'd lost the match but not my chance. Betty seemed to like me. I decided not to assume Kennedy had her for all time—or even that night—just because she hadn't strolled out with me then. Still, I was salving my wounds with saltwater.

I headed north on Fifteenth Street, vaguely in the direction of my apartment. A movie theater advertised its air-conditioning, but I didn't think I could sit through a lousy Eddie Bracken comedy just to lower my body temperature. The last of my grumpiness went into kicking a trampled pork pie hat that lay in my path.

I strolled around the gritty sidewalks without anywhere to go, lonely as a lighthouse and enjoying the hell out of being there. The tumult of city streets still felt delicious to me, with its glad-handing and horn-tooting that you never heard on a battlefield. Birds will sing, and sheep will graze in the presence of Panther tanks, but nobody shambles down the sidewalks or bawls out news headlines in a combat zone. Guys were calling across the pavements to each other or whistling at girls in their summer-thin dresses. Nobody—not even I—was watching out for snipers. The urban uproar was a lullaby.

The war played plenty rough with me. I'd frittered away the year after getting out of the Army working on a Key West charter boat without a responsibility in the world, disproving every pretense I might be the next Hemingway. Turned out Hemingway himself was the next Hemingway. I became a peacetime adventurer and a failure as a drunk.

Dreams of horror still overran my nights. I'd found no ledge to stand on between how much Scotch it took to sleep soundly 'til daylight and how much would make me a lush, and I'd seen guys at the V.A. who had the shakes. My nightmares beat living like that, though they unnerved women those scattered times I didn't sleep alone.

*****

I decided to hike a few blocks up Fifteenth Street to the Jazz Club. It wasn't that I expected to see Jack and Betty there—I was pretty certain where they were headed, despite my pretenses—but I was in no hurry to go sleep alone.

The music I heard at the door was neither as elegant nor spirited as I'd heard the couple of times I'd been there before. The five-man band of somebody advertised as Chazz Dexter tootled away. I almost didn't go in. But the owner, an efficient-looking little man with slicked-back black hair and an eager grin, shook my hand firmly, looking over at my lapel. "Purple Heart. I'd like you to have a drink on the house. I'm Skip Nichols."

He told a waiter to show me to a table near the stage just as the sweaty Dexter brought out his vocalist, a cocoa-complexioned beauty named Nancy Collington. She was as busty as the Statue of Liberty and had that same pale-green eye color. The waiter took my order for Scotch and soda. Nichols ran a unique club for Washington. He hired both white and Negro musicians and opened the doors to dark-skinned customers as well. Nichols had told reporters, "Anybody who'd rather avoid colored folks than hear the world's best jazz can go to a second-rate nightclub. All-white jazz is just mashed potatoes with no gravy."

The music sizzled. Nancy Collington ripped the skin off a dozen ballads the way Jackie Robinson was tearing the horsehide off white guys' balls on the diamond. Her voice mixed cotton candy with more than a hint of pralines. As easy on the eye as on the ear, she wore a low-cut gold lamé gown with a matching matador jacket and a terrific grin. She gave me a jade-eyed wink.

*****

"Mind if I ask where you got hit?" Nichols looked at my lapel again, then at me. The singer went backstage.

"Anatomy or geography?"

He laughed. "Why not both?" He snagged the empty chair.

"Fair enough. Outside Eindhoven. Left foot. Piece of shrapnel just big enough to complain about, but no million-dollar wound. Name's Jack Griffin."

"Eindhoven. The 101st Airborne, right? We flew your air support. P-51s. You know, Griffin, we belong to a relatively small fraternity. I don't know how many men served in uniform, but you and I are combat veterans, a different breed." There was a look to Nichols's eyes I knew. He struck me as a tough customer.

"Guess you're right, Nichols. Guys like us will always know who we are. By the way, I admire what you've done here. The club is terrific. That Nancy Collington is one very talented cookie and well worth whatever the spotlight cost."

Nichols tossed me a Cheshire Cat grin and a nod. I noticed the skinny end of his blue silk tie had been cut off; Nichols was so short he chopped his ties to match his height.

Behind Nichols, over by the front door, was an elevator with red damask walls. You had to get a nod from a Greek-looking guy in a pale-blue dinner jacket to enter it. Nancy Collington disappeared inside it, listening to a porky doofus I recognized as a congressman from the Midwest.

"Beyond the jazz, though, Nichols, I admire your decision to buck all that Southern racial crap. I like your politics."

He chuckled. "Thanks. I genuinely appreciate that. But I don't have any politics. Truth is, I just wanted to own a club that stood out. There's money in that. Besides, the narrow way of life won't last; you can feel it. I'm no saint, you know."

"Hadn't heard you were."

Nichols laughed out loud. "Amazing what a bit of money in greedy hands and some hired muscle can make possible! When you see a blue-eyed, yellow-haired cop hustle a loud-mouthed tourist from South Blowhole, Mississippi, out of here, growling 'Leave the goddam—um—*customers* alone, asshole,' you know you've greased the correct palms."

Paying off rednecked cops to do the right thing leaves you with crooked rednecked cops. "I suppose that applies to the games upstairs as well?"

He raised his eyebrows. "There are a lot of forms of entertainment, my friend. You a gambling man?"

"Not the way you mean. Still—"

"Still, you do what you have to do." He gave me a measured nod. "You take care of your own, Griffin, whether it's your family or the guys you fought beside in the war. You didn't risk your tail for hot dogs and the Pledge of Allegiance, but for your buddies. They took chances to save your life. You did the same for them. And maybe you enjoyed the excitement. Maybe the risks made you feel more alive. All I know is a man who won't kill to protect his family or his war buddies isn't worth dog crap." He flushed. "End of sermon."

I nodded. "Not a sermon. An observation." I hoisted my Scotch and soda and took a sip.

"An observation." Nichols smiled. "What do you do, Griffin?"

I told him I was a private detective.

He raised his bushy eyebrows. "So you're still searching for adventure. Might you ever want to work for me?" He took a cigarette out of a silver case.

My Zippo came out of my pocket. "As my client or as an employer?"

Nichols blew out an arabesque of silver-gray. "I'm fresh out of unsolved mysteries, but I can always find a place for a tough man with brains and experience."

"I'll keep it in mind. But I like working on my own better than taking orders. Thanks, though."

Somebody to my rear caught his eye. "'Scuse me." Nichols grinned again. "Nice talking to you, Griffin."

*****

The club was full of shapely women in fancy dresses and guys in wrinkled business suits. In Washington, tuxedos were for waiters. Men in government worked too late to go home and dress up for an evening on the town, so a gumshoe in a nightclub didn't stand out like a butchered hog in a bridal suite.

Maybe it mattered that the theme was jazz rather than sports or genteel dining. People came into the Jazz Club, and people left it, yet the lid stayed on. All the terrors the Deep Dixie senators warned would come with "race-mixing"—riots, rape, and reefers—failed to materialize at Nichols's joint. Here and there, you could see a pair of white people sitting at the same table with a pair of brown-skinned people and behaving just the way the folks sitting with others of their own hue did. Assorted or plain, customers listened to the music, smoked cigarettes, laughed, had some drinks, chatted. This integration stuff could be boring if people just let it be.

Jazz wasn't what I needed, though, and watching middle-aged men plying gorgeous women with liquor wasn't either. Nancy Collington didn't come back from upstairs. I nursed my Scotch and soda for a bit. Then I gave up. After smiling at a blonde cigarette girl with nice legs and some aging fat guy's dark-haired date with nice everything, I headed back out into the humidity and through the grimy streets to my apartment. There wasn't a hope in hell of D.C. cooling down that night—or the next, as it turned out—so I swam home through the sweaty air.

*****

I rinsed off with cold water around midnight and slept naked on top of my sheets, a cheap little electric oscillating fan almost convincing me Washington was livable in the summer. Before I fell asleep, I imagined making love with Betty Dyson in cool weather on crisp sheets. Maybe I'd at least dream about that instead of having my usual nightmares with the screeching of German 88s, the rattle of Nazi machineguns, and conga lines of Tiger tanks.

Dreaming of Betty was a break I didn't get.

THREE

Aadlund and Griffin Investigations occupied two rooms on the second floor of the old Naval Masonic Lodge Building on Pennsylvania Avenue, three blocks east of the Capitol. I'd forced Harry Aadlund into retirement in June, treating the money he'd embezzled and spent on Bourbon as payment for a controlling share of the partnership and Harry's pledge never to come in again. His last name remained on the door because mine didn't top the phone listings.

I staggered in just before noon Monday morning, a bit grumpy after calling Betty Dyson twice on Saturday to ask her to dinner and wondering half of Sunday whether she hadn't answered because she'd gone off somewhere with the scrawny congressman.

Lana Murphy, our office manager, hunched over the other desk in the cramped outer office. I stuck my Panama on the hat rack and gave her a smirk. "You could steam open envelopes while you walk down the street out there, Lana."

She snorted. "Really, Mr. Griffin, had you forgotten the summers are, uh, *warm* here in Washington?" Fire hydrants came shorter than Lana, but otherwise, they were built the same. Her curly red hair, shaped like a pillbox hat, shone in a vivid hue more Irish setter than human. "And by-the-by, Mr. Griffin, where have *you* been hiding this morning?"

"I questioned Doctor Bivins about the Stephanos disability case. When I showed him those six pictures of Stephanos driving a bulldozer, the good doctor decided his nurse accidentally sent the wrong x-rays and signed a little letter to that effect."

Lana favored the letter with another snort. "General Fidelity will be pleased. Thank Gawd they'll pay. I've been working on the agency's profit-and-loss statement."

"We still afloat?" Numbers zipped past me like tracer bullets, so I kept my head down.

"Barely. At least we've stopped hemorrhaging money since you took over, Mr. Griffin. If we can get a few more good cases, we might make it."

I sank like a heavy dew into my swivel chair. When Harry Aadlund slipped out, and the building manager settled for giving us half the space we'd had, I'd kept the corner office with its odd cylindrical turret hanging out over the sidewalk.

I picked up the morning *Post*. The banner headline,

Dutch Open War in Java

made me wish I had a cup of coffee. The next story said the Republican congressional leaders might finish their year's work—which mostly amounted to voting "no"—before July ended and then spend most of 1948 running for reelection.

A headline near the bottom of page one caught my attention:

"Hide Crime Data as Ordered," Howard Tells His Inspectors

Alarmed at Murder, Robbery Stats, Says "Hold Complaints at Precincts."

A senator from out in Minnesota wanted a full-scale investigation of phony Metropolitan Police statistics. Around three hundred murder and robbery complaints had been "held" for at least eleven months. Police Superintendent James E. Howard, it seemed, told his cops to hold back violent crime cases if they had "a reasonable doubt" the crime occurred. I chuckled. No wonder the District's crime rate dwindled so much in the seven years since Gentleman Jimmy Howard was rewarded for his political skills with the best-paid job in local government.

*****

"Mr. Griffin!" Lana buzzed the intercom while I slit open a letter from my sister Jill in Ohio. "There's a Congressman Kennedy on the phone for you. I'll put him through."

I wasn't sure he hadn't phoned me to gloat about Friday night, but I'd liked the guy. "Hey, Kennedy, how goes it?"

"Listen, Griffin," Kennedy rasped when I answered, "this isn't a social call. Have you seen today's *Washington Post?*"

"Barely."

"I need to hire you." His voice sounded like a prep school boy staring at a physics exam after a night of tossing back cheap gin and smoking Luckies. "Hold on to your seat, Griffin. Somebody raped Betty Dyson and stabbed her to death Friday night."

My breathing stopped, and my voice made a sound like a heavy desk being pushed across a hardwood floor. I sat bolt upright.

Kennedy was still on the phone. "I'd like to walk over there and talk with you. I'm three blocks away from you in the Old House Office Building. Can I come now?"

"Um, sure. Sure." I sat staring a thousand miles away. He told me he'd be right over.

I quickly located the three-inch story headlined

War Hero's Wife Found Murdered.
Flier Stationed at Andrews Field

Read it through three times. It didn't go away. I could only think of the colossal waste… and a husband who sounded very much alive.

Betty hadn't seemed very married to me. I hadn't exactly fallen in love with her, though I'd started to. The truth was, I'd been very much taken with her. She was beautiful and smart. She was funny. She made me feel good. Now, along with outrage and an empty ache, I also felt my teeth grinding. This glowing goddess I wanted so badly belonged to some man she'd made us think was dead when he was, in fact, just another sucker. *And* she was dead. How in hell…?

*****

"We can talk privately in here, Congressman." My office held a desk, a secondhand swivel chair for me, and a small slate-blue couch Harry bought when the agency gushed money and boasted four detectives. The windows overlooking the street were dirty, but neither of us gave a damn whether the rest of the world was still out there or not.

"You can't imagine what a shock it was for me, Griffin, finding it like that on the third page." Kennedy's hand swept toward the paper on my desk. He wore wrinkled khaki pants and a white-and-tan seersucker sport coat that was wet under the arms. Peeling it off, he tossed it on one side of the couch and sat down. His shirt looked as if he'd washed a Chevy with it.

"I'll *bet* it was a shock." I sat down. "Like the one you gave me. Look, Congressman, I've got to ask you a couple of questions."

"Fine. Call me 'Jack.'" He tugged a red silk tie loose.

"Did you kill her?" I heard the guillotine edge in my voice.

Kennedy shuddered. "No, of course not." His blue eyes met my gaze straight on.

"Have you been arrested, or do you expect to be? It's against the law in Washington for me to take your case if either answer is yes."

"I haven't been arrested. I don't expect to be because I didn't harm her. But I can't tell what the police will suspect when they find out I was with her that night."

I told him that would do.

*****

Kennedy winced. "Do you mind if I stand? This couch is murder on—I'm sorry, sickening choice of words—this couch is hurting my back. Look, I, ah, spent some time at Betty's apartment, and several people saw me leave."

I kept quiet. I wanted Kennedy to talk without any clutter from me.

"I'm a new congressman representing a Catholic district. I don't mean to sound as if it were my only concern, but I'd rather not be identified with a rape and murder case. I'm not mentioned, but I have a family whose reputation I'd as soon not drag into the gutter."

"Go on." Keep the ball in his court.

"All right. If the police find the killer quickly, and if they, ah, don't complicate the case by digging into the possible details of what went on that evening between Betty Dyson and me, that would be ideal, both in terms of justice and in terms of what I need." He paused. "I guess it won't be that easy."

"It won't. You may be the best suspect, from the sound of it. The *Post* says she died sometime Friday night. You were there alone with her Friday night, case closed."

Kennedy sat down on the couch again, sat down hard. No surprise. He looked a bit shaky, and I asked if he were all right. He waved me off impatiently. "What will the police do next?"

"Well, they'll take statements from everybody who saw the two of you at the hotel. Once the cops hear your name, they'll get a picture of you and show it around. There'll be a police lineup. Somebody at her apartment building probably saw you. You used cabs?"

He nodded.

"More witnesses. Talk to a lawyer yet?"

"My father made some calls this morning from Boston and asked for what he called the 'best Jew lawyer' in D.C. By ten, I was on the phone with a guy named Abraham Moskowitz—"

"—Whose reputation for shattering criminal prosecutions has made him a celebrity of sorts in the Washington papers. I've never met him."

Kennedy nodded. "He took my case, though I haven't been accused of anything. Incredibly sharp, Moskowitz, I thought. I believe he and my father are both making more calls now, using Dad's name and influence to keep my part in this as quiet as possible."

"Your father is—?"

He stopped, puzzled. "I'm not used to that question." He seemed to enjoy my asking it. "Dad is Joseph P. Kennedy, the former ambassador."

It wasn't as if I never read the papers. "You mean old Joe Kennedy, who's rich as Croesus, the isolationist who Roosevelt fired as ambassador to England during the war—"

He looked as if he'd been slapped. What I knew of the elder Kennedy was coming back to me faster than the tact I tried to show prospective clients.

"This is the guy who lost his oldest son during the war in some kind of secret operation," spilled out of my mouth, "and he has another son who was a war hero of some sort." I stopped short with the realization. "That's you."

"That's me." His expression suggested that he didn't describe his family the way I did.

"I forget what you did that made you a hero. You didn't go into it last Friday night."

Kennedy chuckled. "I've said before that it was absolutely

involuntary. The Japanese sank my PT boat. Dead of night. Sliced right through it before we could get out of the way."

"Sorry, I didn't mean to put it that way—about your family, that is. I just hadn't realized that's who you were. Friday night, I mean. I don't meet a lot of zillionaires."

"It's just as well, diplomat that you are. I'm only a millionaire; Dad's the zillionaire. Let's leave him out of this as long as possible. He makes his own rules."

FOUR

The congressman stood up and walked over to the turreted part of the room with its rounded walls and three narrow windows. The sky was darkening, and it would rain soon. I had the feeling he was looking inside himself, not outside my office.

"Griffin, maybe I'd better ask whether you fell in love with Betty or were jealous of her going off with me. I didn't kill Betty Dyson. I didn't rape her, either. But I don't want you as my private investigator if you're after my ass."

He was tougher than I'd guessed. We glared at each other for a couple of minutes in the gloom of my office. I decided that hiring me didn't entitle him to a heart-to-heart chat.

"Would I have preferred walking out of the dinner with Betty? Sure. She was fun. I liked her a lot. But I can represent you fairly. Also, Jack, I want the real killer found. I gather that's what brought you here."

Kennedy nodded. "I'm a voracious reader, and somebody always had private eye novels in the South Pacific. I don't have any problem with the proposition that the police look for the most obvious suspect and don't like to dig any deeper when it's in a novel. I think I might need to have somebody else solve this case."

Now it was my turn to chuckle. "This is a real-life private detective agency. Aadlund and Griffin doesn't go out and do the job you guys in Congress pay the D.C. detective division for. What do you want a private investigator to do that you're worried the cops won't do?"

"I'm afraid the police will settle on me right away. Members of Congress are immune to arrest for minor crimes when Congress is in session, but not for felonies. If they don't railroad me into jail right away, it can still drag on until some newspaper my father can't influence gets the story. That would finish me even if I'm acquitted. I'm just starting to really enjoy being a congressman. There's so much you can accomplish. And I like making my own way in the world."

"Have you and your lawyer figured out what you'll tell the cops when they visit you in the next day or two? Because they will if the killer doesn't fall into their laps."

"I'll tell them the truth," he said.

"Did your lawyer recommend hiring a private detective?"

"No, I thought of it after we spoke, and I haven't told him yet." He flushed slightly. "Look, Betty and I left Hotel Washington at the same time. I offered her a ride in my cab. She invited me in for a drink. We talked. I left half an hour or so later."

"You didn't have sex with her, or at least try to? That's what they'll ask you."

He stood again and looked me in the eye. "Griffin, I didn't even know Betty Dyson before Friday evening. I didn't rape her. I didn't have a relationship with her. I gave her a ride home in my cab. We talked for a few minutes. She was alive and very healthy when I left her that night."

*****

It began to rain, slowly for half a minute before somebody ripped the bottoms off of the clouds. I jumped up and shut the windows as the downpour swept against them, turning back to my office and staring closely at Kennedy. "Jack, there are just two people you have to level with. One is your lawyer, and the other is your private investigator. Steer either of us in the wrong direction, and we won't be ready to defend you."

The windows had been closed for thirty seconds, and the room was getting muggy already. Washington in July. You expect to see crocodiles waddling down the street, snatching up poodles from horrified little white girls in the nicer neighborhoods.

"I'm not lying." Kennedy spoke through gritted teeth.

"I don't think you are." His jaw eased a bit. "But you're not overwhelming me with the truth, either. *Did* you have sex with Betty Dyson?"

"Of course I did." His eyes blazed. "You knew we would when

we left the God-damned table, Griffin. I wanted her and she wanted me."

"Go on."

He leaned on the edge of my desk. "We didn't have any damned chit-chat; you're right about that. We had sex. We were both hot and hair-triggered. Slam, bam, thank you, ma'am. I really doubt I stayed in her apartment half an hour."

"Why?" I couldn't help asking, and I might need to know the reason. "I mean, she was *not* unpleasant to be with. Or did something else happen to make you leave right away?"

"There was nothing else." His scowl said my question was puzzling. "I, ah, usually leave a girl right after sex."

"Oh?"

"I—The truth is, I suppose, I've never much liked being touched." He spoke very matter-of-factly, his voice flat and a bit nasally. "Touching women, very much so, but *being* touched is rather manipulative, don't you think? And I'm not interested in pretending anything is going to develop. You'd be astonished how quickly women can decide you're in love with them."

"Really." His comment astonished me.

Kennedy smiled. "And, of course, if you don't leave quickly, women can't keep their hands off you. That's when you get drawn into a relationship when all you wanted was to get laid."

He looked embarrassed. "Also, it's very awkward waking up next to a woman when I've had a nightmare about the war. Sometimes that enemy destroyer is crashing directly into me, sometimes I'm drowning as we swim away, sometimes I'm with my brother Joe on his last bomber mission, knowing what will happen."

I nodded. I could have recited a pretty similar storyline myself. I still don't know why I didn't swap bad dreams with him.

FIVE

I telephoned Vince O'Heaney right after Kennedy left. A Washington Metropolitan detective 'til the Army made him a major in its Criminal Investigation Division after Pearl Harbor, he'd gone back to the force as a detective sergeant after the war. Vince would know about the Betty Dyson case.

The War Department stuck me into the C.I.D. with Vince for most of 1942, before I got the notion that shooting at Nazis might be more interesting than arresting pilferers. I'd liked Vince since a young guy named Flaherty and I reported to his detachment. Flaherty and I happened to go out for a bite of lunch on a gray-eyed March day. When we came back, just as we hung up our raincoats, O'Heaney roared into the four-by-four office we shared, fuming mad. He slammed the door. "You guys expect tuh be federal agents? Lemme tell yuh something. Yuh go out on an overcast day, and yuh take your fucking raincoats so if it rains yuh'll have no excuse not tuh come back tuh the office? *Yuh could have been stuck in a bar all afternoon keeping your uniforms dry, but N-O-O-O-O!* And yuh call yourselves investigators!" Merriment danced in his eyes as he stormed out.

I dialed the Metropolitan Police Department. "Still prefer adventure to steady work?" O'Heaney's laugh when he picked up the phone was a big V-8 engine starting up. "What's on your mind, Junior?"

The last thing I wanted was to admit to Vince that I—a private eyeball—was working on the raw edges of the hottest case the M.P.D. had. "I knew Betty Dyson." I heard my clenched teeth, my dry throat. "I'd like to ask you a question or two about what the department knows. I'm upset, and I'm curious."

"I didn't know she was a friend of yours."

"Not really. I just knew her and liked her."

"Sorry, Junior. It's a damn ugly thing to have somebody you know murdered."

"You free for lunch or a drink?"

"Let's say I'll have a glass of ginger ale with you at Moynihan's around two." A chuckle hid in his voice. "Surely you know I don't drink liquor on duty. I'm a *police* officer."

*****

A while after lunch, I strolled westward along Pennsylvania Avenue toward Moynihan's, watching the cheese artists and the hustlers, enjoying the way the city women moved. I stopped at a newsstand I always checked. In his rasping monotone, the mahogany Buddha who tended it told me, "I ain't seen the August *Detective Tales* yet, Mista Griffin."

"I'll live, Carl." I lingered in the shade by picking up a copy of the *New Yorker* with a suburban couple making a brick patio on the cover and glanced at a few of the cartoons. But twenty cents a copy was too pricey. I kept walking.

Washington in July. One of those short, pointless Washington rains that didn't cool the city down for a minute had added steam to the heat. My shirt turned to paper maché as I slogged toward Moynihan's bar.

Washington was never going to win any street-sweeping prizes. Even without a breeze, the grit lining the lanes between the white marble palaces glued itself to my face. By early afternoon, the city's top newspapers and shards of pint whiskey bottles filled the gutters as if the skies drizzled trash. Blazing sunshine ricocheted off the pale sidewalks and flew back up into your eyes.

Long-dead Congresses looking for a town to own invented Washington, a made-up city, a place to hide out from the mobs of New York and Philadelphia. Its only industry was government, its only products laws and regulations. That never kept it from having robber barons or from selling its wares cheap.

It still remained a Southern city, too. Washington had been a Mecca for freed slaves even before the Civil War, and government work during the war had attracted thousands more Negroes. That was one reason the Southerners who ran Congress didn't want the city to vote—the last plantation didn't raise cotton.

Still, for all that, you felt a superficial ease to the intermingling of white and colored people in everyday life. All the city's sounds had a Southern accent, and you got friendly nods wherever you went if you didn't kick any sleeping dogs.

*****

When I tugged Moynihan's door open, cool air flooded out and crested over my chest just in time to salvage my lungs. An oasis of dim light waited inside. Some plaid-jacketed character in a gray straw fedora lounged in a booth at the far end with a dark-haired woman whose back faced toward me.

Vince O'Heaney was a sack of cement in a gray Woolworth suit. He sat at the bar near the front door, facing his drink. I jabbed my Panama onto a coat rack.

"Hey, Vince." I sat down beside him.

"Stupid mick ovuh there." A grinning O'Heaney nodded toward the sulking bartender before I could shake his hand. "I'm not dead sure the bastard didn't get some *whiskey* in this glass. How the hell are yuh, Junior?" He was sitting on one of a dozen mismatched stools. His upper lip had always looked as if somebody'd split it open when the world was younger.

I didn't want O'Heaney thinking I was barging in on police business. "Nothing wrong this air conditioning won't set right." I told the guy at the taps to give me a Coca-Cola.

"Soda pop!" O'Heaney tried hard to look as if he'd just nailed a pervert handing a Whiz Bar to a choir boy. "My, what'd they do tuh yuh in the paratripes, me boy, that yuh won't drink Irish whiskey in the afternoon? Or did the stinking Krauts shoot your guts tuh ribbons?"

Not *mine*, I thought. "You want me to give you a bunch of crap about how I don't make enough money in my pathetic career as a private detective to drink decent whiskey and I'm too refined for rotgut?"

He chuckled as if he'd seen a news item about the King of England having athlete's foot—mildly amused but not much interested.

Or shall I tell you, I thought to myself, *about the nightmares and weird dreams I've had since the war and how I tried drinking to sleep? But there are things a man doesn't say.*

Vince sipped his drink. It did look as if there might be whiskey in his glass.

The scrawny barkeep came over and plunked my Coke down in front of me. "Here." He looked pained at having so much chatter wrenched out of him. His stringy black hair was slicked straight back, his collar buttoned to the top without a necktie.

"Listen, Vince, I don't mind admitting the Betty Dyson thing upsets me." I didn't need to tell him how much it hurt—he'd be uncomfortable with it, and so would I. "Got a suspect yet?"

"On the day after we found the body? The lugs working the case are just starting tuh ask questions today; yuh know that. Six dicks, two sergeants. It's a pretty nasty case, and the newspapers will start yapping if some son of a bitch isn't indicted for it pretty soon. But, yeah, it was upsetting."

"The case?" I'd figured stabbings counted as yesterday's potatoes to Vince.

"Naw, not just that. Guy calls us from Andrews Field out across the Maryland line, a famous fighter ace. Reports his wife was just found murdered in their apartment in Northwest. Says he tried calling her—I guess full colonels have the money tuh talk long distance on the phone from Maryland every Sunday—and she doesn't answer. Doesn't answer three times. So he calls the apartment manager and asks him tuh look in on the wife tuh make sure she's all right."

"And the manager finds...?"

"The blood-caked body of what had been a good-looking woman in her late twenties, stripped half-naked on the bed, her throat slit and a dozen stab wounds. Hell of a shock for the manager, I bet."

SIX

I slapped half a buck on the bar to cover whatever we drank and asked for another Coke. The barkeep nodded. He was new there, but he looked familiar. I decided I hadn't seen that gaunt mug on a post office wall, but I wasn't ruling out his face having been used on the Jolly Roger in some pirate movie.

What else could O'Heaney tell me? "The *Post* reported Betty died Friday night, Vince."

"Prob'ly Friday night, mebbe early Saturday morning."

I thought about Kennedy's version of his time with her. "How'd you decide she'd been raped?"

O'Heaney swigged down what was left of his drink and nodded to the bartender for another of the same. "The medical examiner figured it out. Same way he set the time of death as Friday night or early Saturday. M.E.s do some kinda voodoo, sniff the air, check the Zodiac, consult a Weejee board, gut a chicken and give yuh all these definite answers."

I nodded and lowered my voice. "Vince, did you see the body yourself?"

"Normally, I would have. I'd have sent an M.E., a camera guy, and a coupla dicks over there, and I'da stopped by tuh make sure they didn't screw something up. Yuh wouldn't believe some of the lunkheads they promoted since the war. But it was Sunday. Mary and I took Angela tuh ride the fancy merry-go-round out at Glen Echo Park after Mass. Snilder was duty sergeant. They got me 'overseeing' the case cuz Moon Snilder's such a tub of crap. Thank Gawd I only had to see the pictures."

He reached into his coat pocket and pulled out a pack of Chesterfields, shaking it enough to get the tip of one out where he could snatch it with his lips. "Ordinarily, I'm willing tuh peek at pictures of a naked dame, but yuh ever see any bodies been dead a few days?"

"I was in the paratroops, remember?" The gray dawn dimness of Bastogne under the bared branches of the Ardennes came back to me again. Coca-Cola wasn't the best remedy for that.

O'Heaney nodded and lit his cigarette. "Well, here was what was left of a swell-lookin' dame, flies all over her. Still in her nylons, a shoe still on, a dark dress half-unbuttoned and bunched up around her waist—pushed up from the bottom and pulled down from the top. Her brassiere was still fastened but shoved down, with the straps off her shoulders and her tits bare as could be. Lipstick was so smeared they thought it was blood at first. Little string of pearls around her neck."

I remembered the pearls and the navy-blue dress. I remembered the delicate neck and the full breasts even better. In my memory, Betty wasn't a corpse, and what I recalled of her still made my body itch. Part of me felt like a worm-eaten oak.

"I don't need tuh remind yuh what happens after a coupla days, Junior. Especially in hot weather."

"Okay, Vince, I got it. When's the autopsy?"

O'Heaney snorted blue smoke and shook his head. "There won't *be* an autopsy. Husband said he didn't want her cut up any further. When you're somebody important, Gentleman Jimmy does it your way. They cremated her this morning." He took a sip of whiskey.

"Vince, the husband, didn't want her body cut again, but he ordered her burnt to cinders? Does that happen a lot?"

"Yuh see it all in Homicide, Junior. Yuh see it all."

*****

I needed a close look at the police photos. Still, he'd have figured I had more of an interest than I'd implied if I asked him anything about them. And I truly didn't look forward to going through them.

"Got a good medical examiner on the case?" I finished my Coke to make my question seem conversational, as if I were more interested in how the case was going for Vince and his guys than in what had happened to Betty.

"Yeah." He looked at me like I'd asked if he knew who Eleanor Roosevelt was. "Doc Gregory was available, and he knows what he's doing. Yuh don't risk messing up a case like this one."

"Okay."

"But there weren't any questions, Junior. Somebody'd broken her nose, ripped her clothes half off, screwed the blue blazes out of her, stabbed her with a kitchen knife, and slashed her delicate white throat. Then he cleaned himself up in the bathroom and walked away as pretty as you please. And when we nail the son of a bitch, I've got just two questions for him."

He held up his right fist and then his left. "And if *you've* got any questions of your own at that point, I'd be glad tuh let yuh ask 'em."

*****

After Vince left Moynihan's and headed up the hill toward his office, I needed to kill some time. Vince's territorial nature dictated not letting him know 'til I had to that I had crept into his murder case, so I dawdled five minutes before following him up to the Municipal Building to question the medical examiner.

SEVEN

"People think we're ghouls, you know."

Doctor Gregory scratched his long nose. "Still, a fine time you'd have solving crimes without the Medical Examiner's Office. It takes a strong stomach to look at a man who's got an ax buried in his forehead. Candidly, though, dead patients don't whine like live ones."

I'd expected a cadaverous oddball, some lantern-jawed John Carradine type in a filthy white coat. Gregory was probably in his late seventies. He looked as natty as an insurance salesman, a burgundy silk tie and tan linen suit under his spotless lab coat, his silvery hair brushed straight back.

Doctor Gregory relaxed in his cramped office, surrounded by dark, worn books on dark, worn wooden shelves, the requisite skeleton dangling from a rack in one corner. He was as chatty as a career drunk.

"Well, there's nothing unusual about the Dyson case. Penny-ante rape and murder. You see it all the time. At least I do. This city's major industries are homicide and left-wing legislation, you know. But don't even get me started on Harry Truman."

"Now, why would I want to do that?" I forced a laugh. "But I'm curious how you can tell a dead woman's been raped."

*****

Gregory lit up a cigar the size of a Lincoln Log. It took two matches. Then he chuckled, as if I'd asked if he had an opinion on whether kittens were young cats or not. "Well, first of all, when she's pretty or well-built like this young lady was, and her clothes are all ripped up or askew, you look for it. Sex and rage make a very potent cocktail, Mr. Griffin." He smiled as if I'd just agreed to buy a homeowners policy.

"Look for it—how?" I knew Gregory did necessary work, like garbage collectors and those guys who muck out the stalls at the Kentucky Derby, but you had to wonder about people who seemed to savor it.

"Well, in this case—" he drew in smoke and let it out slowly—"with a married woman in her late twenties, presumably accustomed to sexual intercourse and with no sign of injury about the vaginal opening, it is much more difficult to determine than with a child or a virginal young woman."

Gregory paused, as if savoring his explanation, and dragged again at his cigar. He fitted his lips carefully upon it again and stared at me. "Semen." He leaned back in his worn leather chair.

I waited for him to complete a sentence, but apparently, the word was enough for him. A grimy little window opening onto a light well let in the dimmest hint of a glow behind him. I finally had to ask what he meant.

He chuckled. "When you find semen on the corpse of a woman who has not had sexual intercourse in several days.... Colonel Dyson said he was out at Andrews Field on duty all week. She didn't put the semen there herself, now, did she? No, you see, semen is a colorless but tenacious fluid. We used to think spermatozoa disappeared quite rapidly from the vagina, as they do from the surface of the corpse or from the rectum. Now, if you take a—Well, never mind, not everybody wants to know that."

The mouth end of his cigar was already wet with brown slime. The fire had gone out, but Gregory seemed happier with a cigar that demanded no more attention than a dead patient.

"Actually, the funny little tadpoles have been found days after the act—*days!* I also identify dried semen with ultraviolet light. Both the bedclothes and the dress in the Dyson case bore stains. I was able to recover sufficient semen to determine which blood group the assailant belonged to."

He waited, cigar at a jaunty angle, knowing I'd need to ask what group it was. I obliged him.

Chortling softly, Gregory shifted the stogie with his teeth and lips from the left to the right. "Blood groups being rather large, you cannot use the results to determine guilt, but we often see a suspect cleared because the culprit had type A blood and the suspect is type B.

In this case, even forty-odd hours later, the victim's vagina remained a virtual bucket of the killer's sperm."

I felt myself tugging at my collar. The medical examiner's cheery description of his trade, in relation to a woman I had cared about, started making me angry. "I didn't see the blood type mentioned in your report, Doctor."

"No, of course not. The test results haven't come back from the lab. We should have that answer in two or three hours, and I'll send a copy to the detective in charge at that point."

I leaned forward in my chair. "So you concluded she'd been raped because she'd had intercourse around the time of death. And because she'd been murdered."

"And beaten. Don't leave that out. Her nose, which photos in her apartment indicate was quite delicate, had been pulverized, with a massive contusion surrounding it. And not simply *murdered,* either, but stabbed *and* slashed." Gregory picked up a brown paper folder full of photographs and handed it to me.

After I took the folder from him, I pulled out my notebook and went back over it while I considered whether I wanted to look at the photos or not. I didn't want to see her that way, to forever engrave in my memory the images of Betty beaten and slashed. I also didn't want those thoughts to bring back pictures of the carnage I'd seen at Normandy, Eindhoven, and Bastogne. But I did want to find the guy who killed Betty, and that pushed away, for the moment, Bastogne. *Oh, hell,* the thought went through my mind, *I'll be seeing those portraits long after the last winter in hell passes.*

I flipped open the damned folder.

EIGHT

You could see she was dead. Brutality made the murdered woman look even less like the live one. Bloated and darkening cheeks surrounded the shattered nose, splotched with dried blood and bruises that were a deep gray in the black-and-white pictures. A hideous smile opened on one side of her throat and ended on the other, all black with blood as well. I wished her eyes had been shut.

The smaller mouths were stab wounds; no soldier could miss that. Seven ranged from Betty's left shoulder to the same side of her rib cage, black ribbons trickling from them to follow her topography downward. Two more punctured her left breast.

"What do you think happened, Doctor?" My stomach knotted as if I'd eaten bad eggs. My throat held a stone in it. I closed the folder and set it down softly on his junkyard of a desk.

Gregory's face lit up. I'd asked a violinist for an encore. "When the victim refused sex to the assailant, the man went into a rampage. Rape is an act of *rage,* not simply sexual desire; you can see that. First, he punched her in the face and shattered her nose, as I've noted. A blow such as that is stunning. She might very well have fainted."

I wanted that to be true, but those open eyes....

"The man grabbed a kitchen knife, surely the one that was found beside the corpse. No decent fingerprints, by the way. He raped her. Then he stabbed her repeatedly in his fury, and just to be sure, he slit her throat. Very effectively, too, by the way. None of those stab wounds would have killed her, oddly enough."

"No?"

He shook his head. "They fall in too wide an arc around her heart—the product, I should think, of unreasoning frenzy, perhaps in the moment of sexual release. But the slash across the throat severed the carotid artery an inch and a half beneath the skin. The girl would have been unconscious in under five seconds—had the blow to her face left her conscious at all—and dead within twelve."

As much as I resisted it, Betty Dyson's face came back to me then, laughing at our jokes, the single strand of pearls setting off the beauty of her long neck. I wanted nothing more than a breath of crisp Adirondack air, far from the cheery man whose aftershave was formaldehyde. But I hadn't finished with Doctor Gregory.

"How did you determine when she died?"

"I hate hot weather." Gregory shook his head. I thought he was complaining about the closeness of the stagnant air in his office. "Hot weather is the biggest enemy of fixing the time of death accurately, you know. Well, perhaps you *don't* know that, but to make a long story short—"

"By all means." The dead air and the monstrous photographs made me wish I'd skipped lunch.

Gregory sniffed. I'd hurt whatever feelings he had. "The longer after the death before the investigation, the more imprecise any determination of its time of occurrence becomes. Rigor mortis was complete and starting to disappear. That told me it had surely been over twenty hours and perhaps as much as forty-eight. However, there are corroborating clues, if I may."

I nodded. He relit his cigar, drew on it slowly, and poisoned what air remained in his gas chamber by exhaling his nickel smoke.

"Decomposition begins in twenty-four to forty-eight hours after death. The veins of the skin and the abdomen assume a blue-green coloration. In the extreme heat Washington has been experiencing all summer, an unrefrigerated corpse will attract hundreds of flies in *very* short order, and their larvae will be present within forty-eight hours. I observed these indicators in profusion. The victim could not have been killed before Friday evening or after early Saturday morning."

"No tighter than that?" I wanted a glass of Scotch. Badly.

"No-o-o. Surely not before 6 p.m. last Friday evening or after 2 a.m. on Saturday, but more likely in between. Let us say eight o'clock Friday to midnight."

That didn't let Kennedy off the hook, but it also didn't clearly fasten the blame on him.

"Did you want to perform an autopsy?"

"Oh, not that badly. In the normal course of events, I'd have opened her, just for the record, but there was really no need in this case. I'd proved there was sexual intercourse, and I could have been surer about the *time* of death if I had autopsied the corpse and seen whether her supper was still in her stomach. But there was no question of the *cause* of death. No, it was quite reasonable to respect the husband's wishes in the matter."

I stood up and shook his hand. As fast as I wanted to get out the door, one more question dragged me back.

"Did she fight the guy? Did you check under her nails?"

Gregory tutted as if I'd asked him to solve three minus two and offered him pencil and paper. "Inconclusive. No human tissue under the nails. No blood anywhere except the deceased's. If I'd found skin, I'd know the answer to that and whether the killer was a colored boy or a white man. But there were two fibers, under separate fingernails, of a lightweight wool, a pale gray in color. They could come from clawing the assailant's back. That sort of thing hammers the lid down tight on a suspect's coffin."

NINE

A ten-inch model of a fighter plane perched on Colonel Dyson's desk, and a photo of him standing in front of the same plane hung on the wall beside me. The nose spinner on the model was red and yellow, and the rudder simply red. Above the name "Betty" on the left side were two and a half rows of tiny straight Hitler crosses for German planes shot down. The desk itself was as olive drab as a year in the Army.

I'd driven ten miles out Pennsylvania Avenue, across the Anacostia River on the Sousa Bridge, through Hillcrest with its sunburned children laughing and jumping in the spray of fire hydrants, and then through a brief but convincing thunderstorm, to Andrews Field, headquarters of the nearly-independent Air Force's Strategic Air Command.

A spindly young guard in wilted khakis halted me at the front gate. "Official business?"

"Son, your Colonel Dyson is one of this country's leading air aces, and his wife was murdered over the weekend. I don't suppose there's a lot of business more official than finding the bastard who killed her. I need to speak with the colonel for a few minutes."

Truth was, I needed to get a sense of the guy and find out where he was when Betty was killed. All I knew was what the *Post* printed—that Dyson shot down twenty-four Nazi fighters and lived to tell the tale. Though he and his wife shared an apartment in Washington, Dyson's office was at Andrews Field, and he kept a room in the bachelor officers' quarters there as well. His wife, who'd seemed like a pretty straightforward gal, had given herself to a man she'd just met. I wondered what Dyson knew about her extramarital life. Or what I knew about it.

*****

"I told Detective Sergeant Snilder everything." Dyson had mistaken me for a cop. My other business cards—I gave him one that simply said "Jack Griffin, Investigator" above the phone number—often had that effect.

"Let's go over how you concluded something was wrong. What made you think on Sunday that there was a problem?"

Dyson looked annoyed, even for a thin, balding, hawk-nosed man in his early thirties. "As I've already said, I couldn't reach Mrs. Dyson on the telephone all weekend. That's unusual. We generally speak when I'm out here, which is most weekends."

Mrs. Dyson, he called his wife. "You telephoned her when?"

"I started on Friday evening. I tried once, oh, about seven-thirty and again around nine. I wasn't free until evening on Saturday, about eight and again at ten."

"Did you call from in here?"

"No, of course not. Those were private calls. I used the pay phone over at the officers' club. Finally, I reached the apartment office on Sunday. That, of course, was how I learned of her death, by sending somebody to check the apartment."

"How did it make you feel?"

"I certainly trust the police will examine the evidence thoroughly and bring the culprit to justice. Terrible thing, terrible."

Sturgeon blood ran through his veins, cold and silvery. He was talking about his wife being raped, stabbed repeatedly, and slashed to death. *Culprit?*

I wanted to slap him, but I got a grip on myself. Men do handle grief in different ways, I reminded myself. I'd certainly seen it after battle. Maybe it took a cold fish to shoot down so many planes—not to get caught up in battle fever but just aim and shoot, aim and shoot.

"You ordered her cremated." I scribbled in my notebook as if I'd learned something.

"Well, yes, I did. I don't believe in physical resurrection, of course, and her body was so hacked apart by—when she was killed. And then to let the medical examiner...." He stood stiffly, looking at a gold-framed photo of her on a shelf behind his desk. Maybe he did feel something.

It was late in the day, yet the colonel's khaki shirt and pants were still knife-edge crisp, despite the heat. Perhaps he'd changed them just before I got there, though I hadn't phoned ahead. There were silver wings and some ribbons I didn't know on his chest. One I couldn't identify outranked the Silver Star he wore, from where he'd placed it. No Purple Heart, though. He'd never been wounded.

"Believe me, Colonel, I sympathize with you. I was an infantry officer in the war. This is a more intimate kind of loss. I'm sorry, but I've got to ask you a couple of personal questions because they might bear on how your wife came to have another man in your apartment."

He nodded, looking like he hated me.

"How would you characterize your marriage?"

Dyson jumped up, as if I'd asked him that question in front of the officers' mess. *"If you are insinuating—"*

"I'm not insinuating anything. I don't have any reason to. But there was no sign of forcible entry. She apparently let the man in. Please answer my question."

He sat down again and wrestled his face back into a mask. "Mrs. Dyson was a perfect wife. She wrote me every day, all through the war. My work this past year kept me here a lot. She adored me; anybody will tell you that. If you're asking me whether my wife would have compromised herself, I have no questions whatsoever about her behavior."

"I see." I made a couple more doodles in my notebook.

"But my wife could be very—*innocent.* Because her own behavior *was* so innocent, she could assume it was a benign world. I can only imagine why she would have let the killer into our apartment."

"Why?"

He smirked, as if I'd missed the point. "Just a figure of speech. But when the police solve the case, I'm certain we'll understand what her fatal error was. If you'll excuse me, General Brubaker is expecting me for dinner in fifteen minutes."

"Now? Your wife's ashes are still warm." I hadn't meant to snap at him.

"*Get out.* I don't need a damn civilian to teach me how to grieve. I'm the afflicted man in this case. If the police are thinking of pinning this on me, you'll find I never left Andrews Field on Friday night." He buzzed for the corporal who kept ineffective watch over the inner sanctum from a matching olive drab desk in the outer office.

I walked back to my car and made some notes so I'd look busy.

Dyson didn't come out the door I watched.

The man never used Betty's first name. I drove over to the officers' club and copied down the number of the pay phone. The storm clouds had cleared away, and the slaughterhouse red of the setting sun seared my eyes all the way back into Washington.

TEN

"Salisbury steak's on special, Jack, but I'd stay strictly away from it." Lucille treated me to a smile as she laid down a paper napkin and some flatware. "Stick with the stuff on the menu tonight, except the fried fish is a bit ripe."

It was about seven when I slid into the last empty booth at O'Neill's, up on Maryland Avenue, savoring the new air conditioning. Washington in July was a wilted salad dressed with steam, especially after it rained. I'd never intended to be a soft-boiled detective.

When she came back with a glass of ice water, I asked, "How's Jerry today?" Lucille was married to what was left of Captain Jerry DiMarco, my best friend since we reported to the 101st Airborne together. A Nazi with a grease gun had fired a couple of slugs into Jerry's kidneys one night at the edge of Bastogne when we were being overrun. Kidneys don't heal, and the one he had left just kept getting worse. Jerry was on a downhill slide with no excitement to it. They ran him in and out of the V.A. hospital, and it seemed he was in more often now than a year ago. Two years after the war, Lucille remained the girl waiting for Jerry to come home.

Her eyes sparkled the way they always did, the Mediterranean in sunlight. "I think he was feeling a little bit better this morning." Lucille wore her curly golden hair short. She didn't stand more than five-foot-three, and none of it was wasted.

"Glad to hear it." I'd have felt a little bit better if she didn't *always* say she thought Jerry felt a little bit better. Lucille hoped so hard. "Bring me corned beef hash with a couple of fried eggs over easy on top of it. Biscuits and honey with that, okay?"

"Sure." Lucille smiled, a sunny afternoon in the park.

I liked Lucille. I enjoyed her wit. Four years younger than Jerry,

I met her when she married him in the chapel at Fort Bragg just before the 101st shipped out for England and points worse. "Thought I'd drop in on your husband after supper. Think he'll be up to it?"

Lucille was a lioness when it came to protecting Jerry. If she reported he could handle a visit, he'd be all right. "Jerry'd be really glad you came." Her tomboy grin was a precious national resource. She hovered beside my booth, short as a pixie, hands on her hips, giggling like a glass of Seven-Up. "Jack, did I tell you? I've got a title for my book." She was writing what promised to be a witty memoir of a combat officer's wife in the red tape of Washington. "I'm calling it *My Husband Jumped Screaming from an Airplane.*"

*****

Tired of the insistent images of Betty Dyson's savaged body while I ate my hash, I kept thinking about which classic myth made the best metaphor for the future of the Aadlund and Griffin private detective agency. Icarus plummeting earthward or the self-blinded Oedipus or the Augean Stables that Hercules cleaned all worked. King Midas sure as hell didn't.

I'd taken the five hundred dollars left from my share of my father's modest estate to buy into the partnership six months earlier, having worked there about eight or nine weeks. I knew Harry liked to joke about women's figures, and I knew he downed a couple drinks over lunch. I hadn't paid attention to the finances. Harry ran the agency, which was fine with me.

I'd been an F.B.I. agent 'til shortly before Pearl Harbor, which was when I soured on J. Edgar Hoover, that yapping Boston terrier who posed as a bulldog. Then I'd done my stint as an Army C.I.D. investigator 'til I couldn't stand that any longer and signed up for the paratroops.

The blueberry pie kept Lucille's promise, tasting "not half bad." I gave Lucille a wink before I left for the V.A. hospital. We had our familiar argument over what she called my foolish generosity when I tipped her with a half dollar, but I made her take it, and then I drove over to the V.A. hospital.

ELEVEN

They say Mount Alto, where the V.A. built its hospital, capped the highest spot in Washington. All that tells you is that D.C. is a swamp. The name "Mount Alto"— "high mountain," if my Italian was worth a nickel—was some founding father's joke. I parked on Wisconsin Avenue overlooking Georgetown and went inside, out of the sticky heat.

I hated going to the V.A. hospital. The sight of three hundred guys in ward after ward of white-linen beds—mostly young men who'd be spared the discomforts of old age because their country had needed them very badly—never cheered me up as much as a damned Memorial Day parade. And I hated parades. We'd had no choice but to fight Germany and Japan, and we'd made the world a better place by beating them. It was *still* a sickening waste.

"He awake?"

The one-armed bucktoothed ex-sailor sucking a cigarette by the elevator nodded to me. I'd seen the guy a few times before and gave him an exaggerated wink. Then, with a deep breath and a hard swallow, I marched into the ward to see the man I'd put there.

*****

"Cripes, DiMarco," I grumbled, "are you still loafing around here?"

Jerry saw me and pulled a straight face. "You bet I am! Somebody's got to teach these clowns how to sweat up a set of sheets."

DiMarco always made me laugh. "Well, you're doin' a first-rate job of it, pal. I thought maybe somebody spilled chicken soup on you or something." The ward stank more of men and July than of bedpans and cigarette butts, though I smelled them all.

"Jack, did you drop by to ogle the nurses again, or are you killing time before you pick up some swivel-hipped delicacy and call it a night?"

"I admire your vision, Jerry. Any excitement here today?" I always asked him that.

"Lucille dropped by this afternoon. Lucille left for work. Nothing else notable. Much like yesterday." In Jerry's weather report, the sun rose, and the sun set, and it had curly golden hair.

Jerry and Lucille would have been the happiest husband and wife on Earth if he hadn't had his kidneys shot up. Medicine couldn't cure that. The docs just offered a clear prognosis of the steady deterioration I witnessed every week or two. Jerry never grumbled or blamed me, but I knew what had happened that night—the short hesitation under fire before I threw my rifle company into the breach the Nazis were carving through Jerry's troops. I didn't expect I'd ever let myself off the hook for it.

*****

We talked quietly for maybe twenty minutes before visiting hours ended, and then a little more. Sports and politics, old times, and how Lucille was doing made up most of it. When Jerry dozed off, I went out into the corridor and over to the nurses' desk, where I asked a nurse I'd met a couple of times how Jerry was doing.

"You next of kin?" A smile of any kind would have busted up her rigorous plainness. It struck my mind the vets must've nicknamed her Nettie; it was the only name a face like that could carry off.

"Yeah, I'm his brother."

"I can see that." Her mouth formed an ironic curl. "Captain DiMarco's holding his own. He's doing badly enough to be *here* and well enough to still *be* here."

A more hopeful answer would've been nice, but I hadn't expected it. "I noticed an empty bed in the ward."

"So did I." She sighed. "Southern boy name of Edson Baker. Liver just quit on him like an overworked longshoreman. Of course, he'd let the Japs shoot it up pretty badly on Iwo Jima."

"I'd been hoping when I saw the empty bed that somebody had gone home."

"Young Baker was a Baptist." The ironic twist of her mouth tightened. "So he'd have said that is just what he did." The way she turned and looked back over the ward made me think she didn't want to cry. I didn't either, so I murmured good night to her and drove home.

TWELVE

Heading home alone around eleven-thirty, the conversation with myself began again. Every man my age in America seemed to be getting married, fathering half a dozen kids and buying a bungalow on the G.I. Bill at the edge of some town. I lived alone in a two-room apartment in Washington—three if the bathroom counted. I dated a lot of women and had fun with them 'til they found their calendars full of evenings with more typical men, guys who didn't sit up nights guarding their hearts. My empty private life felt like a guilty secret.

Like most cars in America then, my dark-gray Nash was made before Japan attacked Pearl Harbor. Spending the war years up on blocks in my uncle's garage in Pittsburgh had kept it serviceable. I drove around Thomas Circle, came out back on M Street, and found a parking spot near the Aldon, where I lived. I parked half a block from my apartment and got out. There were hints the heat might finally relax a bit for the night.

A hundred yards or so from my building's entrance, somebody opened up the driver's side door of a dark-colored Mercury and stepped between me and my address. Big guy, beefy guy, with the kind of suit you could buy new for fifteen dollars, only it wasn't new.

"Hey, peeper. C'mere." Coal being shoveled had the same melodic tone.

*****

I knew who he was, and he knew I did. Moon Snilder was one of the crookedest cops ever to grace the Metropolitan detective ranks. The rumor said he'd made sergeant because he had something dirty on Gentleman Jimmy Howard. Snilder was a moose with smelly teeth and no antlers.

"Y'all din't come clean with mah ole buddy O'Heaney when y'all was pumpin' him 'bout mah case." Snilder was growling, fists at his sides.

I stopped short of him before the shadows of the elm trees could block the glare from the streetlight. His voice glittered with malice. One theory of police work is you hire half the criminals in town and give them badges, then tell them to get rid of the other half, whatever it takes. The alternate idea is you pass some laws and enforce them. Snilder was strictly Theory A. I'd heard he was pretty good at getting confessions.

"Y'all *din't* tell O'Heaney y'all was workin' on the Dyson case, an' y'all *din't* tell him y'all was takin' money offa this big shot Kennedy, an' y'all *din't* tell him y'all was goin' to pump the M.E. this afternoon. That's a lot not to tell O'Heaney, peeper, now ain't it?"

I could tell where he was heading, and I wanted to cut him off. "You're right. I'll come in and square it with Vince about it in the morning."

Snilder shook his head. I wondered when the cops had questioned Kennedy.

"Y'all goin' to drop this here goddam case, peeper. An' ah'm doin' y'all a *favuh* tellin' y'all that, understan'?"

"Really? I hadn't suspected you had the gift of prophecy." Snilder was bigger than me, and I stood over six feet. He'd been built like an industrial plant. And I had to play wise guy.

Snilder smiled, his dismal teeth reflecting the dim, distant light that filtered through the leaves. "Yeah. See, the only suspect we uncovered is this here Kennedy guy, a goddam congressman, lots of money. A goddam pretty boy, too. An' it's the case of the year—horrible rape an' murder of a war hero's cutie-pie strawberry-blonde wife. Blood all over hell. Oh, we need to make a quick arrest, an' we're gonna do it."

"Is justice served if he's the wrong arrest?"

"Justice don' need some goddam rich Mick hirin' a fuckin' peeper to confuse the goddam issue here." Snilder rolled toward me like a Tiger tank, huge and loud and dangerous. "We got this goddam case *cracked,* peeper. If ah gotta talk to y'all again, ah'll beat the crap outa y'all in the interrogation room for obstructin' justice. Y'all stay the hell out of it."

*****

Sitting on my worn green sofa, I'd have been glad to own a bit of Scotch. Betty Dyson swiveled into my thoughts, and I figured she'd do to get the smell of Snilder out of my head, as long as she didn't replace it with her police pictures.

I hadn't exactly fallen in love with Betty, though I might have if she'd lived. From Friday 'til Kennedy told me she'd been murdered, I thought she was terrific. Then I learned she was both dead and married. I thought less of married women who screwed around—men, too, for that matter—and I left them alone. Still, nothing I remembered about Betty felt like she was a tramp. The mystery of her death was tangled with the mystery of her life.

In an hour or so, I finally drifted off to sleep, wondering what I really knew about Jack Kennedy. I also wondered how accurate my intuition would prove. My intuition told me he might be a playboy, but he was good raw material nonetheless. Still, did an abnormal psych course a decade ago in college have any real bearing on the inner ticking of the sons of the extremely rich who can do anything? The black ooze overcame me as I recalled that line of F. Scott Fitzgerald's, "The rich are different than us."

A flare went off east of Bastogne in my nightmare, its white magnesium fire spitting sparks as it swung beneath its small parachute. My field phone jumped into the air. "Griffin," Colonel Epping barked, "the krauts are swarming all over Baker Company." Jerry DiMarco's unit. "Hustle your men there *now*."

The ritual nightmare had begun.

"Charlie Company! Get ready to move. They're overrunning Baker Company!" Nazi shells were *krumping* all around us, and you can't throw a hundred men into a fight without grabbing gear and getting ready. But between my men and Jerry's stood a gigantic hourglass, powdery snow pouring relentlessly from the top to the bottom.

"Move out! Double time! Lock and load your weapons."

We raced to fill the gap the Nazis were chopping through Jerry's men. A chrome-coated armadillo scuttled across our path, a naked strawberry blonde waving from its gleaming back. The snowfall underfoot turned to saltwater taffy, sucking at our boots as we struggled to run. Above the explosions, I could hear Jerry whispering, *"Dammit, Jack, where are you?"*

Then the swarming Germans came into sight, a gray-green ooze rolling forward and shooting down into Baker Company's foxholes. We knocked the Nazis over like tiny toys, my Tommy gun spitting forty-five caliber jellybeans into the mix with the rifle and machinegun bullets my troops unloosed. Our artillery joined in the anthem.

Men and things—diamonds and ducklings and dogs—floated through white phosphorus haze before us, and then we ran out of Nazis, the ritual nearly completed. Life showed in Jerry's eyes when I met them, but not much. Somebody'd spray-painted his belly red. A sergeant kneeling to his left glared at me. "Took your sweet time, Captain." Jerry told him to shut his mouth. I woke up yelling out loud for a medic, wondering where the battle went.

Then the sun hoisted itself up over my windowsill and jabbed my eyes until I was wide awake. I lay there soaked with sweat, as glad to see daybreak as I'd been any morning in Bastogne.

THIRTEEN

My phone jangled as I shut off the shower. The boy congressman sounded tense. "Griffin, can you meet me in an hour at my lawyer's office." It was not a question. "There's a new twist to this."

I grabbed my alarm clock. "I'll be there at nine, then. Where?" Glancing out the window, I saw it was raining again, but not very hard.

"The Washington Building, on the corner of New York Avenue and Fifteenth, third floor. The *whole* third floor, Griffin. Moskowitz, Ridgway, and something. Nine o'clock sharp."

*****

At nine-twenty, I was still sitting on a Beaujolais-hued leather sofa in a walnut-paneled waiting room, wearing a light-blue suit that had almost dried once I'd had the sense to come in out of the rain. Coats and ties felt confining as uniforms to me, but Washington's a place where a man who isn't wearing a suit stands out like a stripper in a monastery.

So I sat in the outer office of Moskowitz, Ridgway, O'Malley, and Klein, reading two *Post* articles. The obituary, with a portrait photo of Betty Dyson, spieled out the widower's pompous grief, and the news story spouted stuffy assurances from the superintendent of detectives that the case was receiving "all the attention it deserves." Cute way to put it. The only fresh things were Betty's picture, the catchphrase "the Strawberry-Blonde murder," and a mention that she'd worked for Assistant Secretary of War Stuart Symington, who called her death a "senseless tragedy." It also mentioned they'd hold a memorial service late in the afternoon.

My client breezed into the law office, a few rain spots on his cocoa-colored suit jacket. "Congressman Kennedy to see Mr.

Moskowitz," he told the most deeply tanned cornsilk-blonde receptionist I'd ever seen. "Oh, Griffin, glad you're here."

The lady's skin was warmed caramel sauce, but frost tinged her voice. "Congressman!" She offered Jack her hand. "We are all *so* relieved to see you at last. We were *so* worried when it got *so* late, and we hadn't heard a *word* from you. I'll let Mr. Moskowitz know you have arrived safely."

Kennedy looked properly abashed as I got to my feet and shook his hand. Just as the Norse Goddess of Hoar Frost swished through one of the twin mahogany doors to the right of her desk, a single door to the left opened. A short, elegant Chinese gentleman stepped through it wearing a navy wool suit. He turned and shook Kennedy's hand. "Congressman, I'm Abe Moskowitz. This is your investigator?"

"I'm Jack Griffin, Mr. Moskowitz. But I—"

He laughed at my puzzled stare. "Most people don't expect a Chinese-American to be named Abraham Moskowitz. What I say to get juries beyond it is that during the siege of Peking in 1900, a Chinese woman gave birth to a son just before she bled to death in a Methodist orphanage. The missionary's daughter wanted to raise me, and she married one of the U.S. Marines who broke the siege, a Russian immigrant named Morris Moskowitz. That's the short version."

Just then, the sun-favored receptionist in the fitted yellow dress returned. "Ah, Mr. Moskowitz, I can see how relieved you are that Congressman Kennedy has finally arrived."

Kennedy unleashed that track-'em-down grin of his. "You're Candy. I know your voice from the telephone. Whoever named you was a master of understatement." I saw a fault line for just a moment in her magnificent hauteur. "Mr. Moskowitz, I feel I owe Candy an enormous apology for being late this morning. I can't imagine less than a lobster dinner tonight at Harvey's ever putting me in her good graces."

She tossed her long, straight hair from around her shoulders as if she were in a major huff, but her smile told the tale. "I'll meet you there at seven. At seven-oh-one, I'll either be sitting with you, or I'll be gone."

Kennedy lifted her knuckles to his lips and gave a credible impression of a prince. "My whole staff will be watching the clock today. It's not a task I perform well on my own."

FOURTEEN

"A detective came to my office yesterday afternoon." Jack Kennedy sat next to me on a couch opposite his attorney's massive walnut desk. "He told me in a hillbilly accent that his name was Snilder and didn't ask me a single question."

"He's a slimy detective sergeant." I glanced over at Abe Moskowitz, and we nodded to each other. "Flunked a civil service test in Arkansas but bought a badge here in the District where the pay sounds worth the bribe." A telephone rang once in the outer office.

"'We got y'all *nailed,* Congressman,' Snilder told me." Kennedy's impression of a Southern accent was sabotaged by the Back Bay flat A, but he stuck with it, looking as if he hadn't slept well. "Snilder said I'd talked Betty Dyson into accepting a ride home in my cab, and witnesses had seen me take her inside. Then he said, 'She refused to screw y'all an' y'all smashed her face. Y'all ripped off her unnerpants, pushed up her dress, an' gave her the old whammy. Then y'all slit her throat with a meat knife from her kitchen to shut her up. But we got witnesses to everything, Congressman.'"

"Everything?" Moskowitz grinning looked nothing like the bewigged and bony lawyers in the eight gold-framed and green-matted Daumier drawings hanging behind him.

Kennedy laughed—a strained, inaudible, fugitive laugh. "That was *my* question. Snilder leaned into my face and said, 'Y'all know what ah mean. Ah got witnesses y'all took her to her apartment building, witnesses y'all went in there with her, witnesses y'all left a half-hour later with a knotted blue necktie in y'all's hand an' y'all's shirttail danglin' out y'all's pants, witnesses y'all took a Yellow Cab to y'all's home in Georgetown. *Witnesses!'* Snilder was bug-eyed at that point."

"Did he ask you for a statement or to take part in a police lineup?"

Kennedy shook his head. "Not at all. He claimed that for half a million dollars, my police file could disappear, and some of the key witnesses could be run out of town. I made the mistake of talking with him alone in my office, so nobody else heard his offer."

"Don't ever do that again." Moskowitz was a commanding presence in a sumptuous office with mahogany paneling and wine-red leather-bound books lettered in old gold. The summer-green carpeting was too deep to pass for the White House lawn.

Kennedy nodded. "I told him I'd have to think about it. 'Just ast y'all's old man,' Snilder said. Then he sauntered out, saying he'd be back tomorrow."

*****

"Well, Jack, as your attorney, one possibility is that you could do what he demands. It's not a very good option because you can't enforce a bribe in court."

I nodded. "Look, what do we know about this case? Kennedy drove Betty home. He raced through sex with her and left as soon as he was done. Somebody else came in and broke her nose, stabbed her, and slit her throat before she could either finish getting undressed or put anything on. Jack, if you didn't kill the Dyson woman—"

"I'm getting reasonably tired of that issue being expressed so tentatively." Kennedy's expression was pained, but his temper, if he had one, stayed under control.

"And I'm sure you didn't beat her up either." The lawyer rolled on as if nothing had been said. "You left her awake, Jack?"

"Yes, she was certainly awake, moaning my name as I pulled her door closed in back of me."

"You locked the apartment? Are you sure?"

"Yes, Abe, I checked it as I went out, just to be certain she'd be all right. Not that it helped."

Moskowitz frowned. "Is there any reason to think—any possibility—there might have been somebody else somewhere in the apartment when you got there?"

"Abe, Betty and I climbed all over each other from the minute she shut the door. We sure as hell didn't search the place. But it's a small apartment—a modest living room, a tiny kitchenette off the living room, a bathroom, a bedroom barely big enough for a double bed and a dresser."

I asked if there were closets. Kennedy nodded. "Bedroom and living room?"

"Yes."

"Maybe somebody had a key to the apartment." The lawyer scratched his nose. "Perhaps a janitor or somebody else. Or she might have dozed off where you left her, and then perhaps somebody came in later and killed her. There seem to be a number of possible theories. That could help solve the crime or at least let me introduce a little doubt into a jury's deliberations, if it should come to that.

Moskowitz opened a cedar box full of Havana cigars and pushed it across the glass-topped desk toward us. We took turns clipping off the ends with a little set of stainless steel scissors, then flaming them up with a big gold-plated Ronson table lighter that was vaguely reminiscent of a crematory urn.

I wanted to get back to the case. "So somebody we can't identify murdered Betty very quickly after Jack left. The killer might or might not have raped her. We can't rule that out. But since the semen the medical examiner found could have been Jack's and Jack's alone, we don't even know for certain that the killer was a man, though the evidence and the amount of force the killer used make that seem very likely." I leaned forward. "Speaking of sperm, the cops should have the blood type identified by now. The medical examiner expected test results by yesterday afternoon. If the killer didn't rape Betty and leave semen of his own, the cops'll use Jack's to clear the real killer, assuming the two are from different blood groups."

You could hear the dejection when Kennedy spoke. "They will be. My blood type is AB, the rarest kind. Perhaps one person in twenty-five has my type. When we lived in London, Dad set up a blood bank to make certain there would be AB blood should I need it."

Moskowitz must have played high-stakes poker because he never flinched. "So based on your semen, the police will look for a suspect with type AB blood. Have they asked you what type yours is yet?"

"No, but I—"

"Listen to me carefully, Jack." Moskowitz stood up and bent toward Kennedy. "I'm not advising that you lie. But I'm not certain that you ever learned your blood type."

"Of course I—"

"I'm not certain, Jack, that you ever learned your blood type. Most people don't know theirs."

"Abe, it was on all our dog tags." Kennedy started sounding peevish. "How stupid would I have to be not to know it?"

The lawyer kept a poker face. "How stupid are you? Your service records aren't public information. I can make a case that forcing you to take a blood test violates the prohibition against unreasonable searches and self-incrimination. Buy us some time. I don't think you ever paid any attention to anything on your dog tags except your name. Understand?"

Kennedy did, but he wasn't sold. "I'd look—"

"You're afraid Moon Snilder will think you're an idiot? Try telling him you've got the same blood type as the medical examiner thinks the murderer has, and see if that impresses the bastard. I know it'll impress a jury."

*****

"The police think it was rape," the lawyer summed up, "because of the obvious evidence of sex and because she was brutalized and murdered. That's my guess. They can't prove it in court."

"Let's not plan my legal defense yet, Abe. I'm sunk if they even charge me, if they even link me to the crime because of the semen. Should I head that off by telling them we had sex by mutual consent, which proves I had no reason to kill her?"

Moskowitz shook his head. "It argues that you had no obvious motive—or that concealing rape wasn't it. But it doesn't prove you didn't kill her. It does add to your liabilities, even if the killer is brought to justice."

I agreed. "There's no way Gentleman Jimmy Howard could keep himself from leaking that admission to the newspapers."

Moskowitz nodded. "And I'm sorry, but it's *not* too soon to plan your legal defense, Jack. The cops are speeding to wrap this case up. Griffin's work is cut out for him."

I asked the two of them what they intended to do about Snilder. Moskowitz stared at me as if I'd offered him a nickel for the cigar. "We'll stall while you crack the case and do it in a hurry. If all this gets into the hands of the press, the outcome will be very unfortunate for young Congressman Kennedy."

FIFTEEN

Driving back to the Chesapeake Apartments to question the building manager who discovered Betty Dyson's body, I tentatively ruled Kennedy out as the killer. There was just no motive I could see. I didn't think he could be that crazy and not have it manifest as some kind of high-strung intensity that just didn't fit the guy. And I liked him. Either Jack got caught in a luckless coincidence, or somebody killed Betty Dyson to set him up for a plunge. Those were the only possibilities I could imagine.

A thought stopped me as I parked my car. Who said the killer was unseen? Jack made an obvious suspect because he took Betty home and left without her, but that didn't mean that nobody else had been spotted there, whether out of place or not. I needed to ask a lot of questions at the Chesapeake.

I showed the building manager my card. "Are you a real private eye? You must want to know something more about Mrs. Dyson's murder. My name's Ted Bradley." He pumped my hand as if I were Alan Ladd or General Eisenhower. Bradley had watery gray eyes behind a pair of rimless glasses, with dry rust-red hair slicked back over the top of his head. In his early twenties, he looked all used up.

"Tell me about finding the body, Mr. Bradley."

You could hear the vestigial Southern accent of most native Washingtonians. "Well, Colonel Dyson called me from Andrews Field sometime late in the afternoon. That was Sunday, day before last, oh, about half past five. He told me he'd just come back from a three-day test exercise, flying in those jet fighter planes you see in the newspapers. He'd tried to reach Mrs. Dyson by phone all afternoon and was a bit worried that something might have happened to her. He asked me would I please be so kind as to go up and check the apartment."

"And that's when you found Mrs. Dyson's body?"

He nodded. "I'll show you their apartment like I showed the police." He raised his lanky body out of his chair, a gray heron getting off its nest to find a fish.

*****

Bradley led me down a corridor with old but intact mauve floral wallpaper, and dark, worn oriental carpeting smelled vaguely of cleaning solvents and noodle soup.

While he fished out his heavy-laden key ring and searched it for the passkey, I looked closely at the door to the Dyson apartment. The maroon enamel hadn't been freshened for a couple of years. It showed the usual scuff marks from impatient shoes, but the area around the knob and the lock was neither scratched nor newly painted. No pry bar, no knife blade had forced an entry. Either the killer used a key, or Betty had opened the door. Unless Kennedy failed to lock it.

"I knocked." Bradley showed me how gently he had tapped. "Nothing happened, so I knocked again." He knocked harder, enough to make your knuckles smart. "I called out, *'Missus Dyson?'* No reply. So I slid the passkey into the lock just like this and cracked the door. A *deadly* stench rushed out at me. Took us all day yesterday with electric fans and six bottles of Air Wick just to tone it down. A lamp was burning. *'M-i-s-s-u-s D-y-s-o-n?'* I still got no reply of any kind, so I went on in. Lord have mercy, what I found!"

He pushed the door open as if he were a Barrymore. I followed him inside and closed it. The living room windows had been propped open. Old blood leaves an odor of rusted wrought iron. July in Washington did nothing to improve on it.

"It doesn't smell so much like a slaughterhouse now." Bradley'd seen ghosts somewhere during the war. His pallor suggested he stayed indoors nowadays whenever he could. Red hair and a dead man's complexion aside, I suspected it wasn't fear of sunburn that kept him interned in the building.

"White gloves were thrown on the living room floor—" He pointed. "I found a black high-heel shoe lying over here and a little white hat with a red veil right beside that end table. Her purse lay wide open on the floor right inside the door, as if she'd dropped it when she was unlocking the apartment and hadn't bothered or had a chance to pick it up. Or as if she'd brought it to the door and something happened."

I nodded. That dovetailed with Kennedy's account. "Did the place look ransacked? Had her purse been gone through?"

"Oh, my, no, not ransacked. The apartment itself was neat, except for what I just told you. Mrs. Dyson always kept a neat apartment. You can see for yourself."

So Bradley had been inside before. That was worth noting.

*****

There was nothing masculine about the décor. Small gilt-framed reproductions of Impressionist paintings, none of them more than twelve inches in either dimension, hung in several groupings on walls of pea soup green. Pink and green Persian rugs softened the dark hardwood floors. Both the sofa and a stiff-looking chair were upholstered in rose chintz. I could imagine her sitting there, smiling softly as she read a book.

"You know, Colonel Dyson asked me to pack up everything in here. He canceled the lease right away."

This was the only look I'd get. Novels by Edith Wharton and Jane Austen stood on a narrow built-in bookshelf with four *Reader's Digest* condensed book collections. It also held a slender navy-and-white Chinese vase and a dozen framed photos. One was a wedding picture of Betty younger, her husband a lieutenant then, wearing a summer white Army uniform with novice pilot's wings and no ribbons. The same picture I'd seen in Dyson's office stood next to it—Dyson posing for the camera in front of his Mustang, smiling in the bright sunlight.

Other little metal or bleached wood frames held pre-war black-and-white shots of the two of them or of people I guessed were relatives. The spacing showed one picture missing, but I noted a hand-tinted portrait photo of Betty in her early twenties, with long, heavy hair and a sunflower smile, looking fresh and rapturous, though the pale tints gave the impression she'd lost a lot of blood. I shuddered.

*****

"You'd been in here before?" I pulled my notepad out.

"Well, yes, once or twice." Bradley's long body stiffened. "I manage the apartment, after all. Mrs. Dyson needed help with something in the kitchenette, a light bulb in the ceiling fixture, as I recall. And, of course, you walk through the halls in this job and sometimes see inside the apartments."

I waved off Bradley's need to explain away his familiarity with Betty's apartment. I could come back to that. "You had started telling me about finding Mrs. Dyson's body."

Bradley stayed as stiff as an oar. "I knew something *terrible* was wrong, between the colonel's concern and the hideous odor. I was careful not to touch anything. As I came in, I took a glance into the kitchenette. That drawer on the left was pulled open. I suppose Sergeant Snilder's detectives closed it Sunday evening when they were here. There was nothing unusual to see in the bathroom. But oh my God, when I came in here...."

He led me into the bedroom. "After the, uh, cops left, Colonel Dyson barked at me, 'Have the goddam mattress burned.' Still perfectly serviceable, you know. We bleached most of the stains out of it. There's lots of people all over Washington who can use a perfectly good Sears Roebuck innerspring mattress. It's just silly to waste a thing like that. I mean, burning the damn mattress won't bring Mrs. Dyson back or anything."

I nodded. "A thing like that must be good for...."

"Five dollars. It was almost new, just a bit stained."

I wanted to punch him in the teeth, as if the stupid mattress should have been kept sacred somewhere as a perpetual shrine to the memory of a pretty girl I'd once joked with.

I peeked in the closet and in the maple dresser drawers, a little surprised Dyson hadn't ordered her clothes burned too or that Bradley hadn't sold them. He doubtless provided the *Post* picture I'd seen. That might have netted *ten* bucks. "Mrs. Dyson's body was lying here on the bed?"

"Yep, right on the middle of the bed. She looked so terrible. Her eyes were wide open, with—" He looked as if he were going to faint. "Well, blood had splashed all over the bed, of course, and on the rug, too. Oh, we cleaned that, too. Big blue-bottle flies buzzed everywhere. I found the knife on the floor right over here." He pointed beside the bed, where a right-handed person on top of Betty Dyson's corpse would have dropped it after stabbing her.

My mind called up Doctor Gregory's photos, with the plaintive black mouths dribbling Betty's life's blood onto the wrinkled sheets, the bright sky eyes glassy and staring up at a man who'd long since gone away.

SIXTEEN

Bradley stepped back into the living room and dropped his bony rear end onto the chintz sofa. Nothing I heard or saw in Betty's bedroom raised any conflicts with what I'd already learned or told me a damned thing new. I dumped myself onto the matching chair and narrowed my eyes. "What'd you do when you saw her body?"

"Oh, Lord in heaven! I thought to myself, 'Christ A'mighty, no, not another one of my ladies!' I leaned against the wall right over here. I felt kind of woozy and came close to throwing up. The only thing that stopped me was I couldn't let myself toss my cookies all over her body or in her room."

Not another one of my ladies? I wrote that down word-for-word in my notepad but didn't break his flow with a question.

"I looked her over from head to toe as if I might have found some teeny tiny spark of life left in her, as if that hideous rotten smell was only some tuna fish salad she'd let go bad in her cupboard and I could help her scrub it up. But I knew what it was. I'd known it in the corridor."

"Uh-huh. And then what did you do?"

Cigarettes stood in a white ceramic cup and a heavy Ronson lighter on the end table to his right. He helped himself to both and gestured for me to take one, too. I shook my head.

"I should have called the police right away, soon as I found her cut up like that, or even when I recognized that terrible odor that could only have been one thing. But, see, I promised Colonel Dyson I'd phone him just as soon as I checked to see if his wife was okay, so that was what I did next. The cops—the police—weren't too happy I didn't call them."

"Did you call Dyson from here or from your office?"

"Here. I'd written down the number on a scrap of paper and stuck it in my shirt pocket when Colonel Dyson called me. It seemed only fair to put a long-distance call like that on his telephone bill instead of the Chesapeake's. I picked up the receiver and dialed 'O.' When the operator answered, I told her 'Long distance, please,' and read her the number. 'Person-to-person call for Colonel Donald Dyson,' I said. The call went through real fast, in a couple of minutes."

I nodded again. "How did Dyson react?"

"The colonel yelled, 'Oh, my God, how horrible!' and then he became silent for, oh, half a minute or so."

I interrupted him with a question. "Did he say anything like, 'Are you sure she's dead?'"

"Nope, but I was bluntly clear. I told him she'd been slashed to death. All he said was, 'Don't let anybody into my apartment. I'll call the police from out here. Just *please* don't let anybody into the apartment.' I thought it was a waste of good money for him to call the cops long distance from out in Maryland, but he insisted. It must have been half an hour before they came. Colonel Dyson got here around seven."

Bradley stubbed out his smoke in a delicate ashtray finished in the crackled transparent glaze that was the rage just then. He lit another in quick order.

After a glance at my notes, I looked up. "How long did you know Mrs. Dyson?"

"Close to two years. I met her downstairs just after I got out of the Army." His fingers tap-danced with an unlit cig.

He had a key, I thought, and a tortured look. He'd gone into her apartment before, knew where things were. "How long did she live here?"

"I looked that up for the police, Mr. Griffin. They took the apartment—Colonel and Mrs. Dyson, I mean—in February of 1942, when he was a captain and hadn't gone overseas yet. Prob'ly none of us had. I understand he got stationed at Fort McNair downtown then." The fidgets were gaining on him.

I leaned across the tiny space and into Bradley's face. "What was your relationship with Mrs. Dyson?" I used my stare to suggest that the Grand Inquisitor was in the hallway with a brazier of hot coals in case I didn't get a good enough answer.

The gaunt man looked me straight in the eye, Martin Luther facing Rome unwavering. "You're going to think this was odd." He paused and started over. "Mr. Griffin, were you in the war?"

I nodded. It was answer enough.

"So was I. Army Air Corps, like Mrs. Dyson's husband. They made me a bombardier and stuck me in the nose of a B-24 Liberator. The Nazis shot down my plane near Leipzig, and I ended up a prisoner of war from the summer of '43 to early '45—March tenth, in fact—which is how I became such a scrawny son-of-a-bitch even now. I still can't put on no weight."

"It must've been tough. I've never thought much about being a P.O.W., except that it just barely beat getting killed."

At this, his gray eyes grew even more watery. "We tried to escape, you know? One night seventy-six of us slipped out a tunnel at Stalag Luft III. Oh, they caught almost everybody. Then they hauled fifty of the guys to a field and machine-gunned them. Can you imagine how it feels to be one of the survivors?"

"A bit." I put a hand on his arm, seeing Jerry DiMarco.

"Anyhow, Mr. Griffin, Mrs. Dyson was the sort of woman I dreamed of coming home to. She was beautiful, for sure, but she was warm, too. The lady had a smile she gave away for free, like she had a warehouse full of smiles somewhere. She treated me nice. I don't mean nothing by that, Mr. Griffin; she was nice to everybody else, too, but she was nice to *me*. A guy can fall sort of in love with a woman like that."

"I understand." Better than he thought, in fact. "What did you do about it?"

"Not a solitary thing. Mrs. Dyson was a perfect lady, the wife of a colonel with more decorations than Carter's has Little Liver Pills, while I'm a skinny young ex-lieutenant out of Officer Candidate School who missed half the war in a Stalag. Except that she noticed everybody, she didn't know a guy like me was alive. If I still am."

Bradley looked dried-out, but his cheeks were wet even so.

"All I did, Mr. Griffin, was I sat down next to Mrs. Dyson's naked body until the police got here. I knew I mustn't touch her skin or—or anything. I locked the door and sat in there with her. Dead bodies can't shock me anymore. No, the hardest part of it for me was not throwing a blanket or my jacket over her or lighting candles or anything."

SEVENTEEN

I checked in with Lana before leaving the Chesapeake after questioning Bradley and a few of the Dysons' neighbors. She told me Vince O'Heaney called, leaving word he'd be taking a coffee break at Moynihan's around three. Fifteen minutes. I zipped down Connecticut Avenue. Midafternoon traffic was pretty light as I hooked right on Fifteenth. I parked in a lot on E Street near Seventh, where a guy I'd saved a fortune in alimony by finding out how his long-legged wife spent her weekday afternoons let me park free. From there, I walked to Moynihan's, trying not to think of Betty Dyson being slashed and fed to the flies.

The cars on Pennsylvania Avenue glittered like fish in the afternoon sun. A sheen of sweat turned my shirt into adhesive tape. Ahead of me, a lady with short black hair and Ginger Rogers legs sashayed easily in a faded dress that ended nearer her knees than most post-war ones. It was silky, probably rayon, with a pattern of small purple flowers on a lavender background. The hot hands of a slight, humid breeze molded the filmy fabric to her thighs.

*****

The dead man was still tending bar when I walked back into Moynihan's, my sweaty shirt crawling across my skin. "Coca-Cola, lots of ice." I sounded like a frog. The guy who'd been warming a booth a day earlier wearing a cheap plaid sport jacket and a gray straw fedora was back in the same booth—same hat, seersucker suit, a tomato soup tie hanging dispiritedly from his unbuttoned collar. The woman he was finagling today wore her mouse-brown hair in a bun on the back of her head.

Vince O'Heaney sipped his dark "ginger ale" at another booth, nodding when I glanced his way. After plunking down my nickel for the Coke, I carried it over.

"Superintendent James E. Howard himself stuck me on what he calls 'special assignment.'" O'Heaney spoke without preliminaries, scorn corroding his voice. "I'm s'posed tuh be in charge of rooting out all those missing crime statistics the *Washin'ton Post* caught him burying last week. It shouldn't take me more than a month or two, Gentleman Jimmy tells me through that crocodile grin of his. The three hunnert percent rise in robberies and homicides the *Post* noticed isn't a crime wave or anything like one, oh no, no, it's just that the crime *reporting* system he instituted is so-o-o-o much more accurate than the old way. What this project needs, he tells me, is a'top-flight' man. Oh, he says tuh me, 'and don't worry about the damned Dyson murder case, Vincent, because we've got it all but wrapped up.' Them was his exac' words, *'all but wrapped up.'*"

His face was corned beef.

"You know, Junior, he'd already had the *Detective* Superintendent, Francis L. Blaine, my fashion-plate boss with the Princeton education, chew my ass for talkin' tuh a goddam private eye. 'The Metropolitan Police will solve this case, O'Heaney,' Blaine snorts, 'Not some damn peeper.' But Blaine looked as surprised as me about my new assignment. Uh, my new *temporary* assignment."

I apologized to Vince for getting him in Dutch and admitted I could probably have been a bit more straightforward with him the day before. He mentioned, in a voice that woke a snoring rummy in a back booth, that I was correct—I *sure as hell* coulda been more straightforward with him. "But I don't like having anybody tell me who the hell I can talk tuh about a homicide. And nobody ever jerked me off a case before, Junior. Now it's all Snilder's."

I swigged another sip of Coke. "Did you guys ever check out Colonel Dyson's story? The phone calls, the part about staying on post all weekend?"

O'Heaney snorted, and then he snorted again in case I'd missed it the first time. "And did I put my pants on this morning, while we're at it? Yeah, we checked his story. But the phone company can't tell yuh about calls that didn't go through, so based on phone records, I don't know how many times he tried tuh call her, but she never answered. The call he claimed went through, when he reached that odd duck Bradley—that actually happened, and so did Bradley's call back tuh him at his office from their apartment. We already knew Dyson called us from his office."

"What about where he was all weekend?"

"Well, he didn't sign out, and witnesses saw him there various times throughout the weekend." A fat black fly Vince waved at reconsidered landing on his ear.

"Friday night one of those times?"

Vince tossed me a dirty look. "You trying to slide this thing off on the husband? That's pretty low, after what he's been through, and I can't see it working worth a damn. Christ."

"And the answer is—?"

He showed me the smile I'd seen him reserve for idiot colonels. "Well, so far, nobody spotted him Friday night. He'd been doing test flights of some kind all day—they won't tell us anything about that—and he says he went tuh bed around six. The MPs—I hear they're gonna start calling them the *Air* Police—noticed his car during the night parked in his slot. He ate breakfast early the next morning, around six-thirty. If you and that fancy lawyer wanna confuse a jury with some other fall guy, my advice would be the Fuller Brush Man makes a more likely suspect than the war hero husband."

He finished what he was drinking and signaled for another. Then he stormed toward the john, turning back to shoot me a glance. "Besides, Junior, Dyson's the wrong blood type."

EIGHTEEN

"Your colleague Sergeant Snilder stopped by my apartment building to chat with me late last night," I told O'Heaney when he sat down again. My tactician's brain wanted to avoid the blood type issue 'til I'd talked about bribery. "Odd coincidence, he wants me off the case, too. Now, whose message was that?"

O'Heaney looked startled. "I'll bet Moon got snotty, didn't he? Thinks he's cagey as a fox. Not my message, yuh know that, Junior. And not Frank Blaine's, either, I wouldn't think. He knows what a poor excuse for a detective sergeant that jerk Snilder is. I wouldn't even think the smooth, urbane, butter-wouldn't-melt-in-his-butt Gentleman Jimmy Howard would use a crook like Snilder. Moon's too crafty for either of my bosses tuh trust him."

"But there he was anyhow." My soda straw snickered, and I told the stick man behind the bar I could use another Coke.

"Prob'ly his own idea, now that it's his case. I've been waiting since before the war, Junior, tuh get the goods on Snilder. He's on the wrong side of the bars, and I saw that when he crawled outa Dirt Creek to make some money as a cop. I can't prove it, but I'm sure he deliberately screwed up the Edna Hamilton murder investigation last fall."

I paid for my Coke. "Was that the developer's wife? Shot twice in the face at home?"

O'Heaney nodded. "No sign of a break-in. Her loving husband Rodney, who was so distraught over his rich wife's passing, provided an alibi. He told us 'confidentially' that he played strip poker with his secretary in her apartment until three in the morning—a top-heavy bleach blonde named Stella Gorney. Snilder's squad found the guy's pistol in his garage under a rag on the tool bench, a snub-nosed .32 revolver."

I sipped my Coke. "Nice police work. That must have wrapped it up." I knew it hadn't.

"We interrogated the husband at headquarters. He had some holes in his story, but he stuck with it. Snilder questioned the girlfriend at the guy's office. When he arrived back downtown, Snilder wore a smudge on his fly that looked like cherry lipstick, and somebody lost the goddam pistol before we could run the ballistics check."

I nodded.

"Then the word filtered down from on high that we shouldn't be 'abusive' tuh the poor widower. The builder went free. Married the Gorney bimbo a month afterward. Two weeks later, Snilder bought a new car with money he claimed he won playing stud poker. I wrote him up for gambling, but the Department tossed it out, said it would 'reflect badly on all of us.' I'd sure like tuh nail that bastard, Junior."

"Maybe I can help."

I kept my voice low. "Snilder offered to sell Kennedy the complete Dyson murder case files and scare the key witnesses out of town for a paltry half-million bucks in twenty-dollar bills. He's not too bad at arithmetic, you know, Vince—told Kennedy that'd be two hundred and fifty bank-banded stacks of twenties, which he wants in a new Samsonite suitcase, no less."

O'Heaney spit his drink against the wall and jumped to his feet. "*Police* files? The sonovabitch! That's the bottom of the barrel, Junior, even for that chiseler. Cops start selling police files, we might as well just invite Al Capone and Lucky Luciano tuh police our streets. Let me tell you something, Junior."

He paused and seemed to realize he'd lost his last sip of whatever he'd been drinking that smelled so much like Irish whiskey. He yelled "Hey" at Jolly Roger. Another glass of tea-colored ginger ale materialized on top of the bar. O'Heaney walked over and grabbed it, took a gulp, and sat down as if he were punishing the wooden seat.

"The goddam Dyson murder case isn't finished yet, but Howard's right, the only thing it still needs is ribbons and bows. Your man Kennedy killed her, pal. He raped that war hero's beautiful young wife and then smashed her face and slashed her up."

"So you think even Snilder could solve the crime at this point. What was that cryptic remark on the way to the men's room about Dyson's blood type?"

His split-lipped grin told me Vince had counted on my running another lap around that track. "This'll save yuh a whole lotta work, Junior, not sniffing hydrants the wrong pooch has peed on. Doc Gregory told yuh—as I happen tuh know from questioning him about your chat—he told yuh we'd get the killer's blood group from the 'little tadpoles' Doc took outa the corpse. Seems the bastard who killed Mrs. Dyson had a very rare blood type. *Very* rare."

The part of me that wished I'd become a trial lawyer had to open my yap. "That's assuming the semen came from the murderer."

O'Heaney's eyes narrowed to machinegun slits. "What the hell are yuh trying to say, Junior—the woman was a goddam truck stop? Last Friday was Over Easy Night at the Chesapeake? Or should I think some necrophile ghoul found the body first?"

"Don't yell at me, Vince. We go back too far. You're mad at Howard and Snilder, but I'm handy." I finished my Coke.

His face softened. "Yeh, I am mad. Howard's got a devious reason for taking me off the case, and goddam Snilder'd let it all happen unpunished, the stinkin' bastard. For a suitcase full of cash, that chiseler'd let a cock-eyed fancy-pants murderer get off as free as a blue jay and allow a crime like that go totally unpunished. He'd do that tuh a man who shot down—I dunno, what—twenty-some Kraut planes in combat? Any witnesses?"

"What do you mean?"

I was glad he didn't have my ear in his teeth. "Junior, were there any goddam witnesses tuh Snilder's goddam offer?"

I shook my head.

"Find some. My job now is putting the Department's crime stats in order, if yuh see what I'm tellin' yuh. Get some witnesses when Snilder slinks back tuh see your boy. Young Kennedy is gonna pay off."

"I don't think so, Vince." I wasn't dead sure.

"If yuh think your pal Kennedy is gonna pay him off, remember about what happened tuh that fighter pilot's pretty wife yuh liked, and how much yuh hate crooked cops like Snilder. Then consider about maybe you being the witness."

"Against my own client?"

His eyes bulged. "No, against that bastard detective. Paying the bribe won't prove your client killed her, but yuh can't be party tuh it and keep your license, Junior."

"I thought you were off the case." Where he was jamming me

wouldn't do my reputation as a private detective any good.

"I *am* off the goddam case." He flashed his crowbar grin. "But this, um, *crime statistic* can't get covered up. Don't call me at headquarters, Junior, cuz they don't want me there." He scribbled some digits on a paper napkin. "Blaine ordered me tuh work on this crap assignment at home."

NINETEEN

My loathing for funerals started with seeing my mother laid out in a box when I was a kindergartener. People spouted a lot of somber words about her going someplace better, but all I knew was she'd left me behind again, like three years earlier when she went into the hospital with polio. The only plus in Betty Dyson's memorial service was there was no waxy-looking corpse floating like Ophelia inside a velvet-cushioned coffin.

In all honesty, I hadn't gone to pay my respects or to comfort her mackerel husband. I wanted to see how he behaved, find out who else came, maybe learn something useful.

They held the service at the New York Avenue Presbyterian Church, a wedge-shaped brown brick structure with a white New England steeple. A plaque on the outside wall said Lincoln had gone there as president. It looked like a downtown brick building posing as a white New England church.

There was no money in getting there early and having a row with Dyson. I parked on H Street and watched folks arrive from the shade of a tree opposite my car. The widower came first, alone in a shiny new postwar Lincoln convertible, glancing around as he closed its door. Skinny guys showed off the khaki Class A summer uniform at its best, and his four rows of ribbons and the bullion "scrambled eggs" on his cap brim glittered in the afternoon sun. Even so, he walked from the curb to the church surreptitiously, as if cops, snipers, or perhaps Messerschmitts might be hiding anywhere.

A Diamond Cab pulled up next. The string-bean of a woman who sat up front strode inside while a broad-shouldered blond guy of about thirty held the door for a matronly figure. All three wore black. I guessed they were the mother and brother from Cedar Falls the obituary mentioned. Others trickled in—uniformed men mostly with wives, a few white-gloved women wearing black, a couple of guys in dark suits. Two men with rumpled sport coats bounced out of a Chevy, one lugging a big flash camera.

I glanced at my watch and headed for the double doors. Just as I reached them, a gleaming black Packard rolled up, driven by a young Army tech sergeant with an Air Corps patch guarding his sleeve. A major sprang from beside him to open the door for a tall, solidly-made middle-aged civilian with slicked-back reddish hair. A square-jawed three-star general hopped out the far side.

I held a door so I could watch the parade march past me, minus the tech sergeant who was already reading a paperback book in the sedan. The kingpin in a black worsted suit spoke in a low tone as they floated through the door—so low all I heard was "important for the image of the new Air Force." The skinny major and the brawny general clung to his cocoon of space, attentive as any prince's valet.

People were still milling around inside, some in line to give a few words of comfort to Dyson and the family. I didn't join them. What would I have said to Betty's mother and brother—"I'm so sorry. I wanted to sleep with her, you know."

"It was such a shame," a bulldog voice by my left shoulder murmured. A short, wiry colonel with command wings and a Silver Star was speaking through a brown mustache to two women, one a respectable-looking auburn-haired matron attached to his left arm by a white-gloved hand, the other the bean-pole woman from the taxi. The colonel's voice sounded at once sad and furious, trying to rein in his rage for decorum's sake. "I hope to God the police catch the bastard soon."

"We're all working as hard as we can on that," I told him, turning to insinuate myself into their conversation and willing for them to assume I was a cop. "I had the good fortune to meet Mrs. Dyson at an Army-Navy Club function recently. She seemed very nice." I figured the military connection would lend me a cachet with them that a mere flatfoot wouldn't receive.

The string bean smiled. "Nice doesn't even begin to tell Betty's story, Detective—"

"Jack Griffin, ma'am.

I'd stuck my Purple Heart pin in my lapel, and the colonel eyed it. He offered a hand. "Fred Walworth, Griffin. My wife Anne and our friend Martha Broward. Martha worked with Betty at the War Department 'til about the time we all came home. I met Betty there, at Air Corps headquarters. Air *Force,* assuming Congress passes the Unification Bill before they toddle off for recess."

We all touched hands and made small talk. Walworth had tough eyes. His wife was a dimpled dumpling with a good dye job. The Broward woman sported a nose like a harpoon and a voice with some Texas in it. Walworth said Martha Broward had been Betty's closest friend, and she nodded. Then the minister asked us all to take seats. As we did, Walworth agreed to meet me for a drink the next evening.

Once we'd heard a prayer and a scripture reading, and after we'd sung "Nearer My God to Thee," the minister pitched in a few sentences of his own on resurrection and heaven. The guy clearly never met Betty—he kept referring to "Elizabeth Dyson"—and was so obviously going through the motions so that only his unctuousness kept it from being a Punch and Judy show. Then he burbled that the Assistant Secretary of War, the honorable Stuart Symington, had asked to present the eulogy. The kingpin in the black suit who wore officers for earmuffs commandeered the pulpit, his voice a pipe organ.

"My friends, for the past year or so, I've had the privilege to know Betty Dyson. She was both the devoted wife of one of our Air Force's finest war heroes and the linchpin of my own office. Indeed, because Mrs. Dyson was so devoted to her husband Don, she went to work in 1942 as a civilian employee of the Air Force, committed to support the man she loved and those who flew with him in defense of this Nation and its freedoms. You know, when I think—"

That was the last we heard of Betty Dyson, other than about her generalized dedication to America's finest fliers and the gumption she and everybody else in the Air Force—the Air *Corps* was history to him already—displayed daily in meeting the daunting demands and crap like that. The bereft Colonel Dyson got two more plugs, one for exemplifying the "can-do courage" of the bravest of the brave and the other as the epitome of selfless whatever. By my watch, Symington spent twelve minutes lobbying Air Corps officers and Betty's friends for adoption of the Unification Bill, for which he seemed to think Betty had sacrificed her life. The relief when he finished was as palpable as a hamburger sandwich.

The careerists lined up to pump Symington's hand, and Walworth confided they expected he'd be "upgraded" to Secretary of the Air Force in a few weeks. What had Betty said Friday night about learning "something disgusting and despicable about a very important man" she worked for?

I grabbed a place in the queue for glad-handing, making sure my lapel pin showed. Symington noticed it and smiled. "Did you fly for us in the war?"

"Only one direction. I was a paratroop officer."

He chuckled. My guess was he hadn't reached fifty yet. "Good for you. Nice to meet you."

I stood still longer than his aide expected. "Mr. Symington, I'm working on the murder investigation. We're pretty certain Betty knew the killer beforehand. Could I come to your office and ask you a few questions to help us solve this thing?"

It took him aback, but he seemed willing enough. "Have Major Flanders here set up something. You'll merit our heartfelt cooperation."

Symington had other paws to pump while the thick-browed major whipped out a black-bound notebook. "Tomorrow's out of the question. Call me in the afternoon, and I'll set up a short interview." I got directions and his Pentagon phone number in exchange for mine.

The Broward woman was complaining discreetly to an attractive redhead. "It was self-serving twaddle, Susan; there's simply no other name for it. Inexcusable!" She had steel in her voice. The redhead swiveled off toward a tall major. "Mr. Griffin, if you're trying to solve Betty's murder, I'll be more than glad to help you. Just tell me how I can."

"I'd like to talk to you, Mrs. Broward. Right now, I need a better understanding of Mrs. Dyson's life, and you were a close friend. Could you spare me some time?"

"It cannot be tonight. This was a hideous day."

"You've been through an ordeal, Mrs. Broward. Would sometime tomorrow be good?"

"Well—" She paused. The lady sounded beat to death. "If you'll give me your calling card, I could meet you tomorrow at about four o'clock. I'll phone you. Would that do?"

TWENTY

Kennedy had called a woman named Susan Prebble as a friend I might talk to. She wasn't difficult to pick out of the crowd. Three or four redheads primped beneath the glittering chandeliers of the Mayflower Hotel lobby, but she was the one I'd seen listening to Martha Broward rant at the church. "Mrs. Prebble?"

Her smile was ironic. "Jack Kennedy *told* me you were a nice-looking man. Isn't he just a living doll?"

I was the wrong guy to ask. "I appreciate your seeing me, Mrs. Prebble. I believe I saw you at Betty Dyson's service."

"Wasn't that the most egregious eulogy ever delivered?"

I sat down on the chair facing hers. She shook my hand in a ladylike way and gestured with elegant fingers toward what was left of a Manhattan, as if to ask me what I wanted to drink. "Nothing right now, thanks."

"I'd do just anything for Jack, Mr. Griffin, anything at all. I'm sure he knows that." The Prebble woman turned her head a little bit to the right side, keeping her pale-green eyes on me as she did—that oldest, oldest trick of women. She was still wearing black and glowed in it, pastel freckles showing through her faint sunburn, as if she'd been dusted with cinnamon.

"When I called Jack to ask if he were all right—" She paused. "I mean, I saw him leave the dinner with Betty on Friday night, and then, of course, she was found so brutally murdered. Betty, Martha Broward, and I became fast friends throughout the long, dreary war years. Well, Jack asked if I would mind helping you piece together some things you apparently want to know about her. I told him I'd be happy to answer your questions. This was even before I asked what you looked like, and he said, 'Susan, you'll think he's nice-looking.'"

What made her act work was the faint smile beneath her perfect makeup, her lips held just slightly apart. I decided first-rate finishing schools were a better investment than I'd supposed.

Meanwhile, she looked at me as though I might not be entirely beneath her notice—if she didn't have anything better planned on a given evening. "And then you called this afternoon, as Jack said you would, and you sounded so pleasant I simply had to agree to meet you here. How can I help you, Jack? Do you mind if I call you Jack?"

"Not in the least."

The feline smile returned. "Then you must call me Susan."

I promised I would.

"Let me be blunt, Susan." I leaned toward her.

"I *adore* blunt men. Or is that terribly naughty of me to say?" She smirked and leaned toward me.

I wasn't ready for games yet. "Why did Betty Dyson leave the club with Jack Kennedy?"

Now she permitted herself to snicker, as if she'd tried not to but failed. "Perhaps it is lost on a man, but, as a matter of fact, Jack Kennedy has a *great* deal of charm." She took a gold cigarette case out of her purse and offered it to me. I opened it and let her take one out, then snapped it closed before lighting her cigarette with a lighter that stood on the table. She took a deep drag and exhaled in my direction.

Washington in July. Susan Prebble wore a sheen of moisture that did her looks no harm.

"No, Susan, Jack's charm isn't lost on me. I suppose either a man or a woman could notice that. He's a very likable guy. But the newspapers are full of Betty's war hero husband and the romance of their marriage. Why did she leave Friday evening with *any* man? Did she sleep around?"

Putting a long, white-gloved forefinger playfully against my lapel and pressing it just barely hard enough to dent a freshly-baked jelly doughnut, the Prebble woman finally smiled as if something had actually amused her. "*Surely* you have heard, Jack, that there's been quite a lot of that sort of thing since the war with Hitler and the Japanese began."

"Sleeping around or having a husband in the armed forces?"

"There's not a thing to make the one exclusive from the other." Her face chilled a bit. "It *was* a rather long war."

"I remember." I sounded to myself like a Puritan divine.

She sucked on her cigarette as if she were mad at it and shot the smoke back out through her fire-engine lips.

"*Just* so you understand, Jack, my own late husband Randolph was a Navy flier on an aircraft carrier for two and a half years in the Pacific. He won the Navy Cross in the battle of Midway, and the Japs finally shot him down over Leyte Gulf."

"I'm very sorry. I didn't mean—"

"And also, *just* so you know, it was sometimes very hard for the wives of the men in the war to—Some long, dark, terrifying nights, you think there's no chance the man you love will come home. You get desperately lonely and simply want to have a good time with a man. You get so unreasonably *angry* because they're not where they're supposed to be, lying in bed to snuggle up against in the darkness. Men don't believe women really like sex, you know, but some of us do. And it's wartime, and the boys just want a small favor that you cannot begrudge the poor things before they go off to face death so bravely. Or they simply know how marvelous they look in a well-tailored uniform festooned with emblems of silver and strips of brightly-colored ribbon, or perhaps they.... Am I boring you by talking about women's feelings?" A little arch smile perched on her lips.

"No, Susan, actually you're not. One of the reasons I became a private detective is I like listening to people. And watch them when they're as easy to look at as you are." Her smile softened. "I apologize if I was judgmental. I've been one of those men in need of comfort and passion, and I have no beef with women for wartime caring and generosity. Actually, I've maintained that attitude in peacetime, too."

Now she grinned as if she were purring. "Thank you."

"Do you mind if I ask a couple more questions about Betty?"

Susan flushed a little, as if she'd caught herself being emotional. She shook her head, carrot-colored hair swirling like a dime-store hula skirt just above her shoulders.

"I knew Betty all through the war, Jack. We were very dear friends until she died. She and Martha Broward and I all worked at the Department of War. We went through everything together—the loneliness, the terror of waiting, the ridiculous surveillance, the horrid news. She was wonderful when Randolph was killed."

"You knew her very well, then."

She nodded. "Betty Dyson may have been the most wholesome, the most thoroughly Methodist girl I've met since I left

New Haven for college. I doubt she would *ever* have cheated on Don. She was completely in love with him back then."

"You just said 'back then,' Betty wouldn't have cheated. Had that changed recently? What was your impression when Betty and Jack left the club together?"

She giggled, putting her hand on my sleeve. "I didn't doubt at all she and Jack were going to go to bed together just as soon as possible, which seemed completely unlike her. Betty had the knack of thoroughly enjoying a man's company with her clothes on, though I'd heard men call her a tease. Certainly, she was an accomplished flirt. But I sat two tables away from the door. You could see it in the way their eyes crinkled as they looked at each other, the conspiracy in their bodies as they ducked out before that terribly dull lecture on patriotism. I almost got up to stop her."

"Why would you have done that?" By this time, I wondered what Susan Prebble's apartment might look like. I had no doubt it would be a masterpiece of feminine décor like the Dyson apartment, but that wasn't why I thought about it.

"You may think I was jealous. The truth is that I liked Betty, and I wanted to spare her a disappointing experience." She blushed—it wasn't just sunburn. "A girl sees a man who has all Jack Kennedy's Irish charm and good looks—even if she has no idea he's the principal heir to a fortune King Midas could never even have *dreamed* of—and she thinks what a wonderful lover a man like that would be."

It seemed like a good time to keep my mouth shut.

"But I knew Jack—well, I suppose you've probably pieced it together that Jack and I were lovers briefly in college. He took me home for a few weekends. I knew his mother and his, ah, his father. I knew most of his six thousand brothers and sisters. For two or three months, I was actually in love with him. Most of the time, we simply had fun together, sex together, dinner together, danced and saw movies, that sort of thing. If you want to understand what happened to Betty Dyson, you must let me tell you a couple of things about Jack."

"By all means." *Where in the world,* I wondered, *is this going?*

TWENTY-ONE

The Prebble woman leaned forward, but whether it was to lure my eyes to the dark divide between her sun-pinked breasts or to let her speak softly wasn't clear and made, perhaps, a distinction without a difference. "Jack grew up the second son of a hard-driving wealthy man. Once we got into the war, Old Joe pulled a lot of strings to get Jack a snug desk job in Naval Intelligence."

"I'd gathered the father was influential, Susan. But I thought—"

"The thing is, Jack wanted to prove himself. He pulled strings of his own to get sent to war in a frail little PT boat. That's unusual. And he showed daring and initiative getting his men back to safety after it sank. He's quite a guy."

"I appreciate that." You can get tired of pretty women admiring another man. "So you think a lot of him."

She looked at me with an unapologetic gaze. "Even more than most men, Jack needs desperately to be loved. When he sees a pretty girl, he simply *has* to have her. It's not just that he wants to; it's *urgent* with Jack. But going to bed with her is all there is to it. He's a sport fisherman. A girl submits pretty willingly because he's so cute and so puppy-dog eager. It can be very flattering to have such a gorgeous man dying to go to bed with you."

I was hearing a lot more than I wanted to about another man's sexual habits. Still, I wasn't certain he hadn't killed Betty, so I paid close attention.

"But, Christ, is Jack a lousy lover!" She almost grinned as she spoke. "It's all for the prince, nothing for Cinderella but the honor of being the babe on the bottom. No grace, no caring, no more pleasant chatter. Once a girl gives in, he's all speed and self-gratification. And then he flits away, off into the night lickety-split, while the girl is still thinking about ways she might like to be touched. I'm not suggesting any meanness on his part. Not at all. It's just—Jack has a terrifying hole in his soul."

I felt a bit awkward. "But from what you're telling me, in spite of all that, you've been back to him a few times." I found myself looking into her honest green eyes.

"You simply cannot fathom his charm." She took another long draw on her cigarette and let it out slowly. "It's hard for a girl not to imagine she might slow him down, might make him stay, might win his boyish heart. Because there *is* a young boy's innocent heart in that slender, gorgeous, self-conscious man. I know; I've seen glimpses of it. He can care, he can be wonderful. He's bright, and he's really fun to be with. And he isn't mean. There's no intention to be cruel in all his self-centeredness. Jack is really a centaur, you know—half stallion, racing to topple all the women he can before he dies."

"You say that as if death is part of the equation."

"I believe so. He's had a number of health scares, and the war that killed his brother came within a few feet of killing Jack, too. I'm no psychologist, mind you, but I believe that proving he's still alive is part of his need for women."

I wondered something else—whether to consider the possibility that I didn't understand Kennedy's personality quirks well enough, whether an obsession with dying young could lead to a terrible way of trying to control death that merely surviving the war hadn't satisfied.

*****

I looked her up and down as she stubbed her cigarette out in the ashtray, enjoying the view. Susan Prebble was a very good-looking woman, albeit an expensive one. Neither her dress nor her perfume came from a department store.

"You don't like Jack Kennedy very much anymore from what you tell me, Susan."

"On the contrary." She made one of those unconscious gestures some women make, spreading the fingertips on both white-gloved hands to encircle her breasts, as if to conceal them. "Why shouldn't a woman who has known the man, let us say *extremely* well, still harbor the notion that civilizing Huck Finn could be a possibility?"

"Huckleberry Finn?"

"Look, there's a lot of boy still left in the man. Jack Kennedy's face and fortune allow him to bed as many attractive women as he pleases. Besides, almost as a bonus, he's a congressman who wants to be more than that. Now that his older brother is dead, Jack's the crown prince. Someday he'll settle down a bit. Not completely, I shouldn't think, but a bit. He'll decide his country still needs him, more than it did in the war. He may even find out how to love a woman. It could be a marvelous thing to be that woman."

She hoped Jack Kennedy would settle down to Porterhouse steak and au gratin potatoes when I happened to know he was at one of the best restaurants in town savoring a lobster for dinner and Candy for dessert. I was just getting ready to interrupt her fantasies with some more questions about Betty Dyson because I still didn't feel I knew enough about the murdered woman and what was going on in her personal life at the time of her death. But Susan shifted her green gaze over my shoulder, wearing a sophisticate's Novocain smile.

"Roger, how very charming that you're here. Do you know Mr.—ah—Griffith? He's a friend of Jack Kennedy's."

I turned and faced a Marine lieutenant colonel with three impressive rows of good conduct and attendance ribbons and not a blessed thing to indicate that he'd heard any shots fired outside a movie theater. I grabbed his outstretched mitt as if I were squeezing orange juice. "Jack *Griffin.*" I flashed him my best what-does-she-see-in-you-pal grin.

"Roger Bramford. Susan, I have a driver out in front." He gestured past the gilded elevators and fawn-colored marble.

"Of course, Roger." She stood up. "Oh, just in case either of us should happen to think of anything else, Mr. Griffin, do you have a calling card? I believe you already have *my* telephone number." She gave me a prim little smile and a glint of green eyes as she took my card. "You know, a girl could grow old waiting for Jack Kennedy to grow up."

TWENTY-TWO

The last weak traces of daylight hung above the streetlamps in the moist July stillness. It seemed too early and far too clammy to go back to my airless apartment and make dinner-for-one.

Much of the time, I lived alone and liked it. Quiet was a restful thing at the end of the day. But that night, I didn't want to lose myself rereading a Civil War memoir or listening to jazz records, or sitting between empty seats in a movie. I didn't want to spend the night alone with Betty Dyson's ghosts.

"Ghosts" because more than one of her haunted me. There'd been the laughing war widow Kennedy won in a charm-wrestling match because all he wanted was to get laid, while I was holding back because she'd started meaning something to me. Maybe that Betty wasn't as different as I'd thought from the Army wife picking up guys in a hotel ballroom with her wedding ring hidden away. Somewhere in the mix was a competent professional woman in a key Pentagon position. All of them were lousy company because they were dead.

I might have had some fun with Susan Prebble if she hadn't had a date—she was clearly a coming attraction, and I'd enjoyed the preview. Might have been a good night for a ballgame with the weather a touch cooler, but I couldn't remember whether the Senators were in town or away, and being lonely in a crowd stinks. Still, I tended to be lucky with women, even if I wasn't lucky with love. I drove over to the Jazz Club.

I almost didn't recognize Colonel Dyson in civvies—a tan suit and a low-brimmed fedora—as he burst out the front door by himself. Why'd he change out of his uniform after the memorial service? He nearly wrenched his neck trying to avoid my eyes. I planted my feet astride his path. "Not upbeat enough for you two hours after your wife's funeral, Dyson, or have all the stray barflies found other takers?"

Dyson flashed me a look like I'd vomited on his spit shine. "I don't have to account to you. Get out of my goddam way, or I'll—" It seemed to occur to him that short, trim men ought not to threaten tall, beefy guys. He tugged down the brim of his fedora as he turned his head and followed his nose away from me.

I let him go. I wasn't spoiling for either a fight or an exchange of insults. There was nothing I liked about the guy, but if he wasn't the killer, then he was the poor bastard whose wife cheated on him before she was murdered. Following him crossed my mind, but he'd see me go for my car, and all I'd get would be a long night drive to Andrews Field and back.

*****

Inside the Jazz Club, Nancy Collington in a snug scarlet gown belted out "God Bless the Child"—a gutsy undertaking in a room Billie Holliday'd played—when I reached my table. Her velvet pipes were lifting the joint off the floor by its linoleum. I'd never heard another singer combine the cloudy sweetness of a muted trumpet with the strong, straight-at-you volume of a street vendor, all in the pecan-pie accent of Deep Dixie.

Three tunes later—a Sarah, an Ella, and a third I'd never heard—she took a break. The Tuesday crowd barely matched half what Friday pulled in, so she swerved over to my table in short order. "Honey, y'all came here the othah naht, too. Did ah bring y'all back?" Fire-red lips framed a smile you could have lit Griffith Stadium with if you wanted to watch the Senators blow another game.

I raised my glass. "A magnificent woman with a stunning voice attracts attention. My name's Jack Griffin."

She gave me an appreciative grin. "This is mah first time at the Jay-uzz Club. Deatsville, Alabama's mah home, honey, but why would a pretty girl who can read and write want to stay *theah?* Ah'm singin' at the Cotton Club in Harlem this weekend."

"Don't turn your back on Washington, Miss Collington, though I'm sure your back's as gorgeous as the rest of you."

That was when Nancy turned on the full magnitude of her smile. "Well, Jack Griffin, if you aren't as sweet as candied yams! Ah hope y'all kin stay 'til Ah git off t'naht, maybe in an hour."

My turn to grin. "And all I have to do is listen to you sing like a velvet siren? Nancy, just watching you *inhale* is stimulating."

She loosed a kitten's laugh as she swatted my arm. "Ah kin see yore a terribly wicked man, sugah. Sho'ly it'd be right Christian of me to spend some time tryin' to raise yore spirits. Stick around, baby. Now ah've got to circulate."

*****

While Nancy finished her break, I thought I'd say hello to Skip Nichols. His office sported a secretary with a figure much like Nancy's, though her skin was creamy white rather than mocha tan, and her straight black hair was cut severely short like a sable swim cap.

"Mr. Nichols went out into the club, mister—perhaps upstairs if you haven't seen him." She smiled and batted the long lashes over her olive-flecked eyes. "I'm Millie Kelly, his personal assistant. Can I do something for you?"

Groucho Marx would've raised his eyebrows and asked what she had in mind. In fact, I wondered myself. "I just wanted to say hi. Skip and I had a pleasant conversation the other night."

"Yes, we did." The pink-faced owner breezed over and shook my hand. "*Jack,* isn't it?"

I nodded. "I came to enjoy your featured singer. Just thought I'd say hello."

Nichols grinned up at me. "Well, I'm glad you did. Any further notions on coming to work for me?"

"No, nothing's changed." I thought about the mess the agency was in. Maybe if it folded, I'd ask what he had in mind.

He slicked back his hair with fidgety fingers. "That's fine. Well, thanks for dropping by. If you'll excuse me, I have a couple of important calls to make."

*****

"Why—yore apartment's right *cute,* Jack Griffin!" Nobody'd called it "cute" before. Nancy was admiring a pen sketch of a can-can dancer rather than the blue cotton curtains my sister Jill had sent me when I moved in. With Washington's housing shortage, landing a two-room place was a lucky break I owed to the landlord picking Aadlund and Griffin out of the phone book and being grateful I'd dispelled his suspicions about his sultry wife's afternoon mah-jongg games.

Washington in July. My apartment smelled like a locker room 'til I got a light on and the windows wide open. Still, a fine sheen of sweat only made Nancy glow. I stood the bag we'd picked up in Chinatown on my modest table before she could call it adorable. Carry-out food at my place provided a simple solution to a town where I couldn't share dinner in public with a mocha-toned woman. "If I'd known earlier I'd have company, there'd be more in the refridge than three eggs and some questionable milk. I could've made you something nice."

She waltzed over and laid her palms on my lapels, shrugging off her shoulder straps. "Then y'all'll jist hafta find somethin' *else* to please me with." Being lucky with women wasn't a bad thing.

Her hands slid up to my shoulders as I wrapped my arms around her, the warm heft of her breasts already performing tricks on me. Those flame-red lips tasted tangy, even after she'd transferred most of her lipstick to my face and neck. Her zipper whispered, and so did her red gown as it fell to the floor.

Having big hands meant mine glided over more of her warm, moist skin than otherwise. She moaned softly as my palms found the peaks of her breasts, the tautness of her belly and the golden curve of her hip, the smooth firmness of her thighs, and the midnight grove between them. All the while, I embroidered little kisses on her cheeks, the edges of her ears, and down the sides of her neck. Each time I saw them, her lips and teeth were parted, sending her soft cinnamon breath into my hair and ears.

It turned out we both liked tepid chow mein just fine.

*****

They didn't always start at Bastogne. Just as I plunked myself down into a dentist's chair, lightning shattered an oak out in the waiting room, the prune-faced hygienist trying to ignore rain pelting down on us from neon-orange clouds. I wanted to suggest rescheduling, but the dentist already had his mirror-on-a-stick and a flashlight in my mouth, sliding a huge black monkey wrench between them. Why was he wearing a Panama hat? Because it looked so spiffy with his white medical smock?

The rain started flooding the office. A camel walked through, wearing a frilly green apron. I could barely hear over the thunder boom-boom-boom-boom-booming like a well-fired barrage, the lightning's muzzle flashes revealing the onrushing Nazis. This time my company held the front foxholes. *"Open fire, dammit."* The high-pitched voice screamed from my mouth.

"Wider, please," the dentist grumbled, his coal-scuttle helmet silhouetted against the bursts of light, the muzzle of his Schmeisser against one of my wisdom teeth. I grabbed at it, yelling for somebody to shoot the bastard. But he—"

"Jack, honey, ah'm right heah, baby. Yore aw-right."

I nearly got a hand on Nancy's throat before the flares went off in my brain. I'd done it again. The mortification felt an eighth of an inch better than having a dentist shove a burp gun down my throat. The shaking always took longer to master than the nightmare itself. I'd meant to drive Nancy back to her hotel right after we ate, but our fire hadn't been completely out.

"Honey, it's aw-right." Her voice and her fingers soothed me. "Mah trumpet-playin' boyfriend fought in a tank destroyer company. Anyhow, it's all ovah now."

We just lay there, Nancy snug against my back, for maybe half an hour. Oh, I understood completely why Jack Kennedy never slept with the women he bedded. I hadn't intended to either.

After a while, we got dressed and drove around 'til I could find an all-night diner where they didn't give a good God damn if a white man waltzed in halfway 'til dawn with a colored woman.

The lady had class. Nothing she said or did made me feel like an idiot.

I took care of that task myself.

TWENTY-THREE

Sometime before nine o'clock on Wednesday morning, I walked into my empty office. I glanced through the *Post* while waiting for Lana to show up. The big headline blared that Truman had named James Forrestal, the Navy Secretary, to head the new Defense Department. I was sitting there wondering what the hell a *Navy* Secretary knew about how to fight a war when my PT-boat skipper client called. Since there was nobody out in front to answer the phone, I picked it up.

"Dad arrived in town last night." His voice was all business. "I tried to call you then because Dad wanted a late-night meeting with you and Abe Moskowitz, but I couldn't reach you either at your office or at home."

"I spoke with Susan Prebble then, Jack." More than that about my evening, he did not need to know. "She told me she'd 'do anything' for you."

The boy congressman laughed. "I ought to ask *her* out to dinner tonight, in that case. Anyway, Moskowitz claimed to be busy and offered to meet at his office today at ten. Dad always gets at least *something* his way, so you're going to meet in his suite at the Hay-Adams instead at nine-thirty. I can't come—critical vote this morning. That's half an hour from now, Jack."

"I'll be there."

*****

The Hay-Adams Hotel, with its Grecian-columned stone face and its warm Italian Renaissance styling, catered to wealthy and influential people who didn't own any mansions in Washington but wanted to feel at home in their Nation's capital. The patrician hotel stood just across Lafayette Square from the White House, so you could feel you were the president's guest even if he couldn't shoehorn you in. It was not by mischance that the front door lay only a couple hundred paces from the Treasury Department.

A pudgy house dick in the walnut-paneled lobby stared at me as if somebody'd left yesterday's sturgeon lying on one of the silk-upholstered settees. I told the desk clerk that Joseph Kennedy expected me for a meeting up in his room. In reverent tones, he touched his pencil-line mustache and asked if the house dick would mind taking me up to Ambassador Kennedy's *suite*. The air became rarified as the elevator reached the eighth floor.

I expected the Old Man to be a major league stiff, but the patriarch of the Kennedy clan grabbed my right paw as if he had a million-dollar real estate listing that would fit my needs perfectly. "I'm Joe Kennedy, Mr. Griffin, and I so appreciate what you're doing about my son Jack's problem." I couldn't help thinking his eyes were asking why in the world his son hired a clown in a cheap suit.

The Old Man looked as if he was around sixty years old, but a vigorous sixty. His fine sandy-colored hair showed a lot of white, and he wore it slicked straight back off his forehead. Behind his horn-rimmed glasses, bright-blue eyes set off the Kennedy grin.

You could see the resemblance to his son, from his magnetism right down to the pale freckles, though I didn't spot any of Jack's shyness in him. His double-breasted navy-blue suit, on the other hand, must have cost him about what I'd paid for my car before the war, and it wasn't wrinkled.

*****

Abe Moskowitz arrived at the suite unescorted, immaculate in a French vanilla linen suit and a Panama with a two-inch band of scarlet ribbon, the good quality gross-grain stuff that big-time governments dangle medals from. I interrupted my walking tour of Joe Kennedy's temporary living room to say hello. The Old Man did none of the clumsy gawking over a Chinese guy being named Moskowitz that I'd done a day earlier. Either nothing flustered Papa Kennedy or his son clued him in.

While the financier and the lawyer got acquainted, a slender

Negro in a crisp uniform wheeled in a cart with a coffee service and a tray of pastries and muffins. I looked the living room over. Heavy damask curtains that could probably have shielded the room either from daylight in the Sahara or an atom bomb blast had been pulled back neatly and bound to ornate brass hooks with golden ropes. Between them, a shallow balcony with a wrought iron railing peered out from beneath graceful stone arches and overlooked a sea of summer-green treetops between the hotel and the White House.

Our host tipped the waiter with a twenty-dollar bill, a good bit more, I suspected, than even the Hay-Adams charged for the java and baked goods. He dodged the Negro's astonished thanks, and the man with the cart slid silently into the corridor, pulling gently closed a gilt-trimmed door that sounded like a bank vault's.

"Gentlemen." The Old Man led us to the ornate sideboard where the food waited. Once each of us had filled a gold-rimmed cup with coffee and put a white-frosted pastry or two on a delicate matching plate, he motioned us with his eyes to two brocaded sofas. We set our cargo on the coffee tables.

"First, let's share our latest information. Mr. Griffin, I'd appreciate your leading off. I know we've asked a great deal of you in what has necessarily been a very short time."

I knew both of them were avoiding the same question. "Well, to begin, I haven't identified the killer yet, but I'm beginning to understand the background of the murder."

"'Beginning.'" Joe Kennedy grimaced. "Jesus."

"'The background.' For Christ's sake, Griffin." Abe Moskowitz rolled his eyes. "The cops have Jack's blood type, and we've got nothing."

"How the hell'd they get his blood type? You were going to block that."

"From the semen. No, they probably haven't linked it to him yet. But it's Wednesday. We've held the cops and the press at bay since Monday. We need results now, not background."

"Moskowitz, I can track the days of the week without paper and pencil and without a God-damned criminal lawyer. Let's start with where we are and not with where we wish we were."

He glared. "How many detectives does your agency have working on this case?"

"Just me. My partner's indisposed."

Joe Kennedy's jaw plummeted. "A rinky-dink agency with just one fucking gumshoe?"

I gripped my temper with both hands. "Ambassador, one of the big outfits like the Schindler Detective Agency could fling a couple dozen operatives into the case, but you'd never keep the lid on with all the commotion they'd make."

The ambassador wasn't smiling. "Fine. There's no time to backtrack. We might all keep our shirts on."

*****

I started by reporting what news I had—how the police superintendent himself yanked O'Heaney off the case for talking to me, how Snilder tried to scare me off the job, and how O'Heaney commented, "The only thing it still needs is ribbons and bows. Your man Kennedy did it." I also mentioned my qualms about the apartment manager, Bradley. Finally, I said I hadn't learned much from Susan Prebble.

The Old Man nodded. "'Ribbons and bows,' your detective buddy claims, eh?"

"He was quoting Superintendent Howard."

Abe Moskowitz set down his cup and glanced over at me. "Griffin, Detective Sergeant Snilder called my office late yesterday afternoon. He just wanted to warn me the indictment would go to a grand jury in two or three days, and he'd better get his half-million pretty damn fast if we 'want things and people to disappear,' as he put it."

"Fine," the Old Man barked. "Schedule a meeting with him for noon. He's to bring everything he promised, including a list of key witnesses. I want to know who would testify to what. Tell him I'll have his stinking Samsonite suitcase waiting. I want to see him right here. Make clear he's dealing with me, the rich father, not Jack. I'll talk with him alone."

I kept a poker face, buts Abe Moskowitz raised a question. "Do you actually think he can steal the police files on a grisly rape-murder that's greased to go down the chute and scare off enough witnesses to make the case against Jack evaporate?"

The ambassador roared with laughter. "Do I think a horse's ass thing like that? Moskowitz, I started out as a bartender's son with a lousy job in a lousy bank and had the brains and the balls to turn it into one of the top five fortunes in America. That son-of-a-bitch Franklin Roosevelt may have played me for a sucker a couple of times—he could have sold horseshit to a horse—but no, I'm not that stupid. Still, this nickel-dime asshole cop thinks I'm dim-witted enough to swallow it. *That* pisses me off more than I can tell you. I want to see the bastard here at noon. It's time to make things happen."

TWENTY-FOUR

You can manage remarkable punctuality when you're lifting half a million dollars from a billionaire's back pocket. Despite a suit cheaper and shabbier than mine and a necktie obviously scrounged from a drowning victim, Snilder arrived at the ducal suite escorted by the same out-to-pasture gumshoe who brought me there.

Ambassador Kennedy cooed as he offered Snilder a drink and poured Chivas Regal over crystal ice cubes he plucked out of a golden bucket. The young congressman, he confided, was stuck on Capitol Hill, wrestling with his pea-brained colleagues over how much wealth to take from hard-pressed taxpayers to shovel down ratholes in the next fiscal year. "But that needn't worry an enterprising young man after today." He chuckled and handed Snilder a tall glass.

The senior Kennedy failed to mention that despite his son's absence, the boy congressman's lawyer and private investigator huddled quietly in an adjacent room, along with Moskowitz's stenographer—an earnest-looking woman of perhaps thirty-five Abe introduced to us as Miss Robles—and a professional recording specialist named Marty. The technician had spent the previous hour hiding microphones inside the brass-and-glass floor lamps that flanked the pristine little sofa on which the Old Man asked the crooked cop to sit and guzzle some first-rate whiskey. Ambassador Kennedy introduced himself in a clear voice and made Snilder state his name for the benefit of the recording devices.

*****

"How do I know," the ambassador asked calmly, after he'd looked at the files Snilder'd brought him, "that what you handed me is everything the police have, all the originals and so forth?" He gave a clear impression of a man who understood that you seize the main chance in America unless you're a fool, that he could not begrudge Snilder a lousy half-million dollars out of all the wealth he'd amassed. He said he felt Snilder was simply a hardworking man who saw his opportunity and took it. The sound recording technician smiled, and I heard it all clearly through the earphones he'd given me. Moskowitz grinned broadly.

Snilder explained each of the folders for him. "Y'all don' need the initial crime report, Mr. Kennedy, nor the medical officer's report. Neither one mentions y'all's son, and there's no way to swipe every copy of things like that. Doc Gregory'd just write up a new one with the same stuff in it."

Kennedy nodded.

You could hear how dry Snilder's throat was before he primed it again. "But these here are the only copies of written statements my squad got off the cab drivers who drove the congressman to and from the victim's apartment. Plus the desk clerk and a janitor from the Chesapeake. Plus a dozen other people who seen them leave the dinner together. It's everythin', just like ah said."

Kennedy rustled through the sheets of paper. "These will be missed, I would think?"

I heard Snilder laugh. "Nah, cuz we can close out the case for y'all first thing tuhmorrah morning. We found us a dipsomaniac nigger name of Bulldog Jones who's got a long, nasty crim'nal record an' the same weird-ass blood type as y'all's son. Ah can pull him in for questionin' after leavin' here. Ol' Bulldog did hard time in Maryland a few years back for slashin' a white woman, see, a hooker who wanted her money up front. Ah'll have my boys beat the crap outa ol' Bulldog and keep him awake around the clock, workin' today and tonight, 'til the bastard signs a full confession he broke in, raped the Dyson dame, and sliced her up."

The Old Man grunted.

"See, Mr. Kennedy, nobody wants to arrest a congressman if they got a safer suspect they can pin it on. Y'all's problem is we don't got nobody else until ah do what y'all's gonna pay for." He chuckled as if he were gutting a fish.

"I see."

"By the end of the week," Snilder added, setting his empty

tumbler on a table, "the Dyson murder case gits solved, and nobody in D.C. will ever notice if *this* fuckin' file gets misplaced. A month or so later, ah quit the Metropolitan Department and move outta town."

You could tell just from listening that Snilder had the itch really bad. You could sense he felt the Old Man being maddeningly slow and agonizingly thorough as he looked over the slender file. Joe read aloud the names and addresses of the cab drivers who'd rushed Jack and Betty Dyson to her apartment building and taken him to his home in Georgetown afterward, and the names of a desk clerk and a janitor from the Chesapeake Apartments who noticed Jack there, and a dozen people who saw them leave the dinner on Friday.

"It all seems very complete, Sergeant. So, pardon me if I'm slow, but just to make sure I understand this clearly, what you're offering me is this: If I hand you half a million dollars in cash, you'll beat a confession out of some colored lush who didn't do it but who is a credible suspect because of his felony record. You'll prosecute him for rape and murder in the Betty Dyson case, and you'll sell me *all* the evidence the Metropolitan Police Department has that might suggest that Congressman Kennedy was somehow involved in this repulsive crime. Is that your proposal?"

"Yes, sir," Snilder panted. "Exac'ly."

The Ambassador laughed. "You stupid sack of shit, do you think I would buy stolen police documents in a *murder* case? Worthless documents, to be sure, but police documents nonetheless? That would be a crime, my lad. A crime. Now I suggest you get your stupid ass out of my suite before I decide to telephone Gentleman Jimmy Howard, your police superintendent, and land your ass in the shithouse for keeps. Take this God-damned stolen folder with you."

*****

In the next room with me, Miss Robles touched her short, dark hair and looked discomfited at the ambassador's profanity. Moskowitz leaned toward her. "I need it just as it was spoken." She nodded and wrote fast to catch up. I cracked the door open so I could see.

The detective sergeant sat there as if Joe Kennedy had slapped him across the chops with a mackerel. Snilder grabbed the manila folder off the coffee table with a snarl and shoved it back into his worn briefcase, his jaw stuck forward like a bayonet. "If y'all din't plan to take the deal, why the hell did y'all bring me here, you stinkin' Mick bastard?"

"Why, you fucking asshole, I brought you up to my hotel suite to brief me on the pathetic evidence the police have gathered in this case. You hauled the names of every half-assed witness you have up here, and you let me read their signed statements. I wouldn't drag a case like this one into a God-damn *trailer* court, let alone prosecute a congressman for capital crimes with a wheelbarrow full of shit like this. And at the same time, I've taken my measure of the police officers the capital city has put on this major murder case. I must say that I am not impressed."

The Old Man caught my eye and mouthed the word "now" to me. While he apologized for being rude and asked Snilder calmly if he would please sit down so they could talk more reasonably about what was in everybody's best interests, I told the recording specialist to shut off the tape recorder. He sped the reel back to the beginning and gave it to Moskowitz. They and Miss Robles slipped silently out into the hall by another door.

From behind the door that stood open about half an inch, I watched Snilder jerk stained brass knuckles from a pocket and take a menacing step toward the Old Man. I put my hand on my shoulder-holstered .45 automatic. This situation was a grenade with no pin in it, scary as hell.

Snilder growled. "You stupid old son of a nigger whore. Ah imagine folk'll see somethin' in the papers on this case in a day or two, somethin' like y'all's fancy-ass son gettin' indicted for rape and murder. Y'all'd have a fuckin' heart attack readin' it, you smart-ass rich bastard, 'cept y'all's gonna be in a coma by then." Cocking his arm, he stomped forward heavily.

I drew my pistol and burst into the living room.

"Ah, Mr. Griffin." The Old Man smiled at me. "Is everything just as you and I had discussed?" Snilder almost broke his neck whipping around to look.

I nodded and cocked my automatic.

"Excellent."

"What the fuck's *he* doin' here?" The possibility of being outwitted hadn't occurred to Snilder. "You said you'd be alone. And what's Griffin doing with a fuckin' *gun?*"

Kennedy waved him off. "Sergeant, I asked Mr. Griffin to

listen in on our pleasant little conversation simply as a professional witness. He's also acting as my bodyguard. If you'll look at those hideous lamps right beside you, you'll see I had a sound technician conceal microphones in them. Everything we have discussed was tape-recorded. The technician will also serve as a professional witness. By the way, following my careful instructions, he and several other expert witnesses just left the hotel with the recording."

"Left the fuckin' hotel?" Snilder stood up, quick to assimilate bad news. He started to reach toward his own shoulder holster and then stopped, realizing I was aiming a pistol at him already.

I made Snilder put his hands on his head. "This thing in my hand is an Army Colt .45 automatic, Snilder. Make one wrong move, and I'll blow a tunnel in you they can use to drive cars through from Annapolis to the Eastern Shore, beach traffic through one side and westbound back through the other."

He posed as a gargoyle, stiff and ugly. "Like ah rilly think y'all's got the balls to shoot a cop."

I grinned. "Let's find out. It's no big risk for me, Snilder. We recorded you shaking down a *very* prominent citizen and committing half a dozen felonies. My hunch is if you dropped dead this afternoon, Gentleman Jimmy Howard and Vince O'Heaney wouldn't even bother a grand jury about it."

The renegade cop wilted, an orchid without an oxygen tent. "What do y'all want?"

I looked Snilder in the eye. "Reach slowly with your left forefinger and thumb, and ease your revolver out of its holster. Now lay it by your left shoe and get over against the wall."

I pocketed his pistol and made him strip to his underwear. Then I took the razor from his shoe and the .22 automatic pistol Snilder carried in an ankle holster.

"Let's talk business here," Joe Kennedy suggested. "I have a proposition for you. It's not what you expected, but I think you may be very pleased with it."

Snilder glared and plopped down on the couch.

"You did commit extortion and those other felonies, even if I keep the evidence of it as a personal memento of the need for police reform in our nation's capital. Gentleman Jimmy Howard receives the felony evidence on you only if my son is linked to this case publicly."

The half-million bucks had evaporated. Snilder waited at

gunpoint in his shorts with a strong chance of getting shot, and we had him on tape committing serious crimes. Now the Old Man seemed to be proposing a way out. A steer in the stockyard, he stared at the man with the sledgehammer.

"Here are these, Mr. Ambassador." I'd pulled Snilder's wallet out of his jacket while he listened to the pitch in his boxers, a ratty sleeveless undershirt, and lifeless brown socks. With a grin, I handed the Old Man the cop's shield and police identification card. It seemed like a good idea to stick his handcuffs in my coat pocket.

"Hey," Snilder barked. I turned my pistol on him. Kennedy pulled a sheet of paper from under his desk blotter. I put it on the floor and told Snilder to pick it up.

"I want you to quit the police and come to work for me." The Old Man smiled as if it were Christmas morning. "I pay better. Please read that. Out loud."

Snilder did.

*****

To Whom It May Concern:

I messed up the Edna Hamilton investigation in 1946, making it impossible to bring Rodney Hamilton to justice. I had inappropriate contact with Stella Gorney that influenced my actions. I resign from the District of Columbia Metropolitan Police Department effective immediately.

*****

"*Wha-a-a-t?*"

Snilder was clearly furious. It could get nasty now.

"*Hear me out,* Sergeant," Kennedy bellowed. "I think the part about the *money* may please you. I have a lot of former police officers on my payroll, you know. And I'm famous for making generous offers. Buying off a cop is a criminal offense, my friend, but *hiring* a former police officer at a high salary for next-to-no work is perfectly legal."

Snilder raised an eyebrow. "Yeah?"

The Old Man smiled benignly. "Here's my plan. One, you sign this letter, and Mr. Griffin and I witness it and seal it in this manila envelope. Two, you leave your wallet and guns here in the envelope as a token of good faith. You take that case file and put it back where it belongs. Three, you leave Police Headquarters and meet a man outside—"

"A husky dark-haired guy in a tan suit at the Indiana Avenue doors. Tell him it's four o'clock."

The Old Man went on as if I hadn't interrupted. "—who gives you a briefcase that holds another large envelope containing money, instructions, and an airline ticket. You do not open the briefcase yet. Step four, you take a cab to National Airport and catch your flight. You can open your briefcase in the cab."

"That's it?" Snilder was still waiting for the other brick to drop. "Tickets where?"

The Old Man grinned. "It's not in your interest for Griffin to know where you can be found. You'll be well taken care of, both now and later. I trust you are fond of palm trees, cheap women, and lots of money. I thought half a million was a bit steep, but you'll be amazed how far a hundred thousand dollars will stretch where you're headed."

Snilder was on Kennedy's side now. He signed in a hurry.

"Fine, Sergeant. A large manila envelope inside the briefcase holds a passport and a wallet loaded with cash and identification documents to get you where you're going. You will carry a sealed letter of introduction. The man you'll deliver it to will handle your payoff. Deliver the letter unopened, or it won't be worth a damned dime. Are we clear, boyo?"

TWENTY-FIVE

That wasn't quite the last I saw of that dog's hind leg. When he left, I tailed him over to police headquarters and watched him leave empty-handed eleven minutes later. He didn't see me peering from one side, wearing a cloth cap and no coat.

There were a couple of dark-haired guys in tan suits. One, a car dealer named Joey Como, who you could imagine shooting old women in the kneecaps unless you saw him with his wife and baby daughter, gave Snilder a nod. Joey'd been a machine-gunner in my company from Bastogne to VE-Day. He was the size of a large packing crate. We got together for occasional lunches or ballgames and swapped favors once in a while.

Snilder walked over to Joey and muttered something to him. Joey answered and handed him a briefcase. I snapped three photos, keeping the rogue cop in good focus. Then he ducked into a cab, and that was the last I saw of him.

*****

Miss Robles halted me in mid-stride. "Mr. Griffin? Are you going back up to Mr. Kennedy's suite?"

I nodded. "You, too?"

Though she looked rather plain and gawky, Abe's stenographer had a nice smile. Her hat could have starred in a Hollywood comedy—diamond-shaped with a long, curved peacock feather. "If you don't mind, there is a lot for me to do at the office. Would you please give this envelope to Mr. Kennedy? It has two carbon copies of the list I typed out—the witnesses and what they said, just as he read it into the microphone."

"I'd be glad to, Miss Robles." She nodded and disappeared into the crowded lobby while I hopped onto an elevator.

*****

"Did you leave our friend holding the bag?" The Old Man grinned and asked me to come in again. I handed him the envelope from Miss Robles.

"My man heard Snilder tell the cabbie to hurry to National Airport. Presumably, he's following your instructions, though I can't guarantee he won't change routes."

"Agreed. But Snilder doesn't have much time before his flight, and he can't be certain we're not having him shadowed. Besides, he's leaving his past behind—in here, as a matter of fact." He patted the manila envelope holding the guns, badge, wallet, and resignation. "You take this. Don't give it to your police friend until tomorrow."

I nodded. "For curiosity's sake, where did you send him?"

No cat ever smiled more broadly after a canary dinner. "Ask me that *after* you give your buddy the envelope."

TWENTY-SIX

Lana looked up from her afternoon doughnut and coffee. "Oh, I was just about to telephone my sister Tana at the camera shop. How did the morning go, Mr. Griffin?"

"I'll never get any questions asked if they keep me in meetings. An ambassador and a lawyer. Jeez, can they talk!" I kept the Snilder story to myself.

She laughed, a character from Rabelais. "Oh, the check came already from General Fidelity. Two hundred seventy dollars we need badly. I stuck it into our account this morning." She'd have wagged her tail if she had one.

"Man oh man, you handled that fast. What's our bank balance?" I didn't want to hear the answer.

"I just told you, Mr. Griffin. Two hundred seventy dollars."

"Okay, go back over there now and pull out all but twenty bucks. Pay yourself two hundred of the three-fifty we owe you and bring me the other fifty." I felt like I was rationing out bullets at Bastogne again.

That really perked her up. "Are you sure, Mr. Griffin?"

"Look, Lana, until I get the detective agency back on its feet and have the books squared away, I can't pay you everything, but I'm not going to stiff you. As you say, we can't really afford a receptionist at this point, let alone an office manager. But I won't lay you off as long as we're in business. I need you here, and I can't wait around all day to get messages. When this case is over, let's get serious about who does what."

Lana looked at me shrewdly. "We'll do fine, Mr. Griffin. Really we will. What can I do now besides answer the phone?"

I thought a second. "Okay, look, Ambassador Kennedy got a

list of police witnesses. I'd like you to call each one. Ask questions and write out the answers. You're good with people. See what they know. Everything the police have so far does point to Jack Kennedy. We need to find the real killer fast."

She glanced at my carbon copy. "It looks like I've got a lot of calls to make."

"And I need to follow them up with shoe leather. Give me the names and numbers of the two cab drivers. I'll phone them while you get the others."

*****

My first call went to Major Flanders at the Pentagon to set up a meeting with Symington. I wasn't convinced I needed to talk to him, but there could have been a reason somebody who worked with Betty wanted her dead.

Flanders clearly intended to be Symington's gatekeeper, the guy who kept intruders from wasting the chief's time. "I can shoehorn you in right after lunch tomorrow—Thursday—at fourteen hundred hours. To a civilian that's—"

"To a former paratroop captain, it's two in the afternoon. Do I need a pass?"

"You'll need an escort. Be at the door I directed you to at thirteen-thirty hours, not at thirteen-thirty-one." A dull buzz followed a sharp click.

Next, I reached the cabbie who'd taken Jack Kennedy and Betty Dyson to her place, an expatriate Confederate named Ernest Bland. "Sure thing," his two-packs-a-day throat rasped. "Ah seen 'em outside the Washin'ton Hotel. Ah was glad to pick 'em up. As long as they wasn't no coloreds. Ah cain't *abide* that. Y'all unnerstan' me?"

I did. I was exhausted from understanding these yahoos.

"They was all cooey in the back whilst we wint up Connitikit Avenue. The man paid, an' they got out. All kissin' an' all, saw 'em in the mirruh couple-three times."

Great. Somebody butchered Betty, and I'm still jealous of Kennedy. "Anything you heard or saw make you think the man might have raped her later?"

Ernest guffawed, and I was pretty sure his nose drooled from the sniveling he followed that with. "Ah cain't say how he coulda did that, mistah. Ah cain't see whin she'da stopped him frum doin' *nuthin'* at all, if y'all git mah drift."

Yep, I did. I got it Friday night, though I'd tried kidding myself out of it. At best, Ernest would make a dubious witness—showing Kennedy red-hot but raising doubts about rape and any reason to silence Betty. "Thanks, Ernest."

Lana peered into my office. "I just spoke with a Navy commander named Fisher, Mr. Griffin. He says he told the police he recognized Mr. Kennedy because he'd known him early in the war at Naval Intelligence, and he met Don and Betty Dyson before the war. All his testimony amounts to is that he noticed the two of them laughing through dinner and leaving together."

I wondered if anybody saw *me* at the table. This Fisher didn't, Susan Prebble didn't, and I might as well have been invisible to Betty Dyson.

I turned and stared out the window, imagining what ideas Harry Aadlund would've had, beyond grabbing some cutie's tail. Come to think of it, was there another woman involved in the case, as in did Colonel Dyson have a girlfriend? I didn't get that far Monday before he pitched me out of his office, but why the hell was he outside the Jazz Club right after Betty's memorial service?

I hopped to my feet. "Look, Lana, go ahead with those calls, especially to the people at the Chesapeake. I want to know if anybody spotted Colonel Dyson that night. I'm going to ask some questions at the Jazz Club."

TWENTY-SEVEN

The chairs rested upside-down on tables, and the starched white linens hid somewhere else when I eased through the rear door of the Jazz Club. A hulking man with slicked-back reddish hair and a baggy brown suit was just heading out the front. He seemed vaguely familiar, but I didn't get a good look, and he didn't seem to see me. Millie glanced up from her scarlet nails with a vacant grin. "We're not open yet, mister. Hey, you were here last night."

The owner's door stood ajar. "I was. Is Nichols inside? I need to talk to him." I hadn't slowed my stride, so I was facing Skip Nichols two seconds later.

He smiled. "Well, Mr. Griffin! Pleasant surprise." He looked like he meant it. "Is this visit my business or yours? Have a seat."

I did. "I'm working on an investigation, Nichols. Maybe you've read about it in the papers—the Betty Dyson murder case."

That took him aback. "Well, then, I suppose further pleasantries would be thoughtless. I'd heard the police are close to an arrest."

"I wouldn't know." He offered me a cigarette, but I shook my head. "Listen, last night a man came out of here, maybe around eight o'clock. He was the dead woman's husband."

Nichols shrugged. "I don't recall any officers last night."

"He wore a tan suit and a blue necktie. Kind of a hawk-faced guy, a bit bald on top. Medium height, skinny. I think he may have met a woman here."

"Sorry to chuckle, Griffin, but a lot of men do. There are all kinds of jazz."

"I wondered if I could ask your waitresses some questions."

His jaw tensed. Employers never like that much. "Well, the

waitresses won't be here for a couple of hours. But I think I saw a man like that. Millie, would you come in here, please?"

Another look at Millie was fine with me. She filled a black velvet dress with a neckline that attracted your eyes clear up to your elbows. Nichols gestured to the chair beside me. As she took it, she batted her olive-green eyes my way.

"Millie, Mr. Griffin is a private detective looking into the Dyson murder case we've been reading about."

"Oh, that's—"

"Hear me out, Millie. He thinks the husband came to the club last night, and he may be right—a slender, medium height man in a tan suit and blue tie? It's possible you noticed him upstairs, Millie, when you took Rube his iced tea, is that right? Might have been with a woman. If I recall, he wasn't here long."

Millie narrowed her eyes, a cat watching a mouse relax. Whatever lay behind her vacant expressions wasn't a lack of marbles. "Oh, sure, Mr. Nichols, I remember him. Thin man in a tan suit, a little bald on top? Kind of a big nose? Yeah, I saw him at a game table. A slender, dark-haired woman was standing next to him, but they may not have been together. Ten or twenty minutes later, I saw him pass my desk and leave. You think he was that poor murdered woman's husband? He seemed so sad."

I looked up from my notepad. "Millie, any idea the woman's name?"

She shook her head, and Nichols shrugged. I asked who ran the table and when he'd be in. Millie looked stumped. Her boss asked if it was Carl, and she nodded. Nichols gave me a look as if a ten-pound trout just jumped off his hook. "Sorry, Griffin, he's out 'til Saturday night. Millie, do we have his new home address yet?"

Her black hair swayed as she shook her head.

TWENTY-EIGHT

Lana was just finishing a telephone call when I got back to the half-empty office around three-fifteen. I gave her the "okay" sign and waited 'til she hung up. "Dyson seems to have been gambling at the Jazz Club last night with an attractive brunette. Can you please put in a call to him at Andrews Field?"

"Sure, Mr. Griffin." After she reached the operator, while the call was being put through, she said, "I talked with a Negro janitor at the Chesapeake who saw Mr. Kennedy leave Friday night around nine, and a—oh, your call's ready. I'll put it into your office."

The voice at the far end of the Lincoln Tunnel identified itself as Corporal Richards. I said, "Washington calling Colonel Dyson," and with a snappy *Yessir,* he put me through. Dyson answered with the gusto of a mummy.

"Colonel, we've still got a few questions you need—"

"Who the hell is this? The private eye?"

"A 'private eye' is an actor in a trench coat. Yes, this is Jack Griffin, the private detective. You were identified by two witnesses at the Jazz Club last night."

"You and what other idiot?" I expected him to hang up on me. "I don't want to talk to you."

"Not even about your slender, dark-haired girlfriend?"

That threw his balance off. "I don't—What girlfriend? I don't have any girlfriend, dammit."

"How sad." I might as well needle the guy.

"Look, asshole, *you* saw me there. I was alone."

"Not upstairs at the gambling tables."

The pause could have been for him to figure out what I knew. "I told you I wasn't there with anybody. I also didn't go upstairs."

"What were you doing there, Dyson? And why did you switch into mufti after you left the church?"

"What was I—um, look, Griffin, I—" Even over the phone, you could tell he was sweating. "It's not what you think. All right, I'll tell you the truth. I went there to meet an old friend—a male friend. He was the one with the dark-haired girl."

"What are their names?" I didn't believe him.

"Names. Well, look, I can't tell you their names. He's, um, married, and she isn't his wife. And I wasn't gambling—just watching. I was only there fifteen or twenty minutes."

Lana came in, reflecting my smile. "Dyson, you just confirmed being upstairs at the game tables with a brunette. I'll find her, and when I do, she'll tell me whether you spent the rest of last Friday night at her place."

"The *rest* of Friday night?" His voice sounded higher than when we started.

"Yeah, after you killed your wife. Isn't that what happened?"

That was when he *did* hang up.

Lana had her perky grin on. "You think her husband killed her, don't you, Mr. Griffin?"

"He's still at the top of my list, but I don't want to forget Betty's comment that her Air Corps bosses are hiding something nasty."

TWENTY-NINE

The razzing sneer of the switchboard buzzer echoed from the outer room. Lana grabbed it. "Aadlund and Griffin Detective Agency. May I help you?" Then she pointed at me and put it through to my phone.

The woman's voice held a trace of Texas in it. "Mr. Griffin, this is Martha Broward. We met last evening."

"Oh, yes, Mrs. Broward." The green bean woman. "Thanks for calling."

"You'll have to forgive my not contacting you sooner." Her voice sounded desolate. "My best friend in the world has been murdered. You're trying to identify Betty's killer. The newspapers, as is their wont, have been quite full of lurid details, which have given no comfort to anyone who knew her."

"I still need to talk to you, Mrs. Broward. I'm trying to find out what I can about Betty Dyson's life in hope of developing some leads."

"You're located on Capitol Hill, Mr. Griffin. So am I. Why don't we talk a little about this ugly crime. Perhaps I can help you."

I wasn't sure I had any genuine leads or that calling the list of police witnesses would lead me to a solution any different from O'Heaney's. The Broward woman seemed to need to talk to somebody about Betty's death. I agreed to meet her.

"Give me about ten minutes, Mr. Griffin. Commander Broward and I have quarters at the Navy Yard. I'll be over at the People's Drug Store on Pennsylvania Avenue, sitting at the soda counter, eager to answer your questions."

*****

An ice-cold chocolate malt late on a July afternoon couldn't make Jack Kennedy's situation any worse. I descended into the frying pan like a beaten hound. People swore Satan avoided Washington in July because he couldn't stand the heat.

The drug store was four blocks away. Four blocks away! A skinny, frazzled, dark coffee-colored lady I passed in Seward Square, tending a blonde baby squalling from a pink carriage, nodded as she called to the other milk-white tot she was minding, "Now, William, don't yo' *dast* chase no mo' pigeons!" I grinned back at a nicely-shaped young Negro woman in a thin print dress and red high heels sashaying in the other direction, and she crooned, "Hah y'all doin'?" A white-stubbled Negro sliding a pint into a pocket outside a liquor store made a conspiratorial nod, and a heavy-set tan-skinned lady murmured "Aftanoon" to me outside People's Drugs.

*****

Martha Broward was waiting as advertised, sipping a strawberry shake. A woman apparently uninterested in frills and adornments, she wore neither makeup nor jewelry except for a simple gold wedding band. Her hair, cut at chin level, was straight and Hershey Bar brown.

I ordered a chocolate malt from a wiry soda jerk with salt-and-pepper hair. A big black ceiling fan shoved the hot air around the store to diminish your sense of being a loaf of bread baking past golden brown. We waded through the pleasantries quickly and got down to business.

She started by saying that she and Susan Prebble hadn't been friends since the end of the war, when the redhead made an all-too-obvious play for Martha's husband. Before that, the three women had been great buddies, working day and night at the War Department, sharing most of their meals and most of their fears. Their husbands all fought in combat zones.

I interrupted her narrative. "Susan made a comment to me about all of you going through some kind of surveillance. Was that of any relevance?"

She chuckled. "Neither then nor now, Mr. Griffin. In 1943 or '44, some overeager counterintelligence colonel decided Air Corps

Headquarters might be an espionage target, so he had all of us shadowed for about a month. I believe he was transferred to a radar installation in the Orkney Islands in retribution. Susan and I laughed about it, but Betty found it terrifying. Beautiful women fear being stalked by unsavory creatures."

I asked her the same question I'd asked Susan Prebble: Why was the world's most Methodist married woman trawling for a man and taking one home from the Army-Navy Club dinner? Perhaps I phrased it more nicely for Mrs. Broward.

She sipped her shake slowly and turned away from me, the tide rising in her gray eyes. "Last Friday was a painful anniversary for Betty. She wasn't commemorating her wedding. You see, two years ago to the day, her odious husband packed his Army B-2 bag and moved out on her to the bachelor quarters at Andrews."

This was the first I'd heard of the air ace leaving his wife, though I knew he had quarters at the airfield. The newspapers trumpeted the tragic loss the famed hero had suffered. "Was there another woman?"

"I shouldn't think so." She inserted a Raleigh cork-tip between her dry lips, and I lit it for her.

"Could Dyson have been involved with Susan Prebble?"

Martha Broward shook her head sadly. "I doubt they ever met. Let me tell you a very confidential story since I was privy to it. All I ask is that you keep this story to yourself if you don't need to use it."

THIRTY

"Men cannot possibly know how intensely a woman can love a man, Mister Griffin. Don Dyson always drove fast, flashy cars and always wore expensive clothes. He signed up the day after Pearl Harbor for the Army Air Corps."

"Go on." I sipped my malt.

"The breakneck driver took to flying—*loved* it. He flew well over a hundred fighter missions against the Germans, escorting formations of B-17 and B-24 bombers and shooting down Nazi fighter planes rather like a freckle-faced boy with a spanking new flyswatter, I imagine. It was just as dangerous as anything could ever be, but of course, it was also terribly exciting and important to do. I'm certain Don loved the zooming and the diving and the danger of it. He would write Betty short letters exulting in the Messerschmitts he'd blown to confetti."

She let some oyster-gray smoke drift out of her mouth. "Betty began working for the War Department while Don was in training and so impressed them that she was assigned a demanding job as an Air Corps general's personal secretary late in 1942. She wheedled Don's assignment as a squadron commander out of her boss."

"They thought a lot of Betty at headquarters?" I realized I didn't know much more about her than how she looked, how she laughed, and how she died.

Mrs. Broward nodded. "She waited for Don to come home—dreading from '42 to '45 that he would be killed—and was as chaste as a love song. One day during lunch, she confided to Susan and me, 'I miss Don so much, including sex.' I remember we giggled like junior high school girls, and Susan offered, in her usual snide and ironic monotone, to help Betty 'get laid' before the sun set. That was the only time I ever heard Betty curse."

*****

After another drag on her cigarette, she put a hand on mine, as if to soften what she needed to say to me. "Men can be such uncaring bastards, Mr. Griffin. I'm *not* being unkind. Don wrote her a letter after Germany had capitulated, saying he wanted to get a fighter command in the Pacific for the invasion of the Japanese mainland. Other American fighter plane pilots, he complained to Betty, had scored more 'kills' than he had, as though their names and box scores were on every mouth. 'You've done your part, honey,' she wrote back, 'please try to get some assignment in the Washington area.' But he replied that she had missed his point. There was nothing like the war in the air, he wrote her, and it was going to be over all too soon."

"I see." A red-hot, I thought, but I understood. I hadn't wanted to leave my men unshepherded, and it wasn't only about them.

"Still, Paul Brubaker, who is Don's commanding general now, worked with Betty at the War Department and wanted to do something nice for her. He decided he needed Don on his team at the Continental Air Command when he became operations officer, just before they renamed it the Strategic Air Command."

The Broward woman was heading somewhere with this historical novel of hers. I asked her where.

"Just this, Mr. Griffin. That beautiful girl could hardly endure waiting until Don got back to Washington in mid-May of 1945, assigned to C.A.C. headquarters out at Andrews. She was as itchy as a new bug bite. We kidded her mercilessly for it."

Her quick grin dissipated, smoke beneath a big black fan.

"But then in the weeks that followed Don's return from Europe, Betty would come to the War Office each morning looking more and more as if she'd just received news of his death. I'm not exaggerating about that, by the way—I got to know that look every time the Allies conducted a major military operation, and a few more of our coworkers would become widows."

Martha Broward disappeared into her memories, and I found no words to say. What I pictured was Betty blooming unseen while her husband zipped across enemy skies. I decided I preferred the men's war to the one we'd sentenced the women to.

Martha returned from wherever she'd gone. "Near the end of that July, Betty arrived late one morning looking even worse than before. Her eyes were puffy—red, not blackened—and her fingers jittered as if she were jangling a key ring. I took her into my office and poured her a cup of coffee."

The string bean lady stubbed out her cigarette. I lit up a fresh one for her as she slid it between her lips.

"Don had told her he needed to keep some clothes nearer his office out at Andrews Field so he could work late because there was just 'so much going on and so much at stake.' He moved into a bachelor officers' apartment out there. I asked her, 'Is he involved with another woman?' Betty swore he wasn't. 'A man?' She tried to slap me, but I caught her wrist. I commented that Don didn't have to live that close to his office at the base. He invested longer and longer hours just as the war demanded less and less effort from everybody. But Betty insisted she'd never say a single word that might interfere with whatever Don wanted to do."

*****

"So, Martha, could Dyson possibly have killed her?"

She waved the idea off impatiently. "No, I don't think Don could have killed Betty. He didn't care about her any longer. Passion had become the watery gruel of indifference. He returned all of her letters unopened for two years. His career is going very well at this point, from what my friends report."

I looked at her. "Then why did you tell me all this?"

"I suppose I just wanted you to understand that Betty wasn't a tramp. I suppose I just needed to talk about her. I doubt Betty was ever unfaithful to that loathsome peanut through four years of wartime separation."

"I've been told she was a flirt and a tease." A melodic laugh and dancing eyes cartwheeled through my brain.

Martha Broward glared at me. Then her face softened. "Betty was charming and vivacious. Even talking pleasantly to a man, I'm certain she seemed flirtatious. So many men read a smile as a contract. Other than that, I shouldn't think those comments were true."

I set my teacup on its saucer. "Then how do you explain her taking a man back to her apartment last Friday?"

"Biology." Her ironic smile faded. "What broke the camel's back, as it were, was two years of desertion."

"But last Friday—"

"*Before* last Friday, she started going out with other men. What she did with them I cannot say, though I wouldn't fault her if I thought she'd spent the night with a dozen of them—on separate nights, of course." Her smile was brittle. "Last Friday, Betty finally received a divorce in domestic court for desertion under District law. She sent her used-up husband a telegram informing him about the divorce and phoned me to say she planned to set off fireworks with some handsome stranger."

THIRTY-ONE

Just before five that afternoon, I handed Lana a fat manila envelope holding the guns, badge, and resignation letter I'd taken from Snilder.

"Lana, I want this to go anonymously right away to Detective Superintendent Blaine at the Municipal Building. Walk this over to Ames Delivery Service on your way home, okay?" She looked up from her magazine, nodded, and accepted the package.

I swung by my apartment and read my mail. Then I headed for Chinatown to talk to the Air Corps colonel I'd met at Betty's funeral.

*****

Whoever she was, with her clouds of brassy bleached hair framing the view down her front as she bent over my table in a dress no Sears and Roebuck dared carry, I wasn't interested. "No, thanks, sweetie. I'm here to meet a guy."

Blondie faked concern, her tweezed and penciled brows crumpled. "Oh, honey, a handsome hunk like you shouldn't oughta *swish*. I could straighten you out for ten bucks, if you take my meaning." I did, and sent her away just as Colonel Walworth joined me.

"That's what I love about Mai Fong, Griffin—it's almost as sleazy as Canton, which means the food's what Chinese folks eat, not the Americanized mush you pay more for in the fancier Chineseries away from Chinatown." He folded his khaki cap and stuck it in his web belt as he plopped down across from me. "Been waiting long?"

"Ten minutes—just enough for Blondie to offer me therapy for ten dollars."

"A *stiff* price, if I may say so." He arched an eyebrow to

complement his gruff voice. "Breaks my heart, coming here, but it's the only place I go."

A bony waitress brought us ice water and menus and jotted down our drink order. When I'd called Walworth to confirm meeting him for a drink, he'd suggested Mai Fong. "They've got a cocktail lounge and damn good Mandarin cooking at cheap prices. By seven-thirty, I'll be ready for supper with our booze. You?"

So there we sat—an Air Corps colonel and a guy in a tired suit—surrounded by sleek Chinese businessmen and pallid men in neckties, all seated with white women, most of them young and some even attractive. "Apparently, Colonel, what makes you sad about this joint isn't a shortage of bottle blondes. What's it about?"

"All the hustlers in Chinatown are blonde white women." He shook his head. "For every ten Chinese males here, you can find one female. Except you can't find 'em because, with those odds, even the toads can snag husbands who keep them at home. A lot of the bleached-out streetwalkers live with the surplus Chinese men. You never see a Chinese woman in Chinatown unless she's eighty years old." He sighed like a schoolboy.

Our drinks came—Scotch and soda for me, a gin and tonic for the colonel. We hoisted them silently and took a sip. I must've looked puzzled. "So you're sad for the love-starved Chinese men or for the locked-away women?"

His second sip was a slow one, then he set it down. "Well, since you mention it, neither. No, what I'm blue about is the absence of Asian women—either hookers or decent ones. I adore them. Y'see, I spent the war in China." He tapped his right shoulder and turned it my way so I could recognize the winged cat on it.

"You were in the Flying Tigers?"

"Well, not the old pre-war American Volunteer Group. Fourteenth Air Force. I flew Mitchell bombers. Griffin, I loved China. Oh, it's no surprise the lean, disciplined communists are beating the crap out of Chiang's corrupt and lazy generals. But the people! There are no women as fascinating."

"And you can't find them in Chinatown." I could feel sorry for the guy, though he was taking care of that himself. "Your wife's not Chinese."

"Case in point." He called for another gin and tonic when the waitress came to take our orders. "Quinine water." He winked. "Fights malaria."

I picked pepper steak and chop suey, but Walworth stopped me. "What do you want with that slop?"

"But I *like* Chinese food." He perplexed me, and I let it show. I'd never eaten Mandarin grub until I moved to Washington before the war and couldn't have said whether anybody back in Ohio could cook it.

"If you like Chinese food, let me order. Nobody in China ever heard of pepper steak or chop suey. Then we can chat about Betty Dyson."

*****

Colonel Walworth talked a lot, which was fine by me. I suggested directions, and he explored all the ground nearby. He'd liked Betty and praised her work, noting she never talked about her marriage. He volunteered that he'd taken her to dinner twice and made a pass the second time—New Year's Eve—which she fended off very sweetly.

"A flirt? Oh, God, yes, Griffin. She was beautiful and fun to be with, and she liked people, men certainly included. But a *tease?* No. Not by my book. I mean, her marriage clearly left her alone a lot. Can't say whether anybody else ever scored with Betty. I didn't. But she promised nothing and implied nothing. I took a shot and missed, that's all."

I did know how to use chopsticks. When the food came, I relived the scene in *The Wizard of Oz* when the black-and-white turns to a world of unforeseen color. Shrimp with lobster sauce was edible velvet. The chicken dish was spicy, tangy, and subtly sweet. Once Walworth hacked the head and tail fin off the deep-fried sea bass with ginger and scallions, I *knew* there was a heaven. We chomped contentedly for a few minutes without a word.

"Colonel, let me ask you a question. The day Betty Dyson was murdered, she discovered something she thought was despicable about either Stuart Symington or Bert Orton, probably Symington. How good was her judgment about that sort of thing?"

"Call me Fred. That lady had a great deal of integrity." Walworth met my eyes as he jabbed a crispy morsel of fish into his mouth. "But you're asking for tales out of school."

"I'm asking why a young woman was murdered."

He paused, loaded chopsticks hovering in the air. "I thought it was *rape* and murder."

"That's how it looked on Monday. If she was raped at all, it may have been to mislead the police. But something critical happened Friday involving the man she worked for."

"Secretary Symington or General Orton?" With a sideways glance, he ate the delayed bite.

"Not clear. Maybe both. Aides can be fawning dogs."

He gave me a knowing chuckle. "Strictly confidential?"

"It's a murder investigation. I can't guarantee that. But I'm not a gossip, Colonel." I picked at the fish.

You could see his career wrestling with his conscience. The career won. "No, I guess I don't know anything about that. So, did you miss your chop suey?"

THIRTY-TWO

After a long, brooding walk from Chinatown down to the mall and back I drove home disappointed, certain that Walworth had more to tell than he'd risked. But watching him pick his career over whatever he'd wanted to do if he could cover his rear end reminded me of the nagging question Martha Broward had left me.

Suppose she was right about Dyson having no motive to kill Betty based on a passion that had burned out. There was the woman he might have been with at the Jazz Club, but why murder his wife over a girlfriend if Betty'd already divorced him? Made no sense. Whether or not Dyson had a girlfriend, my instinct insisted that the man's only passion was for his flying career.

Ah, but that's what made the divorce so deadly. A shattered marriage could smash an officer's career, especially in the rarefied atmosphere of ranks above lieutenant colonel. All very well to build the military around competency in combat, but the mass of senior officers were time-serving prigs wedded to iron-willed wives whose social code defined their whole lives. All those fritter-shaped belles and gaunt Yankee biddies knew they could be left to die in the desert if they permitted the men to rotate wives.

That had to be it—Dyson killed Betty to conceal a career-wrecking divorce. In the process, he'd made a martyred hero of himself. He could have the woman he wanted after a token period of mourning. I was sure I'd solved the case.

*****

It was a hazy night, and there was a moon. I dragged myself out of my car half a block away from my apartment and glanced around quickly, feeling a bit foolish. You been in Bastogne, you sweep all the dark places with accusing eyes.

What passed for air was so hot and wet I felt like crumbling crackers into it. I didn't really relax my guard until I was back inside my apartment, where I met two goons I hadn't expected to see. Now I recognized the redheaded ox I'd seen at the Jazz Club. Billy Meechum was a bad-tempered mug I'd known slightly back in my F.B.I. days, when he maimed luckless gamblers and sold information to the Bureau. The guy with him was named Reilly.

"Meechum, Reilly, nice of you to wait up for me."

My living room hadn't been ransacked—that was a good start—but the window over by the fire escape stood wide open. My sister Jill's curtains flapped in the breeze, and somebody'd busted the wood around the latch.

Reilly—I didn't know a first name for him—had the build of a beer truck, a mustache like a black pocket comb, and a reputation for breaking ribs. I knew they'd both spent a couple years beating up union organizers in Detroit until the war put an end to strikes, and Meechum and Reilly drifted down to Washington in a hijacked furniture van. They'd both done graduate studies in a federal pen for that.

The two of them shoved me up against the wall just inside my front door, my Panama brushing the can-can dancer sketch. Meechum came away with the Colt .45 I'd stuck back under my armpit. "Griffin, you got a fuckin' permit to carry this fuckin' thing, or do we have to call the fuckin' cops?" He snapped a bullet into the chamber, not expecting a round to be in there already, ejecting it into a corner. A cigarette hung on to his lower lip as if it trusted him not to smoke it.

"Let's call the cops and report me." My confidence that I'd be glad if they did was ever so slight. What I didn't want was to scuffle with these rodeo clowns two-on-one while Meechum was holding my pistol in his immense hairy hand.

Meechum nodded silently, letting lank red hair flop down over his eyes. Reilly slammed a DeSoto station wagon into my rib cage. The pistol I'd carried in the war stayed pointed in the direction of my head. I coughed hard and caught my balance. "Can I do something for you two guys?"

Reilly's left crashed beside my right ear. I fell sideways onto the bare wooden floor. I rolled onto my knees with my feet away from both of them, deciding I'd listen to the echoing thunder a while before standing up. "I really don't recall either of you owing me this visit. Mind telling me something about it?"

*****

Meechum made the slightest wave with his left hand. Reilly stopped in mid-punch and stepped back grudgingly, as if not slugging me again hurt him more than it could possibly be worth.

"You wanna know what brings Reilly and me over here, Griffin? I gotta say that's a reasonable enough question." They jerked me to my feet. Meechum leaned into my face. "How about if we just tell you this straight fuckin' nose of yours went and jammed itself into business it don't belong in. Better wrestle it outa there and shove off."

You could see why Reilly was doing the muscle work—Meechum was starting to run to fat. I wanted to stall and see if I could figure out why they were there. "My nose is poked into a lot of stuff these days, Billy. That's my job. Do you guys mind telling me what particular business it is that you want me to get out of?"

Meechum whipped a snub-nosed black revolver out of his pants pocket. Then he emptied my .45. He slid the clip into his pocket and mustered enough intellect to jerk the Colt's slide back, ejecting the bullet he'd put into the chamber. He tapped the pistol itself on my nose. When he stared at Reilly and grumbled his name, the goon with the black mustache looked his way.

"The bullets."

Reilly broke a commandment under his breath while he picked up my two .45 slugs. "Somebody I know—somebody wants you to stay out of the case of the sliced-up broad." Meechum taunted me in a mocking tenor voice. "The Metro cops are all beatin' the weeds for the goddam killer, pal. Them bulls don't need no help from a guy dumb enough to give away a perfec'ly good gun. You know the case I'm talkin' about, don't make me name it. Just take up gardening or find some other sensible use for your time, buddy, and Reilly here won't have to smash your hands."

The forty-watt bulb in my ceiling fixture stopped rotating around my head. All that greasy Chinese food decided to stay in my stomach. I put my hands on the wall behind me slowly and got up even more slowly, just faster than a petunia growing.

"Did you need an answer on that now, Meechum?" I gave him

as dumb a grin as I could muster. "Or can I think it over 'til breakfast?"

Meechum laughed out loud. I'd counted on his Spike Jones sense of humor when I phrased it that way. "Hell, I don't need no answer at all. I wasn't askin' no fuckin' question. Just quit the case and mail the old Boston fart a big fat bill for your services. The cops got that one wrapped up—tell him that—and nobody needs you pokin' and proddin' inta it like a farm boy pickin' fuckin' corn or somethin'. Understand what I mean?"

I did. I understood that two thugs the size of aircraft carriers were telling me at gunpoint somebody'd sent them to scare me off the Betty Dyson murder case so Jack Kennedy could be sent to the chair on the evidence the police already had. What I didn't want to do right then was promise Meechum and Reilly anything, or eat any more crow on their account, or get my head stoved in.

"The last thing I need is to keep you guys out late tonight. I know what you want from me, Billy. That couldn't be any clearer. You two like anything else? Glass of milk out of my icebox, maybe?"

Meechum put the muzzle of my empty automatic against my forehead. "Here, this piece is yours. No, I think we understand one another, pal. Nice place you got here, Griffin. But you oughta lock the fuckin' windows."

And then they left, a bad dream I'd had while wide awake.

*****

For another hour or so, I sat up playing solitaire with a well-worn deck of cards that had a meaningless pattern on the back, thinking about my various visitors. Somebody else besides Snilder wanted me off the case now, wanted Jack Kennedy sealed up and delivered. Just when I'd decided Dyson killed his wife to forestall a divorce, two thugs I couldn't imagine him knowing told me to butt out. I was in no shape to figure out how they were involved, so I didn't call either of the Kennedys. Finally, I dogged out on the couch, dropping half the cards on the floor.

The nightmare I wanted to put off barged in anyway. It started with me floating through the sky, a dandelion seed in the breeze. A psych professor at Ohio State once told a class that dreams of flying are actually about freedom. I'm not sure that applies particularly well to former paratroopers with no parachutes.

At any rate, I was flying along a bit nervously when a bumblebee the size of a Panama Clipper came after me. Then suddenly, I was the bee itself. Rising like a hot air balloon was a tall, skinny clown with an undersized derby. I saw his silhouette surrounded by thumbtacks and long hatpins. "Get off the fucking case, Griffin," the clown brayed as if he'd said something uproarious. "Get off the fucking case. Get off the fucking case. Get off the fucking case." I hadn't known gargantuan bumblebees could shudder.

In the nightmare, I sweated like a pork roast in a gas oven. Now the gunmetal sky turned black, and a flare popped above Bastogne. Now Colonel Epping ordered me to reinforce Jerry's company. In this dream, it occurred to me that if Jerry died, Lucille would be available. We took forever, but Jerry clung to life. His goat-faced sergeant croaked, "Took your sweet time, Captain. Out chasing dames?" Another flare lit Lucille's tear-washed face. Then she was gone. The sergeant faded, too, and Jerry as well.

Dawn broke slowly, and with it came consciousness. It was about five-thirty when I woke up, gray dimness lurking in my room like fog. The dream always played out worse the times I decided to let Jerry die so I could have Lucille, and I always wrestled afterward with what had really happened.

THIRTY-THREE

When you wake up at dawn in July, you've got nothing but time to kill. I loafed in bed for a while reading General Sherman's account of Vicksburg, shaved as leisurely as possible, and daydreamed twenty minutes in a tepid shower. Once I'd dressed, except for my tie and jacket, I fried some bacon and half a dozen flapjacks while the coffee perked. The radio promised the mercury'd stay below seventy-five.

Before I left my apartment, I made a couple calls. Jack Kennedy's office and home phones didn't answer, and I wasn't calling the Old Man that early. The police should have received Moon Snilder's resignation packet by then, so we'd probably headed off a headline in the evening papers saying

Detective in Kennedy Murder Case Missing;
Police Fear Congressman Killed Officer

or something of that sort.

Then I made myself take a long walk before the day heated up. My intermittent efforts to stay in shape pretty much resolved themselves into doing calisthenics in my living room once or twice a week or reminding my legs I'd been a foot soldier. I hiked as a way to think things over. By that morning, I was better at remembering Betty smiling than Betty dead. Songbirds chirped like schoolgirls. I *did* miss a step when a woodpecker started drilling before I realized it wasn't the chatter of a Browning machinegun a couple hills away.

I wanted to tell the Kennedys what I'd learned about Dyson and spend the day cracking his alibi. That remained my lead theory. If the flyboy killed Betty, somebody saw him leave the base or return to it, and somebody'd remember seeing him in or near the apartment. By the time I'd gone a good mile—down Thirteenth to Pennsylvania Avenue, around the back of the White House, up Seventeenth to M again and home—I'd mapped it all out. Then I drove to my office around nine-thirty.

*****

Lana looked up from a cherry Danish pastry and coffee when I got to the agency. "Good morning, Mister Griffin. Can I get you anything?"

"Anything but another suspect. Yesterday Kennedy seemed to be the only conceivable killer. Now Betty's husband looks probable. Dyson abandoned a gorgeous and loving wife to be closer to his office than anybody thought was needed. He went with a brunette to the Jazz Club Tuesday night after the memorial service."

Lana washed down another bite of her roll. "What about his alibi?"

"That means nothing, Lana. If he murdered Betty, the alibi's phony and I'll find the holes in it."

Her grin was infectious. She loved winning. "Are you sure he did it?"

"Not quite. It makes sense, but I've got to root out the evidence. And I haven't ruled out Secretary Symington and his aide. The guy I shared dinner with last night wants to talk, but he's scared of something—probably whatever they're hiding."

"You're happy it isn't Mr. Kennedy, aren't you?" Her coffee and roll left no trace but the mug she rinsed and the waxed paper she tossed into the trash.

*****

Jack Kennedy jerked the office door open a minute or two later, looking like an expectant father who feared a second set of quintuplets. His red-and-yellow striped tie dangled crookedly, and his hair was a bird nest.

"God, Griffin, I'm sliding down the rabbit hole. Dad's gone over to the *Washington Post* to give Phil Graham a warning not to be hasty. Did you read the newspapers yet?"

He waved the front section at me and pushed it into my hands.

We walked into my office and I sat on the edge of my desk. There it was, bottom of page one.

Congressman Is Questioned
In Strawberry Blonde Murder
Kennedy "Not a Suspect Now"
According to Police Superintendent

"All the article actually says is that the police questioned me late yesterday afternoon as somebody seen with Betty Dyson Friday evening at the Army-Navy Club dinner. But Superintendent Howard carefully left himself room to suspect me later on. That isn't what's shaken me, though. I gather you don't know about *this*."

He snatched back the paper from me and folded it open to the third page, pointing with a shaky finger.

DC Woman Found Slain
In 16th Street Apartment

My guts turned to concrete. Somebody raped and murdered Susan Prebble around ten o'clock, the *Post* reported—slashed her throat and stabbed her repeatedly.

The paper's editors hadn't thought to link it to the "Strawberry Blonde Murder" yet, except for the comment that it was the second rape-murder in less than a week in Washington. The paper didn't give much detail at this point, but they'd make a connection—you could smell it. Susan had carrot-colored hair, but she'd become a strawberry blonde in tomorrow's headlines. I stared back at Kennedy.

*****

"I—I took Susan out to dinner in Georgetown last night. People spoke with us there together. We caught a cab back to her apartment for a drink afterwards and never had the drink. One thing followed another in rather quick succession, and I—ah—we made love in her living room on her couch. I left by nine-thirty, perhaps somewhat earlier."

I remembered Susan's ironic smile, the near-drone of her low-pitched voice, the sun-pinked pale skin disappearing into the V-neck of her funeral dress. "It says here the police were summoned after somebody called the manager and reported hearing screams coming from her apartment. Did she scream when you were—well, while you were there?"

"No, she didn't." He was pale beneath his tan. "I feel as if I've become Death himself, dressed in a black robe, carrying a scythe in my pants."

The second murder had shaken Kennedy badly. Me, too. I'd found Susan very appealing. Kennedy couldn't bring himself to sit down, but he was still very much in control of himself. "Look, first of all, Suze was a good friend of mine before the war, Griffin. Sex, yes, but she was also a woman I could have conversations with. I used to talk with her about problems with other women, and she'd sympathize. For Suze to die this way sickens me. And it's a shock, as well, for anybody I know and care about to be murdered so viciously."

I could see that clearly in his eyes. His jaw was rigid with anger. I let him talk while I started sticking the odd Tinker-Toys of his behavior together.

"But this is *not* a terrible coincidence." Kennedy continued pacing. "In the past week, I've taken two very willing, fine-looking young women to their homes after having dinner with them. We enjoyed sex in both instances. Each time I headed back to my house in Georgetown alone, and each time somebody else slashed their throats and stabbed them again and again. The *same* somebody, I should say. These two outrages are identical, Griffin."

"Yes, they are, Jack." I found myself wondering if his veneer of sanity could be a cracked transparent glaze like the one on Betty Dyson's ashtray. "Identical right down to your being there both times. Right down to your taking them to bed. The first question I've got to ask myself is this: Did Jack Kennedy kill these women? Is there any history of mental illness in your family, Jack? Is there anything about visiting their apartments you can't explain to yourself?"

His voice sounded low and steady. "Once again, I did not kill Betty Dyson, and no, I did not kill Susan Prebble, either. And no, I'm not crazy."

"Jack, would you know it if you were?"

THIRTY-FOUR

That question stood him up straight, Nathan Hale with the noose over his head. I bored in. "Look, just to toss all the possibilities onto the table, some murderers have no recollection of their crimes. For one thing, the war didn't leave any of us who fought in it unscarred mentally. If you were—well, with some mental conditions—look, a man with, I don't know, I'm not a psychiatrist, Jack, I just took a couple psych courses in college. I've worked on a few weird cases. Some men could do everything you say you did, then go into a homicidal rage and kill a woman, and afterward block out any recollection of it."

"I'd remember." Kennedy looked damned angry.

"*Would you?* The conscious mind, Professor Barker always taught, is a minefield. A guy I know—an officer—was ordered to relieve his buddy's unit that was being overrun. They arrived a bit too late. He doesn't remember dawdling, but in his *dreams,* he delayed moving his men because he hoped the buddy's wife would be available afterward. He doesn't know which version to believe."

Kennedy started to interrupt, but I waved him off. "As you say, this can't be a coincidence." My mind raged, as if I were a drunk waking up in a burning house. In that moment, I couldn't imagine he *wasn't* the killer, and I wanted to break his neck.

*****

The congressman stared at me angrily. Then his jawbone relaxed, and the bonfire in his eyes burned out. "If you think I haven't been ransacking my brain over this, looking for any clue that I might have done what you're asking me, then *you're* the lunatic, Griffin."

The lake-blue eyes searched for help, close to desperation.

Myself, I was a gutted building. I wanted to feel how horrible it must have felt for him, the connection between desire and death, the marble floor of the Capitol turning to quicksand beneath him. Instead, numbness oozed through me. I was an hourglass filled with ashes.

"Griffin, all the while they questioned me yesterday afternoon about Betty Dyson's death, I knew I hadn't killed her. I hung on to that like the bottom rung of a rope ladder hanging over Hell. Then I read about Suze Prebble during breakfast. Everything this means hit me at the same instant: the twin murder charges I'll never beat, the two loving women who died so monstrously for some reason connected to sex with me, and the coincidence so impossible I'm questioning my sanity as much as you are."

He walked over to the window and looked nowhere.

"In the last two hours, Griffin, I've pored over and over every minute I spent in their apartments, over and over the *consecutiveness* from each moment to the next one, searching for the slightest gap I can't recall. I can account for every minute to myself, Griffin, but I keep rechecking it, wondering if I could have—have killed them while in a delusional state, thinking something normal was going on. Questioning your own sanity around a horrible coincidence that cannot be a coincidence is more terrifying than you can imagine."

*****

The fingers of his left hand examined the fingers of his right, his mind surely unaware of it. His eyes searched mine again, as if something he'd misplaced might be in them.

"Congressman, I think—"

Kennedy glared at me. "You think I could be a psychotic killer."

"Actually, no, I don't. I think something a lot more sinister than that is going on here."

Kennedy stepped back to the window, staring out toward the shade trees for a minute or two. I could tell he wasn't focusing his eyes on the leaves or the sunlight or anything else outside. Finally, he turned back to face me. "What do you think it is?"

"Ever since Betty was murdered, I've been thinking that if you didn't do it, her death had to be about her. Now I think it was about *you*."

"But you just said—"

"You're right, Congressman, there has to be a connection. Either you killed them both, or somebody's setting you up."

THIRTY-FIVE

Kennedy and his father and Abe Moskowitz agreed someone was framing Jack when we met half an hour or so later in the living room of the ambassador's suite. A coincidence was out of the question. We also ruled out Jack as the killer, whether out of madness or to protect his reputation, though I still had doubts.

Likewise, Susan's death pretty clearly eased Colonel Dyson off the hook—he had an alibi for the first murder, and I could check whether he had one for last night. Susan didn't meet the description of the dark-haired woman at the Jazz Club.

But *somebody* had slaughtered two attractive women within a very short time after the congressman had been seen with each of them, after he'd marked them with his rare vintage genes. "No question I'll be identified." Kennedy looked resigned but not desperate. "I waved to dozens of people while Susan and I were at dinner. I rode cabs both ways. I joked with the desk clerk and an acquaintance of mine we ran into in the lobby coming in, and again with the clerk as I left."

"Somebody followed you." The Old Man and Moskowitz nodded agreement with me. "Somebody who might know you don't stay long after sex. Whoever it was waited 'til you left—'til he *saw* you leave, in fact—and somehow got into each of their apartments. Then he killed the women and got out, apparently without being seen or heard."

Moskowitz nodded. "The victims let him in. Did Betty Dyson and Susan Prebble know the killer? Was he dressed as a cop or a handyman? Was more than one guy involved? *Was* it a guy? A jealous woman? Most of all, why did they let the killer in?"

Pretty clearly, at this point, the murders had nothing to do with the two victims. By then Dyson's place in the whole affair no longer seemed even marginally relevant. Ditto Ted Bradley, the haunted apartment manager. Symington might have had the resources for a complicated murder, but what tie could he have had to Susan or to Jack Kennedy?

The ambassador shook his head wearily. He seemed pretty worn around the edges that morning, although the news of the second murder hadn't come in time to cost him any sleep. He'd combed his hair back hastily, and his eyes were King Lear telling a tragic tale. Someone had marked his second son to die.

*****

Moskowitz looked up from writing on his yellow pad. "It must be somebody who's got it in for you, Congressman. Or you, Mr. Ambassador. Somebody who wants one of you destroyed."

We'd had better appetites the day before. The ambassador's blueberry Danish lay unharmed on his fragile plate, and Jack had taken two discernable bites out of another one. Half a bran muffin waited in front of Moskowitz, and I'd left part of a pecan roll. On the other hand, we'd hit the coffee the way Joe Louis hit Max Schmeling.

The Old Man snorted and stood up, pacing as he spoke. "I don't think it's an attempt to get me. Look, I've made some enemies in my time, probably made some recently, as a matter of fact. But my heyday is essentially over. And how could it be Jack? My son has no enemies of this sort. He's a war hero, and he won a congressional election, but that's all. He can't keep his fly buttoned any more than I can. But you don't frame somebody for rape and murder so you can send him to the gas chamber just for screwing women."

"Electric chair. It's the electric chair in D.C." I'd been staring out the window down into Lafayette Square while they spoke, watching sagging people sweat as they sauntered through the park below. Washington in July. If you can't walk like a Southerner, you'll look like a rag mop. The flag over the White House was a nylon stocking drying over a shower curtain rod in some woman's bathroom.

I'd been listening to the conversation, thinking about Betty Dyson and Susan Prebble. You got so used to seeing men lying dead in the war, in all the ingenious variations on the theme of death by unnatural causes. You got so hungry just for the sight and the sound and the touch of a pretty woman. More than the shock of how brutal their deaths had been, Betty and Susan had been soft and bright and full of life, but they'd disappeared from the world of the living as if they'd been daydreams. It left me sad and leaden.

I looked up. "Well, Mr. Ambassador, as Abe says, somebody's working awfully hard to set Jack up for a long fall. Unless the murderer has a lot more brains than Moon Snilder, it isn't simply an extortion scheme. But we still don't know what the killer or killers are after."

"I believe we'll find that out today." Moskowitz, crisp in a dead-white linen suit and a deep-green necktie, looked as fresh and starched as the tablecloths at the Mayflower. The cufflinks riveting his sleeves were small, the most elegant use of gold and emeralds I'd ever seen. He lit a slim, dark cigar with a heavy table lighter, and the three of us waited while he dragged in and finally let out a long puff of acrid smoke. "Call it an intuition, if you like. Griffin's moving ahead steadily, isn't that right, Jack?"

"Sure. The only things I still don't know are why somebody killed Betty Dyson and Susan Prebble or who did it."

Moskowitz kept rolling. "Meanwhile, two things have become clear. One: Congressman Kennedy needs to visit his home district in Massachusetts and attend to pressing business there for a few days. Two: he needs to be as celibate as the Mother Superior of the Poor Clares for a while."

"That's simply impossible. Leaving town, I mean." He wore a chagrinned smile for an instant but didn't indulge it. "Look, this session of Congress is in its final days. We'll vote on dozens of significant, controversial issues—including the Unification Bill, one of the most sweeping changes in our history. Several bills face close votes. It would end my career to go visit my mother in Hyannis this week just as surely as it would if I were to be arrested for rape and murder."

"That's up to you." Moskowitz leaned forward, resting his cigar in a crystal ashtray. "But if I were our beleaguered Superintendent of Police with all the evidence he's got, I'd arrest you for both murders within the next twenty-four hours."

THIRTY-SIX

Two plainclothes cops waited in Kennedy's cramped two-room third-floor office in the Old House Office Building when Jack, the ambassador, and I got there around noon. A bony detective sergeant I didn't know murmured that his name was Cook. "Congressman, I've got instructions to take you directly to the superintendent's office. I can obtain an arrest warrant in half an hour if you want to stand on ceremony, sir."

The ambassador started to step between the congressman and the two cops, but Jack touched his father's shoulder. "Yes, this would be a good time for me to meet with Superintendent Howard because I expect a number of important votes later today. Besides, I've just been discussing the case with these two members of my legal team. They can ride down to the superintendent's office with us."

Without a pause, he turned to his worried-looking young secretary. "Mary, call Abe Moskowitz and have him meet us over at the police superintendent's office." He grinned. "I'll be glad to consider that my one phone call if you like."

What the soft-voiced detective sergeant *didn't* like was taking directions from a mere mortal, but he surely knew the man he was bringing in for questioning was a member of the committee that owned the District. The last thing Cook wanted was to have to deny legal representation to a United States congressman who oversaw his job. It's in the Constitution, for one thing. Cook didn't need trouble.

Heading down the marble stairs, Joe Kennedy whispered, "Griffin, are you truly a lawyer?"

"Of a sort. Used to be in the FBI, and you had to be either a lawyer or an accountant to get in. One of Hoover's few useful ideas. I hate both math and writing other people's real estate contracts. Passed the bar exam here in 1940, though I never practiced law. But are *you* really a lawyer?"

He chuckled. "Actually, I was awarded *honorary* law degrees from Oglethorpe and Edinburgh. People assume that a big shot like me must be an attorney. By the way, Snilder stepped off his flight in the Dominican Republic, and customs officials took him into custody immediately. Somebody tipped the authorities he was smuggling a large amount of cash in a package addressed to a leader of the opposition to Generalissimo Trujillo. Probably won't get to the cheap liquor and easy women for a long while." He flashed me a death's-head grin. "Foolish thing for him to interfere with a Latin American dictator, wasn't it?"

Unperturbed. Impressively impassive.

*****

Superintendent Howard—formally "Major and Superintendent"—posed as an Anglo-Saxon Buddha behind a polished mahogany desk the size of a Sherman tank. He didn't blink when Congressman Kennedy strode silently into his dark, paneled office with a three-man squad of putative lawyers. Gentleman Jimmy's lush white hair didn't ruffle, and his florid jowls wouldn't have flapped in a hurricane. His custom-tailored navy suit didn't wrinkle, and his shirt was fresh-fallen snow.

"Congressman, we've met before." Howard's French horn voice was melodious. He rose from his burgundy leather swivel chair to shake hands as if a college buddy had just strolled into his Pullman compartment. "I introduced myself at the hearing last month on public safety in the District. It's good to see you again, Congressman, though under these unfortunate circumstances...."

Howard stopped sucking up to his murder suspect and gestured to the two matching leather sofas. We took seats, Jack on the right, next to his father, and Moskowitz and I on the other one.

With a studied carelessness, Howard began stuffing a briar pipe with black, oily-smelling tobacco. "I received a call this morning." He paused to pass a gold-plated Ronson over his pipe, puffing a few times—less for the pleasure of smoking than to draw out the tension and to command the situation. "A citizen tipped me that you had been seen with Susan Prebble last evening. I assume you know Mrs. Prebble has been murdered."

Kennedy nodded. "I read it in the newspapers."

There was a deliberate oppressiveness to the mahogany desk, the burgundy furniture, and the dark-blue drapes. You were supposed to feel buried alive in the superintendent's office, but like the gesture with the pipe, it was so overdone it canceled itself out. The smoke smelled like smoldering creosote.

"I had already decided I would issue a warrant for your arrest in the Betty Dyson murder case this morning." Howard stared Jack in the eye. "I dispatched a team of my best detectives to the Prebble woman's apartment right away. We just received the autopsy report and the lab work. No question it's the same killer. I'm certain I don't have to tell you the Prebble woman was raped as well as viciously slashed to death, do I, Congressman Kennedy?"

"I also read that in the papers." Jack kept motionless. So did I. Moskowitz laid a hand on the Old Man's forearm, but whether to comfort him or to keep him quiet, I couldn't tell. "Congressman, I've been trying all morning to think why I shouldn't simply have you brought before a grand jury this afternoon and charged with capital rape and murder in both cases. You not only know what you did, Congressman, but you must also know that I have overwhelming evidence in each case." He passed the glittering Ronson over his pipe again, sucking the flame down into it. "And by the way, I've located six very solid witnesses who can place you at the two crime scenes. Four of them are white. We can fry you with their testimony."

THIRTY-SEVEN

Moskowitz snorted. "Short of eyewitnesses to the crimes, you have enough circumstantial evidence to fry an egg, but not anything like enough evidence to convict a war hero before a jury, whether your witnesses are white men or kangaroos."

Howard snorted. "'*War hero!*' Oh, how careless of me not to have reckoned with that! Do you think we don't arrest 'war heroes' every day in Washington—for every crime in the book, from sodomy to shoplifting? You might have pulled that 'war hero' dodge on a local jury two or three years ago, Moskowitz, when the war was still going on, but not now. No, I'm afraid the war's been over for a long time."

Maybe it has for you, I thought.

"I didn't harm either of them." Kennedy's voice stayed level. "I did not rape either woman, and I did not murder either one."

His father cut him off, leaning forward and smiling as he spread his hands apart, his palms facing each other. "Let's look at this reasonably for a moment, Superintendent. The evidence *is* circumstantial, however damning it may appear to you. Mr. Moskowitz is correct about that. And my son Jack *is* completely innocent of these crimes. But let's forget all that for now. You and I are practical men, Superintendent."

The Old Man sounded as if he were about to offer Howard a sum of money that would astonish everybody. I started to cut him off before he committed a serious crime, but curiosity got the better of me. I wondered whether the ambassador would do it and how Gentleman Jimmy Howard would respond.

"There aren't more than five men in America richer than I am, did you know that? I'd like you to imagine the legion of legal talent—no disrespect to Mr. Moskowitz here—that I will assemble to represent my son in a courtroom. Imagine the hordes of private investigators I will be able to unleash to check the background of every potential witness you have and to look for the real killer while you piss away federal revenues on a glamour trial in which you will lose. Imagine the *Washington Post* and the House District of Columbia Committee discussing how sound your judgment has been."

Buddha vanished, replaced by W.C. Fields. "Now just a—"

The Old Man overrode Howard. "I'm not suggesting your witnesses will move to other cities to take new and more lucrative jobs or that they'll sun themselves in Haiti during the long months your trial is being conducted before a packed and disappointed courtroom. I'm not suggesting that all your witnesses will become amnesiacs or that your underpaid detectives might doctor your files. No, Superintendent, I wouldn't predict any of those things. I'm an honest man, and I assume other people are honest and civic-minded as well."

The ambassador was a Hollywood showman enjoying his own performance. He smiled like a dance band maestro. "But let me suggest that you imagine the highest caliber psychiatrists in the nation telling a jury of mothers, fathers, veterans, and very attractive young women what tragic effects the war might have had on my son's mind, both losing his older brother and being injured himself during close combat on the unforgiving sea."

The edge of a sob tinged the Old Man's voice, but he mastered it. "So you need to understand, Superintendent, that sending my boy to the electric chair is a hollow threat."

*****

"You're—You'd lock your son up in St. Elizabeth's Hospital for the rest of his life?"

"I don't like having my sons killed, Mr. Howard."

"Mr.—ah—*Ambassador* Kennedy, *you* may find St. E's preferable to watching him make his last confession to a priest and then sizzling immediately afterward." He looked directly at Jack. "I can assure the congressman that St. E's is no place for a handsome young cock hound to spend fifty years."

Jack's face turned ashen. For that matter, I hadn't much liked the ambassador's suggestion of hiring "hordes of private investigators." And clearly, making Jack out to be a lunatic veteran might spare his life, but his career, his freedom, and everything else he enjoyed about being alive would be gone. My client sat still, his eyes a zoo animal's.

I liked Jack Kennedy. I wanted him to be innocent. It wasn't just his boyish charm. He was bright, which frankly was not something most congressmen are accused of. He thought about things and could entertain conflicting ideas. He was King Croesus's playboy son whose father had sent him to a desk job early in the war, but he'd finagled his way out of it to go fight. My sense was Jack would find his footing if he got past this, and we'd be glad he was in Washington before it was over.

"Never mind the insanity defense." Abe Moskowitz scowled. "The congressman's rationality is not at issue in this case. Superintendent, Jack Kennedy did not murder those two unfortunate women. Somebody has been setting him up."

"Really." The superintendent sneered as he set the black briar pipe on his glass-topped desk. "And who might that 'somebody' be, Mr. Moskowitz?"

I had no idea, myself. Moskowitz smiled as if the toughest question on the exam turned out to be what year they started the War of 1812. "I expect an answer for you in three or four days, Superintendent. Our investigators haven't been led astray by the simplistic solution the real killer dazzled you with. It would save you a great deal of embarrassment to wait until we conclude our inquiry."

Moskowitz bluffed like a champ. Gentleman Jimmy Howard's expression told me he knew it but couldn't be sure.

"As I say, Congressman Kennedy, I have been trying to think why I shouldn't haul you before a grand jury this afternoon." The richness of his voice sounded bittersweet, a horn fugue in something depressing by Wagner. "This whole case became clear to me on Monday, even before you murdered the second woman. I told my detectives, 'Let's say Jack Kennedy killed the girl. That fits all the evidence, and it makes sense, as much as a crime like this *can* make sense.' And then an idea occurred to me this morning, Congressman, while I was reading the autopsy report on Mrs. Prebble over a cup of coffee right here at my desk. There might be another possibility."

I was sure he wanted money—boatloads more than Snilder asked for, probably more than the District's annual appropriation—and I thought the Kennedys and Abe Moskowitz expected that as well.

Gentleman Jimmy picked up his briar pipe and did his routine with the gilded lighter again, as slowly as he'd done it before. "I'd like to speak privately with the congressman, if the rest of you don't mind waiting outside."

Moskowitz started to object, and so did the ambassador. I wondered if Howard would dare to send a congressman downstairs to be beaten up. Jack raised his hand and silenced us.

"Five minutes. I'll give you five minutes, Superintendent. After that five minutes, I will leave to take care of critical legislative business on the Hill. Or you will arrest me, if you prefer, and I will demand to speak with my legal team present again."

Jack looked pretty calm for a thirty-year-old first-term member of Congress facing utter ruin. The electric chair wasn't at all out of the question—no matter what Joe Kennedy had argued—if the prosecuting attorney yelled loud enough about who in the hell these rich pretty boys think they are.

But something—perhaps all those dark nights of the soul patrolling in a flimsy wooden boat in the South Pacific—had put steel in Kennedy's spine. There were limits to the terrors Gentleman Jimmy Howard could spread before him.

THIRTY-EIGHT

Without a word to one another, the four of us filed out of the Municipal Center five minutes later and rode silently in a red taxicab over to the Hay-Adams. We didn't speak on the elevator, nor in the carpeted corridor leading to the ambassador's suite, nor before the heavy gilded door had swung closed with its brass-on-brass whisper.

"It isn't money that he wants." Jack looked bemused. "Howard told me there's a meeting coming up on Friday afternoon—tomorrow, before Congress adjourns this weekend—that's important to him, a House District of Columbia Committee meeting. I knew about it, of course, but he's *very* well informed about it. Howard tells me he is 'deeply concerned about the tenor' of a bill that will be voted on during that meeting."

"A bill?" Jack might as well have told the ambassador that chickens' beaks were made of aluminum. The idea that Gentleman Jimmy Howard had legislative rather than monetary goals was incomprehensible to him.

"I'm a *congressman*, Dad." Jack seemed to need to let his father know he worked for a living. "And I'm a member of the D.C. Committee. We oversee everything about government in the District. We are the government here."

"How exciting for you."

"It is for Howard. We've held a number of hearings on the Metropolitan Police Department this year. We suspect the statistics on quite a few murder cases are being suppressed. Police officers get paid off to leave murders unsolved—you saw that offered yesterday in this very room—and whenever something like that happens, money seems to float upward. Important evidence disappears from locked rooms, detectives scratch their heads, and *honest* cops end up pounding the pavements in the July heat and January cold out among the Negro wards in Congress Heights."

The ambassador shrugged. "Jack, this happy horsecrap goes on in any number of cities. What the hell—"

"What makes it unusual in Washington, Dad, is how much it happens and that Congress might decide to deal with it. The bill Howard's afraid of was introduced by Representative Owen Tollafsen, a particularly stiff-necked Republican from rural Minnesota, a man with no tolerance for cities, vice, crime, or corruption of any kind. He really hates Washington. His bill would set up a select panel with unprecedented authority to hire staff and investigate, to make sweeping recommendations for reform, and take individual cases to a special grand jury the bill would create. The Senate has already adopted an identical measure. If the House passes it, Truman's pretty sure to sign it into law."

The Old Man snorted. "That would no doubt be embarrassing to Howard, Jack, but that's no—"

Jack waved his father's condescending objection off. "Dad, if that legislation is adopted, I think Howard could be indicted as an accessory after the fact in murder cases he's let be quashed. Apparently, the superintendent found an informant on the committee staff, someone who has taken a tally on how the various committee members plan to vote on this thing. It's extremely close."

His father finally listened.

"Chairman Dirksen would like it to pass, Dad, to embarrass the Democrats who controlled Congress so long before this year. A number of Republicans don't want to spend the money for it, though, and some Southern Democrats want the District left the way it is, with its cheap liquor and its cheap whores, a home away from Dixie where a champion of racial purity can get his hands on a well-built Negro girl without any Daughters of the Confederacy finding out he did."

"Where does that leave us?" The Old Man lit one of his cedar-boxed Havana cigars and passed the box around.

Jack took another and bit the tip open. "I've made it very clear I think it's a good bill. The Nation's capital needs to be a city people feel safe in and can be proud of. Having murderers finance the ineptitude of the Metropolitan Police is simply not acceptable to me."

He passed the heavy gold Ronson across the open end of his cigar. Pungent pale-gray smoke haunted the coffee table. Moskowitz nodded and took the lighter from Jack. When he finished, he passed it my way, and I lit a cigar, too.

Moskowitz spoke first. "What does our urbane friend want, then, if it isn't money?"

"Superintendent Howard wants me to skip the committee meeting on Friday or else vote *against* the Tollafsen measure. Either way, the bill would fail, and the full House won't get a crack at voting on it. The Senate version will die without a bill passing the House. It may not come up again next year if it fails now—1948's an election year. If I do as he asks, Howard promises he'll bury these two murder cases and stall the newspapers until after the committee votes. If I cooperate with him, he says, 'probably some lunatic will come forward to confess and spend the winter taking the rest cure at St. Elizabeths.' He offered it as plainly as that."

You could have heard a worm crawling inside a velvet bag for a minute or two. Joe Kennedy glanced around through the spectral air, turning from his son to the elegant lawyer and then to me with a little mocking grin.

"What," Moskowitz asked at last, "did you tell the superintendent you would do about his proposal?"

Jack Kennedy looked very young in that moment—a prep school boy smoking one of his father's cigars after being caught screwing a dimpled waitress from a roadhouse across the tracks. "I don't know yet what I'm going to do, Abe. I'm in favor of that bill, and I've said I'm planning on voting for it. Being blackmailed, especially by Washington's head law enforcement official, makes me furious."

Moskowitz murmured his agreement.

Jack leaned forward. "And I didn't murder either of those women. But even being linked with this in public is going to hurt me. I don't imagine the Eleventh Congressional District would like to hear I only screwed a hero's wife and a war widow just before they were murdered. And the evidence the police have got could ultimately send me to the electric chair if I faced the right prosecutor and the wrong jury."

*****

A breeze flowed through a half-open window, and we all used it as an excuse to be quiet for just a minute. It was Moskowitz who broke the mood. "Did anybody else notice the topic Howard *didn't* bring up, at least not to all of us?"

The two Kennedys and I all used the phrase "blood type" in the next five seconds, with Jack adding, "As much as I expected it, he never mentioned it when I was alone with him. Frankly, I thought he'd try to badger an answer out of me."

I made a face and shook my head. "You're thinking Howard's trying to solve the case. What he wants is to make you jump through his hoop. He alluded to lab reports proving it was the same man, so if you were the killer, you could figure all he needed was a sample of your blood to put you away. But if he pressed it and you had only a coincidental connection to the crime, he'd have lost his leverage."

Joe Kennedy grinned. "Griffin's right, boys. And what it means is Howard isn't too sure Jack murdered those poor girls."

"The question remains," Moskowitz repeated with only the slightest tone of irritation, "what did you promise the superintendent you'd do?"

"Well, I did *not* say what I just laid out for the three of you. I told him again I was not guilty of any crime and that I'd have to think further about the situation. Dad, I simply can't afford to duck out on that committee meeting at this point. I'm already being called a playboy, a lightweight, in some quarters. I'd have to use Howard's phrase and say that 'I'm deeply concerned about the tenor' of the bill."

Moskowitz glared. "You agreed to that, knowing there was probably a tape recorder somewhere?"

"No. What I told Howard was I'd need to look carefully once again at the language of the Tollafsen measure to make certain that Congress wasn't being hasty. I'm sure he *took* that as my agreement. Perhaps it bought us the rest of the week."

As much as the haze in the room permitted, everybody looked everybody else in the eyes. Moskowitz blew out a thunderhead of smoke. "Jack, you're better at this than I expected. That was well done."

The congressman grinned shyly.

Moskowitz did not smile. "Jack says his committee meeting will probably take place Friday afternoon. We all agreed earlier that he's been set up. Now we know who did it and *why* he did it. Griffin, you've got not much more than a day to prove all this."

THIRTY-NINE

Moskowitz and I rode down on the elevator with the Kennedys and hailed them a cab. After they sped away, the lawyer turned to me with a grave expression, sweat starting to bead on his forehead even in the shade of a sycamore tree. "Griffin, you don't think Howard was behind the murders, do you?"

"No, I don't. Even if Howard ordered somebody to kill Susan in the manner of Betty's death, I don't see how he could have anticipated the opportunity for that first killing. I doubt there's anybody on the Metropolitan force both corrupt enough and competent enough to do this for him. Howard's using another man's crimes to his own advantage."

"Any idea who might have done it?" Moskowitz looked a bit haggard.

"Yeah, I see some possibility Betty Dyson's death was connected to her job with the Air Corps Assistant Secretary of War, so I wangled an interview."

"Stuart Symington?" Abe suppressed a cough. Clearly, I'd surprised him. "He owns a reputation as a man who makes things happen. I've heard he's cagey rather than particularly bright."

"Both women used to work in that office, Abe. Susan could have been the source of the dirty secret Betty learned, or Betty could have confided it to Susan."

"If nothing else, it might be something I can use to cloud jurors' minds." Moskowitz had a criminal smile. "When do you question Symington?"

"I've got to drive over to the Pentagon in forty minutes. I doubt he's behind it, though he's the only connection to both women that we have."

Crossing Lafayette Square, both of us seemed to be glancing around as if we wanted to make certain nobody lurked within earshot. The sidewalk we shared curved beneath a dozen oaks and maples, the dappled shade warding off the worst of the heat.

I checked my watch and took another look around. "Abe, we're operating under the premise that Jack didn't kill those women, that somebody's setting him up. How strongly do you believe it?"

He glanced back toward the hotel. "Privately? I'll be damned if I can tell. It's as hard to believe he's innocent as it is to envision him doing such a thing. Even if he did, it's difficult to imagine somebody with so much wealth and power standing trial for it. But a man's entitled to a lawyer, and if he's tried, all you'll hear from me is dead certainty he's being framed. My only hope would be raising enough doubts to hang the jury rather than Jack. How about you, Griffin?"

"About the same. I keep remembering the rich are different. Jack nurses ambitions mortal men don't dream of. Protecting them could motivate desperate acts. I haven't let myself think much about that." We started walking again.

"You could be right, Griffin. That crossed my mind, too." Moskowitz gazed at me intently. "It's a question neither of us wants to examine, but we'd better at least consider it."

I nodded. "The one person we can identify who was with both women at the times they were butchered is our client."

The lawyer glanced around to make sure nobody was nearby. "Griffin, you've been worked over and threatened with worse. I'm their lawyer. Both of us could be in danger. What if we're wrong, and that earnest young man did do it? Joe Kennedy's a case study in ruthless ambition. He'd do just about anything to protect his son, whether Jack killed them or not. The Old Man made a police detective vanish with neither a trace nor a question left behind."

Moskowitz must have been frightened—he usually held his cards snug against his three-piece suit. I asked him to go on.

"My greatest qualm, Griffin—if Jack turns out to be the killer—is that the crimes and everybody connected with them could disappear into the thick air of Washington."

"True, Abe. And Gentleman Jimmy Howard has the moral fiber of soggy corn flakes." A dozen pigeons scampered to avoid our feet.

"Exactly. Jack votes against the police reform bill, and Joe makes Howard a good offer. The police dispose of the murders. The press papers them over. Some hapless bastard goes to the chair or St. E's, and that's that."

I shrugged. "This is all pretty tenuous, Abe. If Jack killed them, why is everybody trying to scare me off the case?"

"Maybe because you cared about the two women. Maybe the fix has been made, and the last remaining danger is Jack's hotshot private detective concluding he did it. Maybe Joe Kennedy bankrolled Meechum and Reilly's visit. Everybody believes the Old Man has underworld contacts."

Next thing I knew, I was looking around us. "Sounds a bit like *you're* trying to warn me off the case, Abe."

He shook his head. "You and I know some inconvenient information, if Jack takes Howard's deal—guilty of murder or not. I'd like not to be the next Snilder, but who'd raise a hue and cry if a lone wolf private eye and a Chinaman disappeared?"

FORTY

"Unconscionable. Simply unconscionable." Whenever Stuart Symington opened his mouth, a sonorous voice broadcast a canned statement. "I asked my aide, General Orton, to join us because Bert was Mrs. Dyson's immediate supervisor. Wonderful woman. Exemplary."

Orton turned out to be the square-jawed stiff with three stars and a trim mustache who'd been at the memorial service with Symington. He was my height, tanned with graying hair combed back from his forehead. The Eighth Air Force patch on his right sleeve meant he'd flown B-17 bombers in the war, and the wreath on his wings suggested he'd commanded some of them.

I'd arrived at the Pentagon fifteen minutes early and waited half an hour to see him. We sat in Symington's large, sunny office in deep-blue upholstered chairs, theirs facing mine. Framed photos of fighters and bombers soared on the paneled walls, and the desk and bookcases all sported models of planes. I got the point.

"Mr. Symington—and I'm glad you're sitting in on this, General—we're looking into the possibility the murderer was somebody Mrs. Dyson knew because there's no sign of forced entry and nobody heard anything. Many of her friends were women. Her relatives all live in Iowa. That makes male coworkers worth a look. There may also be a connection to the murder last night of a woman named Susan Prebble, who worked in this office during the war."

Neither man reacted visibly. Symington's thick fingers brushed his hair back from a sharp widow's peak. "Well, I haven't heard that name before, but as to Mrs. Dyson, she'd have known several dozen men here. Bert, wouldn't you think she saw a lot of men every day?"

"Yessir." Orton was quick with that stuff. "Probably twenty or so every day, the same ones, and another twenty or thirty less often. I could have a list of names drawn up. I'd also be glad to find out when the other woman was on staff. Susan Prebble, you said?"

"Yes, I'd appreciate that." Fifty guys to sift through with no time and just me on the case. "Did she see any of them socially?"

Symington shrugged. Orton filled the gap in his tenor voice. "Well, I wouldn't necessarily know. Mrs. Dyson was married, of course, and had a spotless reputation."

I kept silent—it made people uncomfortable and kept them talking.

"As I told the secretary, she sometimes went to lunch or dinner with one or more people. I've taken her to dinner; you'll find that out. It—well, it can be a good way to establish bonds with staff." Seemed like his chair got hot.

"How recently?"

"How recently what?"

"Did you take Betty Dyson to dinner?"

"Well, several days—probably a week or so ago."

"That's perhaps one to three days before she was murdered. How many times did you do it?"

He glanced at Symington. "How many times did I do what?"

"Go to dinner with her. Are these questions too complicated?"

Symington let him flounder.

"Well, no, but—Look, you're conducting a murder investigation, and you seem to be implying—"

I shrugged. "Not at all. That's in your mind, General."

*****

His gray eyes narrowed. "I took her to dinner three or four times. I wanted to pump her." He flushed. "No, that sounds terrible. Look, the secretary appointed me as his new aide three weeks ago. I wanted to pump Mrs. Dyson for information. She'd worked here longer than anybody else, and she knows—knew—how this office works. People talk more freely one-to-one. That's all I meant. I'm a married man, Detective—"

"Jack Griffin." I was skating on the rusty edge of impersonating a cop by not clearing that up. "But, just to finish that line of questioning, General Orton, which of you two did she actually work for?"

Being included brought Symington out of his thoughts. "I suppose you could say she worked for both of us. Certainly, Mrs. Dyson was a key member of my personal staff and often brought issues directly to me, especially before Bert came aboard. But he directed her day-to-day work. Is it important?"

Orton took out a pack of Luckies and offered me one. "The secretary's cutting down," he murmured with a wink.

I waved him off. "It could be important, Mr. Secretary. The night she was killed, Betty Dyson told two witnesses she'd just learned something 'disgusting and despicable' about a very important man she worked for. That sounds as if she meant one of you."

The memorial service hadn't been as quiet as Symington's big bright office got. A brass clock in a rosewood case ticked softly a dozen times.

Symington tugged at his ear. "Privately, we may have to ignore the old doctrine that you never say anything uncharitable about the dead. The truth is, Detective, Mrs. Dyson was one of the most principled people I ever met, but to a fault. It made her rather judgmental, a bit holier-than-thou, if you will. For the record, both General Orton and I qualify as 'very important,' though I suppose I'm more likely to fit that term. Even so, I can't think of anything I've done that's 'disgusting and despicable,' and we vetted Bert rather carefully before he was selected."

Orton tossed another chip in. "If I may, sir, that particular assessment of hers is remarkably vague. She could have been referring to something she didn't like in somebody's personal life, which would have been a matter of moral viewpoint and none of her business. Mrs. Dyson could be something of a prig, too—though I've also heard men call her a high-powered flirt and a sexual tease."

"Bert's got a point, Detective. She could have disagreed with a policy or personnel decision—somebody she disliked being hired or somebody she did like being reprimanded. It's also very possible she gave credence to a rumor with little or no factual basis." He was steering away from sex and morals.

Orton took another turn, his voice high and tense. "In any case, sir, I'm concerned that Mrs. Dyson would share so opinionated a comment with anybody outside this office. Obviously, that's a lapse of security and good judgment, Detective Griffin."

Much as I hated to, if I didn't clarify my position the third time it came up, big shots like these could rip my license into shreds. "General, perhaps you didn't hear me mention at the memorial service that I'm a *private* investigator, not a police detective." They hadn't heard it because I hadn't said it.

The two men looked at each other in shock. Symington nodded to Orton, and the aide looked at his watch. "Mr. Secretary, you've got that meeting in three minutes."

They both stood, and Symington reached out his shovel-shaped hand. "Well, *Mister* Griffin, I'm glad we were able to help. Major Flanders will escort you out of the building."

*****

Moskowitz came on the phone right away. "How was your meeting with Symington? Find out anything useful?"

I stood in a gas station phone booth near the Pentagon. "Let's say a feeling of forthrightness didn't ooze out of Symington's pores. His aide, General Orton, was slick and shifty-eyed, though glancing in every direction may be something all fighter and bomber pilots do. I learned enough to keep that line of thought open, but no more."

"Why do you say that, Griffin? What's the possible connection?"

"Last Friday, Betty mentioned to Jack and me that she'd discovered something 'disgusting and despicable' about her boss." I remembered her disgusted frown. "That was all she said. When I told Symington and his aide that, hell froze over, and Betty skipped from being the homecoming queen of the new Air Force to an unreliable scold."

The lawyer wasn't a quick sale. "Did you expect one of them to say, 'Oh, I'm the bastard she meant?' and describe some odious thing he'd done?"

"Yeah, and confess to the murders, too. No, but the general admitted taking Betty to dinner a few times, including a day or so before somebody cut her throat."

Moskowitz thought for a moment. "Lunch seems more credible for talking shop. You take a woman to dinner when you're making a pass. Was there more?"

"There's some dirty secret one or both of them want hidden.

They explained it away without explaining anything. Symington's also involved in a lot of money and power. Somebody might have wanted Betty killed if she was a threat, but it's harder to imagine who'd do the actual killing. These guys aren't foot soldiers. I could see Symington or his aide ordering a thousand deaths, but not one. Besides, Susan Prebble had no connection with them unless she was Betty's confidante. Which is possible."

"Well, Griffin, if nothing else, Symington's been deeply involved in all that cutthroat bureaucratic in-fighting with the Navy over merging the armed forces."

I knew that. "Yeah, the newspapers say nasty stuff's going on in the shadows. He wants to make his Air Corps equal to the Army and Navy."

"More than that. Griffin, these men are creating a new empire. Fortunes are going to be spun out of fear and your tax dollars."

A dump truck roared into the gas station. I asked Moskowitz what he meant.

"Stu Symington doesn't just want to make the Air Corps *equal.* Most of the sniping in the corridors is actually over who'll be given primary responsibility for delivering the atom bomb if need be—the Navy or the new Air Force, the aircraft carriers that dominated the Pacific War, or the heavy bombers the European campaign depended on."

"Got it. Whoever wins'll need tons of stuff nobody's invented yet. They'll have to dump zillions of bucks into it, won't they?"

"Hundreds of zillions. And you can hire somebody to slit a throat in this town for ten dollars. See if there's more to this angle, okay?"

FORTY-ONE

Chippendale hadn't manufactured comfy chairs, but a two-minute wait on striped silk upholstery felt fine after hoofing my way to the Navy Yard in the noonday sun. "Mistah Griffin, Miz Broward will see y'all."

I was on my feet by the time she walked through the doorway. "It's so nice to see you, Mister Griffin. Please come in and have a seat with me."

"Thank you, Mrs. Broward."

"Effie, bring Mister Griffin and me each a glass of lemonade, please. It's a beautiful day, Mister Griffin, though these horrid stabbings have quite unnerved me. Poor Susan."

I sat on the edge of a chintz-clad sofa next to her. "My recollection was that you disliked Susan Prebble."

Her eyes were moist. "No, Mr. Griffin, it was impossible to dislike Susan. She had a certain charm and wit, and of course she was quite physically appealing. I broke off our friendship when she tried—unsuccessfully, I might add—to bestow her gifts upon my husband. But her death saddens and sickens me."

The maid brought in tall tumblers of lemonade. I murmured my gratitude. "Mrs. Broward, I really appreciate your kind response to my phone call. You're the last connection I have who knew both Betty and Susan. I'd about given up hoping that somebody in either woman's apartment building saw something suspicious."

She sipped her lemonade. "I wonder, Mr. Griffin, if you specifically asked whether anybody saw an Air Corps general with slicked-back hair and a mustache."

"Bert Orton?"

The Broward woman had a thin-lipped smile. "I shall be frank,

Mr. Griffin, as this is *not* a social visit, though I find you pleasant and polite. I think Bert Orton might be the murderer."

"Why do you say that, Mrs. Broward?"

She placed her empty glass on a wooden coaster next to mine. "Well, that spineless rodent is more than simply oily. Orton has a predator's instincts. During the war—I'm going to say it was probably 1943—he spent a few months in our office. Susan thought him repulsive, yet she had a fling with him that involved a weekend in Baltimore. She refused to explain herself. Also, a pretty stenographer told me several months later that Orton coerced her as well, and she had been forced into grotesque sexual acts—she needed her job rather urgently because she had a baby and was married to a soldier serving overseas."

"Nice guy." *Where did these creeps come from?*

"Then, just before he left for England, the wretch pawed Betty in his office with the door closed. She told me she slapped him, and he slapped her right back. Of course, she stormed out. I wanted her to report him, but Betty couldn't bear ruining a badly-needed officer, a colonel headed for a bomber command. She thought it served him right. 'It will be hard for him to pull his shenanigans with only men to boss around,' she said, and she laughed, so I hoped it would be the end of it."

A stern-faced Navy officer kept watch behind her, preserved in oil paint and framed in gilt. The gag about iron ships and wooden men flitted through my Army brain, but Commander Broward's expression and ribbons portrayed a steel-spring ship captain on a gray-painted bridge, shell bursts and a flaming kamikaze over his broad gold-striped shoulder.

I looked back at Martha Broward. "You're quite certain, then, that Orton was sexually involved with both women—had an affair with Susan and tried to land Betty?"

She nodded grimly, as if signaling a headsman that it was time. "There could be corroborating witnesses. It would astonish you how many women who work for Bert Orton would be willing to see him plummet into the abyss."

Actually, that was no surprise at all. Still, Orton was a long way from toppling. I had no evidence whatsoever that he'd killed either woman. But I had a suspect with a dirty connection to the two murder victims—a suspect who wasn't Jack Kennedy, with a connection that could wreck a career. At that point, I wanted it to be Orton, wanted him broken like a matchstick.

Martha Broward's story may have been old news, but it bore traces of a motive. People climbed the Matterhorn with skimpier handholds than that.

FORTY-TWO

I'd just turned out the lights in my office when Fred Walworth called. "Ever eat Peking duck, Griffin?"

"Got something you'd like to share?"

"Uh-huh. Same place, half an hour?"

*****

The empty eyes of the bottle-blonde bimbo who'd tried to hustle me the night before followed me from behind a wall of mascara to a table by a window where Walworth nursed his gin and tonic. She shook her head in pity.

"I just ordered for us, Griffin—Peking duck and spicy orange beef. Here comes the girl to see what you'll drink."

"Coca-Cola, lots of ice." I smiled at her. "Thanks."

She tottered off on heels stupidly high for hoisting trays, but sexy legs brought bigger tips. The background murmur in the restaurant whispered like waves lapping ashore somewhere cooler. "Hell of a day, Fred. Thanks for getting back to me."

Walworth nodded. "I know there was another murder that looks related. I may have found a connection."

My Coke arrived in a tall cylindrical glass sweaty with cold and stood on a little paper napkin. I swallowed a third of it right off the bat. "What did you find out, Fred?"

"Look, when I heard that this Prebble woman worked in our office, I checked dates. She left in January 1946, over a year before the current deputy secretary arrived. Prebble's husband was a flyer like Betty's, but Navy. No link to Secretary Symington."

The food came then, and both of us dug in. Probably

Walworth didn't want to talk with the numb-looking waitress at our table. We dove headfirst into the crisp-skinned Peking duck over rice with its seductive aroma—why perfume companies didn't use food smells to lure men always baffled me. During those first few bites, you could have set my hair on fire without getting my attention.

When we'd emptied our bowls, Walworth slopped more rice into his and topped it with orange-flavored beef. "These little doodads are strips of orange peel, cooked, and sweetened in the sauce. But *these* things that are the same size and color, but a bit tapered? *Very* hot chili peppers. I love 'em. You may not."

"Got it. But as tasty as the duck and beef are, I assume we came here to talk turkey."

"Tenacious, aren't you? Okay. Susan Prebble and Betty Dyson both went to work at Air Corps HQ early in 1942. Then in 1943, when General Orton was just a bird colonel, he served on staff for four months before he could wangle a combat command."

"Uh-huh." Martha Broward got the year right.

"Two horrid, dull, nosy women with gray hair in buns insist Orton tried to make some time with Betty Dyson. I'm told he acted so fresh just last week in his office that she slapped his face."

I almost spurted out the tea I was using to rinse chili pepper off my tongue. "Last week? Somebody saw this?"

*****

For a moment, what he'd said paralyzed me. Early last week was just days before Betty's murder. Walworth crammed a bit of beef into his maw. I was still staring. "No wonder Orton was so uncomfortable when I questioned him about taking her to dinner. Mentioned being married, as if it were proof he never noticed she had sex appeal." Once more, I could see her laughing.

Walworth nodded, dumping more Peking duck into his bowl, a grain of rice nesting in his mustache. "The office gossips say he asked her out on the pretext of discussing work, expecting to dive into her pants."

Maybe more soy sauce would rinse some of the pepper off the beef. I splashed it on the way a fading hooker doused herself with perfume. "What makes you believe it?"

"I'm not a snoop, Griffin. But they keep slicing our office

space smaller, with thinner and thinner partitions. My cubby hole sits next to Orton's office. I don't usually hear him, but Friday afternoon, he was yelling. At Betty. First, it was loud but unintelligible, and I was writing a report. Then I heard her voice. She sounded furious. 'I won't do that!' My assumption was he'd pressed her for sex."

"What then, Fred?" I helped myself to more of the duck—it didn't fight back.

"His voice said 'goddam pure.' There was more, you understand, but that's what I made out. She yelled back, 'First, your filthy rumor file. Now this! The answer is no.'"

I'd have asked a question, but my mouth was full of duck.

Walworth went on. "Orton was practically growling by then. Something something 'stinking moralist in 1943.' Betty shot back, 'Damn you, General, and damn your filthy photograph!' That's when she stormed out."

The colonel had kept his voice soft, but he glanced all around. Mai Fong's was busy, but it was the least inquisitive crowd I'd ever seen. Behind him, two men in pale linen suits—one built like a cigarette, the other a fat cigar butt—murmured quietly. I could hear the sailor at the table behind me crooning, "Come on, baby. Aw, come on, baby," as if he were a backup vocalist for Frankie Sinatra. The four strapping Southern boys around the table to my right debated whether Lana Turner or Jane Russell would be better in bed, as if they'd ever find out. And the bimbos at the bar were enjoying a gin break.

"Well, Griffin, I followed Betty into the corridor and told her I could see she was upset. She says, 'You make one stupid mistake, Fred, and somebody nails you. Should I go to Secretary Symington?' Before I can reply, she heads to the women's john. I never saw her again."

I laid my chopsticks down, crisscrossing their tips. You could practically sculpt the cigarette smoke in the room, but that wasn't why my eyes were moist.

"What 'filthy rumor file,' Fred?"

FORTY-THREE

Walworth twitched his mustache, dropping a five and a ten on the table while nodding his head toward the door. "Dinner's on me. If I'd told you what I knew the last time, there's a chance the Prebble woman'd still be alive—*if* there's a connection between the two dead women and your question. Let's walk."

With the hazy orange-pink sun tucked behind low-roofed buildings, the scorch disappeared from the day. What breeze there was staggered under its load of Chinese aromas and auto fumes, but the sidewalks down toward the mall had emptied. The city's businessmen headed home to dinner by then, the office workers had fled, and the tourists were safely ensconced in their hotels ahead of nightfall.

We kept our silence, Walworth musing over a White Owl cigar, for five or so minutes. Nobody was close enough to hear when I asked again about the dirty rumor file.

"Griffin, if this gets tracked back to me, I'll be cleaning the latrines at a weather station in Greenland with a small toothbrush. How aware are you of the political infighting between us and the Navy over this Unification Act?"

"About the way I follow sports. I can tell you the Yanks beat the Dodgers in the World Series last fall and that the Senators weren't in contention, but I don't know the score of any given game or who Rizzuto plays for."

"That's fine—the basic outline's enough. A couple of items of gossip posing as issues showed up in Drew Pearson's radio broadcasts over the past two weeks, hinting that the Navy's top leadership was too shaky to entrust with serious tasks like using atom bombs—that Forrestal, the Navy secretary, is showing signs of too much stress in his life to head the new Defense Department."

"Is he?"

"How much is too much? I've participated in negotiations with him. Remarkably tough man. He directed the Navy all through the war and now this. The job was created as a storage locker for stress."

We waited for a cab to pass before we crossed D Street. Glancing over my shoulder, I spotted the two guys in pale suits from the next table at Mai Fong walking briskly, as if they wanted to keep up with us. "And the rumor file?"

"A three-star general I won't name"—Walworth showed a gold-capped wisdom tooth when he grinned—"ordered Betty, Tom Lefferts, and me to create a file of memos recording odd things anybody ever heard Forrestal say. The general said the secretary wanted it, which would be in character—a man who doesn't have any personal loyalty doesn't command any. 'Odd things.' Define that in Washington!"

"It sounds fuzzy, doesn't it? Would you include taking bribes or turning them down?" The two yo-yos behind us had split up after I looked. The fat one was half a block away. The skinny guy crossed the street and hung farther back on a parallel track. Was I getting paranoid?

"The nameless general commented that if the remarks weren't made recently, the memos could have 'approximate dates for when the comment might have been made.' He laid out an invitation to fabricate." Walworth seemed unaware of the two men. "He kept calling Forrestal 'high-strung,' which he clearly used to mean the guy's a fruitcake, but it ain't so."

We didn't break stride for the hennaed hustler who asked if we were looking for fun. "You're saying Orton ordered three staffers to create a file of faked or real hints the guy's nuts."

Walworth had a shark's grin worthy of the Flying Tigers. "You didn't hear *me* suggest that. It's *your* conclusion—a reasonable inference. A lot of chips are riding on this unification thing. Frankly, if the civilian head of the Air Force is caught defaming the civilian head of the Navy—well, it's like having the wind change while you're pissing in the woods."

My next backward glance found the fat man looking at the window of a darkened shop. His buddy was nowhere in sight. Had they seen me look at them?

"If you were guessing, Fred—and I'm sure you're not—would

you think a guy like Orton would leak nasty stories on Forrestal to the press on his own initiative?"

He cackled. "Bert Orton doesn't possess enough initiative to pull his pants up on his own. You'd probably guess he takes all his marching orders from his boss. I wouldn't comment on that."

Another look told me the fat guy was chatting with the hooker in the false red hair. The second hadn't reappeared. We trotted across Constitution Avenue and slowed to walk between the Federal Trade Commission and the National Archives. All the parking spots that had been hen's teeth during business hours stood empty. A fear-faced spinster with a rag-end of a dog on a brown leash watched her mutt crap on the sidewalk. I saw it, but my eyes were searching for the guys behind us. I didn't spot them. Maybe they weren't shadowing us after all.

"Fred, I'm still trying to see a connection here. It isn't Symington having his drudge leak some snotty stuff about his chief antagonist. How does Susan Prebble wake up dead as a result of that?"

"That's the question, Griffin. And if the same bastard killed both women, it probably wasn't Symington."

"You're sure about Orton, Fred? The wartime affair with Susan and the two humiliating rejections from Betty, now and then?"

"My two horrid gossips don't generally embroider their stories, Griffin. And I heard what I heard."

*****

Still unclear whether the mismatched men from the restaurant had been following Walworth and me or had simply walked behind us, I parked my Nash in the shadows out behind my apartment. There was a strong chance Meechum and Reilly would demonstrate their disappointment in me for sticking with the case, whoever paid *their* fare. My automatic found its way into my hand as I stepped out of the car.

My snug little living room was empty. Nobody hid in the kitchenette, the tiny bathroom, or the cramped bedroom. I thrust myself into each space, a foot soldier clearing a building in a town at war, my pistol sticking straight out in front of me and all my moves like throwing hand grenades.

Once I'd cleared the Ghosts of Evenings Past out of my

apartment, I jerked the windows open. I could follow up with Walworth's "two horrid gossips" in the morning. Finally, I relaxed by reading Captain Harmon Root Hubbard's memoir of the Illinois cavalry, savoring the interplay between a massive struggle that shaped my world and the individual stories that were the singular form of "massive struggle."

Dog-tired, I finally crawled between the wrinkled sheets, wishing even more that I'd won Betty away from Jack that night, because if she'd been killed just to get at Jack Kennedy, then she'd still be alive, and maybe maybe maybe.

But all the maybes had been slaughtered Friday night, whoever did it, for whatever purpose. It took me a couple hours to get to sleep. When I did, no matter what Macbeth may have thought, it didn't knit up any God-damned raveled skein of care for *me.*

*****

Every time Old Joe Kennedy spoke, pearls poured out of his mouth. Six of us, all men, gathered tranquilly around a poker table in a drawing room that had sumptuous walls of bottom-of-the-ocean blue-green. The other players looked elegant in white tie and tails, their upright starched collars bent sharply at the tips. I wore a baggy brown suit, and my necktie hung crooked as hell. At least the dream missed Bastogne this time.

We played seven-card stud with the low hole card wild, a tricky game. I hadn't peeked at either of my two hole cards. What I held face up in front of me after the last card had been dealt was a pile of crap. I hesitated.

"You gonna bet, Griffin? The rest of us haven't got all day." A blond man I thought was named Morgan glared at me. The others chortled as if Morgan's remark were wit of martini dryness because none of us were going anywhere.

Then Old Joe Kennedy spoke again. The pearls of his speaking swarmed upward like fat bugs toward a pale ceiling three miles above us. Then I remembered we were sitting together on the rear deck of the *Titanic* the morning after its legendary plunge. We half-dozen poker players had not survived.

"Play... the... cards... you... have," Old Joe Kennedy advised me. I watched his green-white bubbles of wisdom float up and drift away.

"You're a millionaire, Mr. Ambassador." I noted with some alarm that there were no bubbles at all when I spoke. "You're a God-damned financial genius. But even so, we're *still* at the bottom of the Atlantic Ocean. Why should I trust you?" Old Joe Kennedy waved my words aside.

Still, I hesitated to bet. A man I now recognized as Lieutenant Colonel Epping, my battalion commander at Bastogne, finished drinking his watery whiskey. "Griffin, did you come here to study the damned *odds,* or are you prepared to *gamble?"* He touched two fingers to a ruby hole between his eyebrows, half an inch below the helmet I just noticed he was wearing with his tux.

The snow lay all about us on the ocean floor now—as it did whenever my dreams touched on Bastogne. Old Joe Kennedy tapped on my sleeve before the green baize table could fade away. "The cards you've got showing here look like shit, boy. Every one of us was dealt better. But you haven't touched your hole cards yet."

Then a hundred thousand Nazis opened up as they charged from behind a forest of seaweed. Panther tanks and Tiger tanks roared down at us, steel in an avalanche, all their guns belching blue flame. I flipped over the cards I'd been keeping face down: the Queen of Hearts and a train ticket out of there. I was still floating upward toward the surface when the alarm went off. It was seven-thirty.

I lay there gasping for breath on damp and gritty sheets, coming slowly out of my terror. The *Titanic* nightmare visited me now and again, the result of having a stepmother who'd survived the sinking, followed by some joker named Darnstadt loaning me *A Night to Remember* while our own troopship crossed the U-boat lanes on its way to England.

As I washed up, after I'd shaved and scrubbed my teeth, I mined the dream for any nuggets I might have missed while I was held spellbound by my fears. We—the two Kennedys and Moskowitz and I—were at the bottom of the ocean. If I had any hole cards at all, I sure as hell hadn't seen a trace of them. I didn't think there was a single facet of the case I hadn't flipped over in my mind. What was there to do other than play the lousy cards we'd all been dealt?

But Colonel Epping was right. There wasn't a God-damned dime in studying the odds.

I was going to have to gamble.

FORTY-FOUR

If I had hole cards I hadn't checked lately, it was Vince O'Heaney. I dialed his home telephone number. We met for breakfast at the Tastee Diner, an out-of-the-way eatery across the District line in Silver Spring.

The Friday morning newspapers were still spouting stories about the last days of the congressional session before the August recess and, for that matter, before Christmas, too. The House D.C. Committee scheduled a vote that afternoon on the Tollafsen police reform bill. The story rehashed charges about Howard's "alleged" willingness to ignore a number of murder cases, with just the faintest suggestion he'd either helped himself to a few big chunks of cash or yielded to some other influence that wasn't named in printer's ink.

Vince slid onto the stool next to mine. Once the waitress doled out coffee, my French toast, and his bacon and eggs, he dabbed at his bald forehead with a paper napkin.

"So?"

"You're an honest cop, Vince."

He snorted. "Time tuh hold on to my wallet."

"Gentleman Jimmy Howard sidelined you Tuesday with that 'special assignment' to root out those missing crime statistics. Know anything about the Tollafsen bill?"

"The who?"

"A piece of legislation that comes to a key vote today. If Congress passes it, they'll create some kind of select panel to make recommendations for reform and to send cases to a special grand jury. The superintendent's scared to death of it; tried to blackmail Kennedy into opposing it."

Vince's jaw dropped open with egg inside it. He swallowed.

"Howard connected this bill and the murder case tuh Kennedy?"

I nodded. "Vince, I just want to counsel you to keep your eyes wide open the next few days. Don't let whoever he's assigned to your crime statistics project set you up as the fall guy for a cover-up. Why not take the Strawberry Blonde files home to review them?"

That won me a split-lipped grin. "By the way, Junior, your old buddy Moon Snilder quit the force."

"You're kidding. Why?" He looked for my reaction. I seemed to get away with it.

"Don't know why, but he mailed Blaine his guns and badge with a signed letter admitting he screwed up the Rodney Hamilton murder case last year. Claimed he had a 'lapse in judgment' and 'inappropriate contact' with the Gorney broad. I think he skipped town. Know anything about it?" I was decidedly getting the fisheye.

"Yeah, Vince, one thing. It won't wreck the department."

I'd played one hole card.

*****

Lana's coffee wasn't brewed for royalty, but nobody ever fell asleep drinking it. I handed her my notepad. "Last night, I got two leads—women who worked with Betty and Susan during the war and know some office gossip. I'd like you to get their home phones. Hazel Ditters lives in Alexandria, and Minerva Quayle is in Washington. I've got to make a couple other calls."

"I'll get right on them, Mr. Griffin."

*****

"Moskowitz," I muttered into the receiver, "I know it's Friday morning, and Kennedy has to decide in the next few hours whether he's going to accept Gentleman Jimmy's solution or not. I haven't solved this God-damned case, but I think I'm close."

"Griffin, who have you got that we didn't have yesterday?"

"One—we can probably rule out the husband. There's no known connection between him and Susan Prebble, and he didn't care about his wife any longer. She was granted a divorce last Friday based on two years' desertion."

There was an audible snort. "Griffin, who can we rule *in?*"

"Her boss."

"Symington?"

"No, but his married aide monkeyed around sexually with both women. He slept with Susan during the war and apparently tried unsuccessfully to nail Betty both then and last Friday."

"You're pretty sure he did it?"

"I'd bet you dollars to doughnuts on it. I've found two witnesses I want to question before I confront him."

"Frankly, Griffin, there's no time. If you can corner the guy this morning, we might keep Jack from making a decision that would put him in other people's hands for the rest of his life."

*****

The tenor voice sounded officious as ever. "Senator Vandenberg, this is General Orton. How may I help you, sir?"

"General, I'm not sure how your secretary concluded I was Senator Vandenberg"—I knew damn well she'd thought that because it's what I told her—"but you and I need to talk in the next hour about what you did to Betty Dyson last Friday. I've identified witnesses to every piece of it."

He spluttered. "But—This is—Is this—?"

"Jack Griffin, the private detective you bounced out of Symington's office yesterday. I'll be at Sherrill's Restaurant on Capitol Hill for the next sixty minutes. It's quiet but too public for you to pull anything stupid. After an hour, I take my information to police headquarters."

I hung up without waiting for an answer, hoping I'd sounded like a blackmailer.

FORTY-FIVE

It was almost a quarter to eleven when the harried general arrived, so most of the tables at Sherrill's were still empty. He ignored the couple near the door and the two middle-aged women in the booth opposite where I nursed my coffee. His broad face was splotchy red. "See here, Griffin, I don't know what kind of drivel the office gossips have fed you, but I have nothing to hide."

"And that's why you came running." I jerked my head sideways and down, and he took the seat opposite me. "I told you and Symington that Betty Dyson complained the night she was killed about the 'disgusting and despicable' thing the man she worked for had done to her that day. I have more details now, ranging from the Forrestal dirt file to your sexual demands."

People don't literally blush beet red, yet Orton came close. "What is it you want?" He glanced warily at the two women, but the tall one in the broad-brimmed straw hat stayed bent over her book while the short one kept writing on a legal pad.

I flashed him an oily smile. "Tell me about the Forrestal file. Your idea or Symington's?"

That brought his color down. "Uh, his. But it's a legitimate national security concern."

"Which is why you feed that stuff to Drew Pearson? To protect America's security? That's a news story in itself, and I'll bet he made *you* do all the dirty work."

Sherrill's ceiling fans weren't quite adequate for the heat of the day, but I wasn't sweating the way Orton was. "I—I swear I did nothing wrong."

"That brings me to Betty Dyson. Did you expect her to hoist her skirt and lie on your desk, or did you mean later?"

Whatever he replied was inaudible.

"Speak up, Orton. You were loud enough when you tried to blackmail her sexually. I know about what she called 'your filthy photograph.' What was the source?"

"How could you—? Look, she wasn't Simon-pure, okay? She had an affair back in 1943 at a time when she was under surveillance. The investigator jimmied the hotel room door and snapped her screwing a sailor."

I'd guessed it was something like that when Walworth quoted Betty on making "one stupid mistake."

"I simply pulled it from her sealed personnel file and showed it to her with the comment that she'd made herself available before. I don't want that broadcast, but I didn't do anything lots of other managers haven't done."

My jaw clenched mercilessly. "Not in daylight, you didn't."

His face went stupid. "What does that mean?"

"That means you went to her apartment Friday night, knowing she'd be alone because you knew her husband abandoned her. Then what, Orton? Did she do what you demanded, and you killed her anyway, or did you blow up when she laughed in your face?"

He toppled back against the booth so hard his head banged behind him, and he tore at his pomaded hair with both hands. "You think I *killed* her? No! No, there's no way I could have. I'll admit to everything else, but not that."

"Did she let you in, or did you force her?" I wanted to snap him in half.

"No, you're totally off base there, Griffin. Friday evening, I flew on an Air Force transport to New York City with Secretary Symington and General Vandenberg—the senator's nephew, a rising star in the Air Force—to spend the weekend in meetings with several newspaper publishers. Three junior officers and the flight crew can attest to our being on that flight—it left before seven o'clock. Half a dozen reputable men spent Saturday and most of Sunday with us."

*****

At the booth across from us, Lana looked up from her legal pad and shrugged as Martha Broward silently closed her Graham Greene novel. I held Orton's attention. "I'll need proof of your alibi, General."

"I turned in my receipts for reimbursement on Monday. They can be produced quickly." He rubbed his mustache and allowed himself a feeble grin. "You thought you'd blackmail me for murder, didn't you, gumshoe? Thought I'd pay a fortune, right? What—ten thousand? Twenty?"

"No, we can't all be blackmailers. I discussed this case with the D.C. police superintendent yesterday, and he's waiting to see what I uncover. We're all strolling down the street to my office to handle some paperwork, then we'll drive to the Pentagon. Ready, ladies?"

Orton jumped sideways in his seat when Martha Broward swept off her straw hat. He recognized her right away. I gestured toward Lana. "You haven't met my office manager, Lana Murphy. She takes excellent dictation."

Lana grinned. "And your shrill voice carries, General. I jotted down every word."

At the agency, I subjected Orton to Martha Broward's extended opinion of his behavior toward Betty while Lana whipped out a transcript of the restaurant conversation and fetched Murray, her pet notary, from down the hall. I told the general that the document would show my client how I knew Orton *wasn't* the killer. He was so terrified he'd be tarred with the murder that when Lana, Martha, and I swore to the transcript's authenticity, he did, too.

FORTY-SIX

My watch read eleven-thirty when Orton and I stormed the Pentagon. His secretary, a haggard redhead, handed him a manila folder. "You asked for this on the telephone, sir." He handed it to me. I burned up five minutes poring through receipts, flight manifests, and a lengthy memo for files detailing the meetings he described. It all fit. Orton had an unshakeable alibi—he absolutely couldn't have done it.

"You're off the hook for Betty's murder, General. I could bust your jaw for the rest of it. Now let's tell the secretary I've cleared both of you."

Orton shell-shocked so easily I wondered how many missions he'd actually flown. He led me into Symington's ducal office. "Excuse me, Mr. Secretary, but Griffin here has finished his investigation of the Betty Dyson and Susan Prebble murders, and he's giving us a clean bill of health. I thought you'd want to know right away."

The sour look Symington gave me intensified. "I never thought we were suspects. Is that all?"

"Barely half." I watched his head jerk toward me. "I documented the 'disgusting and despicable' business I asked you about. Give this a quick look." I handed him a notarized carbon copy of the transcript Lana had typed, reaching past a dumbfounded Orton.

Symington didn't let his jaw drop very readily, I imagined, but he made an exception this time. I followed his eyes down the sheet, the corners of his mouth puckering. He turned to his aide. "Get me the file you have on Mrs. Dyson. *All* of it."

"Yessir." Orton's expression registered the dimming hope that his boss would enjoy the photo. He scooted out the door.

*****

"What rock did you find that bastard under, Mr. Secretary?"

Symington shook his head mournfully. "I ordered a very careful background check done."

"They missed something. What was Mrs. Dyson's opinion?"

He looked non-plussed. "Why would I have asked her?" The wariness in the edges of his eyes showed just long enough to confirm Betty'd warned him, though. But Symington *wanted* a weasel for the job, a crafty creature who'd do whatever his boss asked without explicit instructions.

I stifled the urge to say as much—the creep I wanted was Orton, who'd shoved Betty into the mud. "Is his third star permanent?"

The assistant secretary's brows saluted, and a hint of a grin crept onto his face. "No, it's brand new." The look on his face denoted a man who pondered death warrants pretty carefully before signing them.

"I'm sure the Forrestal file is nothing you'd condone."

His eyes narrowed. "No, of course not. Scandalous idea."

"Exactly, yet Orton claims you ordered him to do it. If that became public, combined with his perverse mistreatment of a war hero's wife the very day she was brutally raped and murdered...."

Symington shook his head violently. "It would do the Air Force incalculable harm at this juncture. Incalculable." He sank into his leather desk chair.

He needed a solution, though he may have wanted it to be somebody else's idea. I offered him one. "I assume the Articles of War still punish conduct unbecoming an officer."

We heard a tap at the door, but Symington ignored it. "Still, Griffin, he served his country. Not heroically, though the bomber wing he commanded established an excellent combat record."

"He's done enough, then. Still, a court-martial would be disastrous for the Air Force." Symington would hear "disastrous for *you.*" I held up my hand. "That's why you allow officers to resign their commissions."

Symington nodded curtly and called Orton back in. The assistant secretary showed enough class to burn the photo in a heavy glass ashtray without looking at it, while the general scrawled out the letter that made him a civilian.

I'd been able to play the Queen of Hearts after all, but she'd cost me my only remaining suspect—other than my client.

FORTY-SEVEN

When I'd talked to Moskowitz earlier, I'd been positive Orton killed both women. But he couldn't have killed Betty, so there was no reason to think he'd killed Susan. Now I'd run out of leads as well as time. On the way back to the office, I stopped at a gas station to call Moskowitz and let him know the score. Another nickel put me in touch with Lana. "I torpedoed General Orton, but we're out of suspects."

"Well, Mr. Griffin, what you accomplished this morning was still good. A man like that!" It was hard to get Lana down, and I needed a note of cheer. "Mr. Griffin, if there's nothing else you can do, why don't you take your friend Jerry DiMarco a nice lunch and share it with him? I'll tend the store while you're gone."

*****

"What's in the paper bag, amigo?" Jerry sat propped up, looking better than the last time. "Stop at the hardware for some nuts and bolts?"

I picked up his tone. "It's a Mussolini candy dish. I knew how much you wanted one."

"Bet you got it cheap." We both chuckled as I handed him the sack. "Holy smoke, that's the best-looking peach I've seen since my wife left here last night. Where'd it come from?"

"Well, I'd have brought you a corned beef sandwich or something, on the off chance you're tired of hospital food, but I know how strict your diet has to be. I swung by Eastern Market and grabbed you this. You can eat fruit, right?"

"Can and will. Thanks, amigo. Hey, no kidding, a guy on the

radio an hour ago mentioned the House might vote today on a bill requiring police commissioners to do a 'top-to-bottom review' and report back to the Congress early next year. Christ, Jack, who'd want to review the bottoms of D.C. cops?" He'd lost a kidney, but Jerry still had his Looney Tunes laugh.

We joked some more about baseball and Congress, two realms where the Senators were incompetent. I was on my way to another crack when Jerry let the chuckle fall from his face, his gray eyes gazing steadily into mine. "Jack, has something happened between us, something gone stale, something I said that was out of line?"

That caught me flat-footed. I remember cocking my head the way a puzzled dog does. "What makes you ask that, Jerry?"

"You come by to see me, and all I hear is wisecracks and weather. Maybe you see me as a dying man, and it's easier to pull away. Just seems to me we haven't talked about anything serious since Christmas or so—especially your end of the conversation. We joke, we talk kinda politics and sports, you keep it all cheery, and if Lucille's around, you fade away. I don't know more about your actual life than the outline of a few cases. We used to talk about everything."

It felt as if he'd slapped me because I knew he was right. "We did, Jerr, and we don't anymore. I'm not sure what happened. I haven't even told you I half fell in love with a woman who was murdered the night after I got back from Los Angeles. I just didn't figure you needed sad news. No, it wasn't anything you said."

"God, Jack, that's terrible. I'm so sorry." He took a sip of water from a glass with a bent glass straw in it. "My hunch is we're not equals any longer. We went through hell together as airborne captains once, and we could do anything. Now you're a loner in good health, and I'm slated for an early grave. That must be hard for you, Jack."

I'd avoided talking about anything more long term than his current symptoms for quite a while. "Jerry, you're *not* dying. You've got time, and they're working on things that will help."

"They are, Jack, but you don't wanna face facts." He laid a gaunt hand on my arm. "Yes, there are hopes. One bunch of researchers is developing a mechanical kidney of some sort they'll hook you onto and clean your blood, but they're not far enough along to test it anytime soon. Another bunch thinks one day they'll be able to salvage kidneys and other organs from fresh corpses—healthy people killed in car crashes, for instance—and replace damaged parts like mine. But I *don't* have time to wait, Jack. I doubt I'll be here a year from now."

My God, how I didn't want to hear that! You really *can* feel the blood drain out of your face. I couldn't have looked much better than he did, and realizing it made me see he was right. "Does Lucille know, Jerry?"

He gave me a rueful smile. "Does she know? Sure. Does she *accept* it? No way in hell. If love and willpower could heal me, I'd be dancing. You see Lucille as the girl next door, but she's twice the fighter you and I were."

My eyes stung, sitting beside my closest friend in a room full of marked men. "All right, Jerry, if a year's your outside limit, let's not waste it. I'll stop tiptoeing on eggshells when I'm here."

He laughed. "Good, cuz you're not naturally light-footed, Griffin!"

The bastard made me chuckle. "Okay. Yes, damn it, you're right that it's hard for me. I feel responsible."

DiMarco gave me the fish-eye. "Really. Then I guess the Nurnberg trials were a crock, blaming the war on the poor Nazis. Dammit, Jack, I'm a *casualty*. People get hurt in battle. You didn't order them to attack."

Guilt has talons three feet long. "Yeah, but I should've gotten to you sooner." It was one of the hardest things I'd ever needed to say. I knuckled a tear off my cheek.

"Jack, I was out in front of my foxhole checking my men's positions when the Nazis opened up on us. They hit me right off the bat. I was one of three survivors in the bottom of the hole, and a scar-faced Kraut with a Schmeisser was sneering down at us when Charlie Company opened fire."

"Believe me, I remember. But, still—"

"And a minute later, you had a medic working on me. I remember asking you to tell Lucille I was sorry I wouldn't be able to buy her a house, and you said, 'You'll have to do that yourself, you sonuvabitch, because you're not dying on me. I can't tell Lucille I let you die.' And damned if I'm not still here two and a half years later."

"Yeah, and you're still dying."

A soft hand touched my shoulder, and I turned to see Lucille standing by my chair, a shocked look blanching her face. I'd have sawed off an arm not to have spoken the last words I'd said. Her eyes were teary.

Jerry reached for her other hand. "Hi, sugar. Can you imagine it—Jack thinks he's responsible for what happened to me."

Lucille pulled back and stared quizzically. "Why, Jack, you *are* responsible for what happened to Jerry. You saved his life. He'd have died for sure, shot up like that, if the Germans ran the rest of you out of there. Every minute we've had together since Bastogne is a gift from you." She bent and kissed him. "Jack, I'll never be able to repay you."

I stood up and wrapped an arm around her shoulders. "I think you just did, Lucille."

FORTY-EIGHT

Talking with Jerry and Lucille hadn't done a damned thing for Jack Kennedy, but *I* felt a hell of a lot lighter when I floated back to the office. Lana was chattering on the phone to her twin sister Tana. She finished up and asked what came next.

I shrugged. Then a question about one of the loose ends slid through the foggy valleys of my brain: why the hell had Meechum and Reilly—two thugs with no known connection with the police or Gentleman Jimmy Howard—busted into my apartment, slugged me, and told me to get off the case? I understood what Snilder'd done, but he was grifting for himself. I more or less ruled out a tie to Howard, but what if he'd called in a few chits with some big-time crook those two goons worked for—it could be the answer. Meechum and Reilly weren't working for themselves. That would have made no sense at all.

But who *did* they work for? Was there a tie to Joe Kennedy? I'd spotted Meechum two days earlier at the Jazz Club. Nichols himself seemed to me to be a right guy with some shady connections. What he was doing about race had my respect. Maybe he could give me an idea who Meechum and Reilly worked for. I drove over to find out what I could.

*****

The service door to the alley in the back of the club was open. Outside the owner's office, his decorative personal assistant sat at her black art deco desk on a matching black chair in a black satin dress that gleamed softly like her precision-cut hair.

"Nice to see you, Millie. Nichols here?"

Millie licked her red lips and awarded me a less-than-innocent smile. "Sure, mister." She showed me in.

Framed and signed photos of a couple dozen jazz artists covered the wall, more of them Negro than white—Louis Armstrong, Duke Ellington, and Sarah Vaughan were the faces I knew. There were also some pictures taken during the war stuck in among them—one of Nichols grinning in glaring sunlight from the cockpit of a P-51 Mustang fighter with the name "Inside Straight" painted over seven little Nazi crosses, and one with a beaming group of guys clustered together in front of a Mustang. A polished mahogany end table standing by the wall under the photos held a chess game in progress.

On the broad, ludicrously tidy wooden desk stood a hand-tinted picture of a delicate dark-haired woman and a baby in a fuzzy pale-yellow outfit. They both had teacup complexions, tentative grins, and amber eyes. The mother wore swirls of auburn curls. The little girl toddling crookedly beside her had Nichols's round face and fine, straight black hair.

"You found my wife Arlene and Thumbelina—our daughter Marie." The man who owned the Jazz Club strode across the room like a bantam rooster to shake my hand. "Just a couple of shots of me. The only jazz riffs I ever played were improvisations with six .50-caliber machine guns, three in each wing of my Mustang, Griffin. I heard you gave up on that murder investigation."

Nichols brushed his dark hair back from his forehead, above the baby-pink complexion and the ready grin. A saffron silk tie with blue diamonds brought his slate-blue suit to life. He motioned me to a tufted leather chair.

"You read the daily papers, Nichols, so you know they found a second woman slashed to death this week, Susan Prebble. I've been trying all day to figure out why two thugs named Meechum and Reilly tried to scare me off the case. Can you tell me anything about Meechum or Reilly that might help me out?"

His grin faltered, but he wrestled it back into place. "What makes you think I can help you, Griffin?"

"Well, I'm not really certain you can. I saw Meechum here last Wednesday afternoon. He's a big ugly redheaded moose who hires out as muscle. Reilly has black hair and a mustache like a comb."

Nichols nodded noncommittally. "I know the men you mean, Griffin. I guess I'd think anybody who'd been warned to do something by those two cement trucks would pay close attention to his message." He laughed, a little too much. Neither of us seemed to think he'd said anything funny.

That puzzled me. It never flitted through my brain that Nichols himself might somehow be involved in the case. But there he sat, getting steadily more fidgety as we spoke. I'd heard he'd used hired muscle, and he'd told me as much. Maybe he feared that having some kind of connection with the two killings would hurt business.

He reached casually over to the shiny black intercom on the edge of his desk and pressed a button. "Millie, send Billy Meechum in here right away."

I didn't want to chat with Meechum. Before I could react, Nichols pulled a small nickel-plated Colt revolver out of a desk drawer and aimed it straight at my chest. "Don't try anything cute, Griffin, will ya? You've made a serious mistake, my friend."

*****

I could see his point for myself and didn't need to hire a private detective to explain it to me. I was that clever. Billy Meechum burst through the side door to the office, smiling broadly when he saw me—the kind of smile a man makes when he's been expecting a baloney sandwich on stale store bread, and somebody brings him a big juicy Porterhouse steak.

His gnarled right hand filled with the pistol he'd shown me Wednesday night at my place, and he jabbed its muzzle hard into my ear. Then he reached into my suit jacket and helped himself to my .45 automatic. Nichols, still smiling as if we'd signed a business deal, kept me covered from in front.

The receptionist's voice sounded tinny on the intercom. "Mr. Nichols, there's a—Sir, you can't go in there now. *Sir!*" But the door popped open, and Jack Kennedy strode into the room, starting to say something to Nichols. I kept my eyes on the dapper little man with the gun.

"Nice to see you, Congressman Kennedy." Nichols kept his silver pistol pointed at me. "And could you just push the door closed, please?"

So Kennedy turned out to be chummy with Nichols, the link to Meechum and Reilly. Then he *did* do it.

I hoped for enough of a diversion for me to try something. Sitting down with Meechum behind me and his gun in my ear made a feeble position for launching an attack.

"Meechum." Nichols gave a chop downward with his head. I tried to move before the big guy did, but he caught me just above my right eye with the butt of my .45. I didn't feel the floor when it reached up and broke my fall.

FORTY-NINE

I knew what was wrong almost immediately, even before the fog drifted away. Some sneaky bastard had drilled a tiny hole in the top of my skull above my right eye. Then he'd tied half a dozen knots in a strong braided cord that he was jerking through the hole to find out how much pain I could feel. But when I finally shoved my eyelids open, I couldn't spot the guy.

God, it hurt all around the upper right side of my face. I could see flecks of dried blood on the side of my nose. My hands wouldn't move at all. Awareness and focus were two snails vying for the Slowness World Cup. Gradually I realized I was tied to a crude wooden chair in a strange, spacious place I hadn't been in before. The gray beneath me was concrete, not fog, and the dark irregular walls were boards nailed carelessly to two-by-fours. What air there was carried a pervasive smell of eternally rotting fish and primordial mildew.

I could hear water lapping softly as a cat behind me. When I eased my head sideways to look, the knotted cord treatment began once more. What startled me was finding Jack Kennedy tied to another makeshift chair right next to me. Now I remembered what had happened at the Jazz Club, whenever that was. So Kennedy *wasn't* in on it!

"You're awake, Griffin. Thank God. They gave you a nasty gash over your eye. I worried they'd killed you, or you'd be paralyzed."

"Both." My mouth tasted dusty. "Did they clobber you, too?"

He shook his head. Some wavy brown hair flipped down to bother an eye. "When I watched you fall like a dropped brick, I told Nichols I'd do what he wanted. There was a pistol in my ribs. They tied my hands first and then yours—tossed a tablecloth over you and stuck you in the trunk of a Studebaker."

No wonder my spine felt old. I grunted.

"Right now, they're holding us in an isolated little boathouse somewhere down on Maine Avenue where they clean fresh fish and oysters for the Jazz Club's kitchen. Meechum went to pick up a motorized skiff of some sort. When he gets here, the two of us will disappear. They're going to drop us into the Potomac. I think Nichols and Reilly are still around, outside watching on the wharf for the skiff to get here."

I kept my voice low. "Why the hell did you go to the Jazz Club?"

Kennedy snorted self-derisively. "I think I told you that the other night when I took Susan back to her apartment, we ran into somebody I knew in the revolving door. It was Nichols. The Jazz Club's a popular place, and I'd met him once or twice. He rode up on the elevator to the sixth floor with us. Susan didn't know him. I introduced them, and we joked a little. Then Suze and I went into her place, and Nichols claimed he needed to find number 610, which was down a different hallway."

That pierced my slug's brain. "Nichols was at Susan Prebble's apartment?"

Kennedy made a boy-can-I-be-dumb grin. "This morning, the bright idea popped into my head that Nichols might have seen somebody hanging around there or something. But when I found you between the assorted pistols and Nichols ordered me into the room at gunpoint, I realized *he* could have killed Susan."

The gods were still jerking their knotted rope through my throbbing skull, but the drizzle-gray haze started lifting. "They're going to fasten something heavy onto us and drop us into the Potomac." I still felt slow on the uptake.

Kennedy nodded. "Yes, I suppose."

"Why have they left us alive, then, Jack? It would have been a lot easier for them to kill us at the Jazz Club than to do all this. Avoiding bloodstains?" I tugged at the hemp ropes on my wrists. Nice job, I thought. Evidently, an Eagle Scout tied them.

Kennedy was talking. "I offered Nichols money, lots of it, but he just laughed. Still, he liked my idea enough to see what he could shake Dad down for."

That didn't mean anything. Nichols was afraid we knew too much. We did, though most of it was still a *New York Times* crossword to me. Number one down was: if Nichols didn't know Betty or Susan and he didn't rape them, why did he kill them like that?

Kennedy kept his voice down. "Nichols called my father at the Hay-Adams from a pay phone. He said I was a dead man if he couldn't pick up a million dollars in unmarked hundred-dollar bills in a satchel this afternoon at four. Of course, he warned Dad not to call the police, and put me on the phone. I told Dad they had you, too. Dad promised to pay for both of us."

Nice of him. It wouldn't matter, though, except to buy some time.

"Nichols told Dad he'd call back later and tell him where to have the money delivered. I'm fairly certain Nichols plans to have both of us drowned in any event."

I agreed with him. "Leaving either of us alive would be monumentally stupid, Jack, if Nichols was involved in the killings. Murder's a hard rap to flee, even with money. You kidnap a United States congressman at gunpoint, you're pretty certain any foreign government—even Joe Stalin's—will send you home to stand trial."

Still, when Meechum and Reilly warned me off the case, I had no idea Nichols was involved. But the chess player in him knew I'd inevitably find the connection once I'd started asking questions about Billy Meechum. Nichols started out two moves ahead of me.

What the hell could have been in it for him to kill those two women or to have it done for him? It wasn't something Joe Kennedy wanted, not with Jack tied up next to me. Was it a botched extortion job?

The homemade chairs they tied us to stood on the edge of the dank concrete floor, right beside the narrow slip for the motorized skiff to pull in. They could simply kick us into the water while we were tied up and not leave bullets that could be tagged to specific guns by any ballistics whiz in the country.

Nichols gave the Old Man a four o'clock deadline. I asked Kennedy what time it was. He chuckled. "Actually, Griffin, it's hard reading my wristwatch from here."

We both laughed as if he were Bob Hope.

But he'd made me think, headache or not. "Hey, scoot your chair farther away from the water and turn your back toward me. I'll do the same. Maybe one of us can reach the other's knots."

You didn't need to give Jack Kennedy an idea twice. In half a minute, we were back-to-back. I couldn't reach his ropes, but he started working on mine right away. "I sail boats a lot. I know knots."

Time oozed away as he kept picking at my bonds with his fingernails. It felt as if more hours went by than we had. Einstein could probably have used these drawn-out moments to explain his theory of relativity. Actually, Kennedy finished quickly, but he'd only been able to reach the rope that bound me to the chair rather than the one on my wrists. Our feet weren't tied, though. As soon as I was free of the chair, I stood up and stretched a couple times. I hurt all over and felt wonderful. We just might survive this mess.

FIFTY

Then I squatted down again quickly to see if Jack could finish undoing the ropes around my wrists. But the sagging door on the river side of the boat house made noise, and I got back in my chair, quick. Then it jerked open. Reilly came strutting in, a rooster armed to the beak. He clutched my Army .45 in his left hand and his own automatic in his right.

Reilly noticed immediately that we'd moved our chairs closer to one another. "Have you been holding hands, little girlies? Are the both of you all lovey-dovey queer on each other? Or are you just scared you're gonna die when Billy gets here? 'Cause frankly, I can't see Nichols letting you two darlings go free."

I kept dead still and didn't give him the satisfaction of reacting. Punks hate that.

Reilly loomed up closer, pointing his own pistol at me and holding mine as if he wanted to slap me across the face with it. "Yeah, you queer little sweethearts have just got to be punished for getting so cozy. Being a faggot is against the law in Washington, you know."

"Shove it, moron!" Forget about wit—I wanted Reilly exploding with anger. He didn't have the voltage to be pissed off and know what he was doing at the same time. Taking a wide step to get closer, he reached his left arm back to wallop me with my pistol.

I didn't wait for it. Thrusting myself up onto my feet, I slammed my chest against his. That got me past Reilly's pistol. In the same motion, I kicked as high and hard as a Rockette between his legs with my knee. The impact knocked him on his back. His twisted face was purple.

Some people have a novel idea that kicking a man in the crotch will put him out of action long enough for you to squire your girlfriend to an expensive French restaurant and savor a four-star dinner. Actually, the effect is intense, but it doesn't last. And a lug who's accustomed to pain gets *really* annoyed. I didn't wait for that, either. My hands were trussed like a rabbit in a stew pot. Reilly still held guns in both fists. He'd blast us if I didn't kill him immediately.

That's when I recalled the trick a short, wiry British commando from Liverpool taught me. Jumping as high as I could, right up over Reilly while he tried to catch his breath, I came down feetfirst onto his chest, kicking downward hard with both feet together. My heels snapped straight into his breastbone just above his heart. With a hideous sound like dry sticks being broken inside a velvet bag, his chest caved in.

My commando jump-kick ruptured Reilly's heart. His fingers fell open as his ruined lungs filled with blood. He was dying very fast. I jumped to his left and kicked my .45 a bit beyond his reach, then did the same thing with his gun.

It was a wasted precaution. Red foam oozed out of his mouth. Reilly was past trying to reach anything. The commando trick worked perfectly except for the strangled screech he'd made when I kneed him in the crotch.

My pistol lay half-cocked beside Reilly. That meant there was a lovely fat bullet in the chamber ready to fire. I flopped down onto my left side and rolled over the heavy Colt, grabbing it with my hands still tied behind my back and fitting it into my right palm, cocking it fully.

I flopped onto my side so I could shoot toward the door over Reilly if I had to. No hope for aiming. I kept my voice low. "Jack, force your chair over so you're flat on the floor, too." Kennedy got it—a sitting duck is, well, a sitting duck—and wrestled his crummy chair to the concrete. Either Nichols would come inside in a minute with a gun in his hand to see why Reilly had screamed, or he wouldn't.

He did.

*****

"What in hell is all the—"

Nichols froze when he saw his gunman gurgling on the floor. He snapped off a hasty shot at me. I felt it *thunk* into Reilly. Nichols blasted a couple more my way, too hot-tempered to simply aim.

I fired maybe five or six fast shots in his general direction. Nichols toppled like a wobbly vase. His nickel-plated revolver clattered onto the floor as he fell. He didn't land very close to it. His belly oozed a Bloody Mary, and his right hand fumbled without luck to staunch the flow.

Nichols wore a funny smirk on his face. I kicked the shiny little pistol farther from him. He turned pale and sweaty. "I knew I made a stupid mistake on this whole thing."

Nichols's bleeding didn't look heavy enough to kill him. Still, you don't want a bullet in the gut. You could die pretty slowly, and it could hurt a lot. I'd watched a couple dozen soldiers go that way. It wasn't fun even when they were Nazis.

When would Meechum show up with the skiff?

*****

"Griffin!" Kennedy's yell startled me. "We've got to get loose quickly." I'd lost track of him being there. I spotted a filet knife on the fish-gutting table.

Rolling to my knees, I hopped to my feet and grabbed the knife. My first thought was to flop next to Kennedy and cut him free. But the idea of two marginally mobile men using a razor-sharp blade between the veins in our bound wrists without being able to see what we were doing struck me as damned risky.

Stabbing the fish knife into the top of the bench, I rubbed the rope against its edge where the knots crossed my wristwatch to keep it away from an artery. I wasn't too badly nicked when I got free, and I cut Kennedy loose in less than a minute.

"Go back to Capitol Hill and vote on some God-damned bills or something, Jack. Just get the hell out of here. Don't mention a word about any of this unless the cops ask you point-blank. Go."

That was another idea I didn't have to hand him twice.

FIFTY-ONE

Skip Nichols didn't look much healthier than Reilly. I holstered my pistol, snatched up the phone, and called O'Heaney at home. "You know that crappy-looking boat shed where the Jazz Club keeps its skiff and guts its fish?"

"End of Maine Avenue, with the fancy red and white sign."

"Yeah, that one. Hustle yourself over here with an honest cop or two, if you can find that many. Maybe a competent police stenographer, too. Have someone send an ambulance along. Make it fast, Vince. I caught the killer we've both been looking for in the Dyson case. He's not gonna last too long."

I knelt beside Skip Nichols. I'd liked the guy. He came home from actually fighting in the war and did some fairly principled things in a pretty unprincipled way. I still didn't understand how he figured in the two murders. "Kennedy was right, wasn't he? *You* killed Betty Dyson and Susan Prebble. Why, Nichols? Why in the hell did you kill them like that?"

"Funny thing." His eyes were hooded. "Clever ideas don't always work out the way—the way you think."

Half a pack of Chesterfields peered out of his sport coat pocket. I took one out, lit it, and stuck it between his white wax lips. He gave me a grateful little nod.

"Nichols, what the hell was so God-damned clever about slashing Betty Dyson and Susan Prebble's throats?" There was a butcher knife in my voice.

A good-sized piece of an old tarp lay in the corner. I spread it beside Nichols and eased him onto it, pulling what was left of it over his chest to keep him warm. He seemed hurt worse than I could see. I didn't want him going into shock.

It was muggy in the shed—Washington in July—and the rotten fish smell just hung there like Macbeth's head on a pike, an ugly and disgusting presence. I helped myself to one of his cigarettes, though I usually didn't smoke.

His gray eyes were already turning to glass. "I'm not going to make it, am I?" His forehead didn't feel much warmer than the concrete floor.

I shook my head. "No, I don't think so." Not much blood oozed out of him, but my bullet probably ripped a hole in something important. Whatever I'd hit would fill his body cavities with black blood. I tossed my suit coat over him, too, as if that would slow down the shock I watched closing in around the edges of his eyes, a wolf pack in winter.

Two cops burst through the door Kennedy'd left open. They wore uniforms, so they weren't O'Heaney's. *"Holy Christ!"* One of them pulled out his service revolver and cocked it. "Stand up slowly."

I did exactly that, my empty hands floating up into view.

The other cop drew his gun slowly. "A scrawny guy in a rumpled suit waved us down a block from here. Tells us he heard shots and yells coming from the Jazz Club's boat shed. Then he waves down a Yellow Cab, hops in, and skedaddles."

There was an urgent whisper down at my feet. "Griffin. Make you a deal."

The cops were still forty feet away. "Let me talk to him." The shorter one nodded to go ahead. Neither one relaxed his pistol.

Nichols looked terrible. Wherever his blood was, it didn't make him pink anymore. "I'll tell them what you already know." All he had left was a whisper. "You might prove it once—once I'm dead, but—not easily. I'll take the fall—for everything—just when the cops are all ready to—to arrest your pal." He coughed, and it hurt him. "But one thing...."

"What's that, Nichols?"

"My wife and—Thumbelina. Do something with—with Kennedy's old man—to take care of them—will ya?"

I nodded my head.

Just then, Vince O'Heaney came pounding through the door with two young detectives I didn't know. A dumpy middle-aged woman carrying a steno pad ran right behind them. The door opened again behind them as soon as they'd slammed it. A short fat guy I knew named Grady Burgess who wrote for the *Evening Star* joined the party, carrying a big black press camera in his left hand. I could see O'Heaney thinking about running Burgess off. He decided not to.

Nichols wrestled against slipping into the abyss. The sweat on his face came as much from exertion as shock and the July heat. The cops and the newsman huddled around him. O'Heaney told me softly that there was an ambulance on the way. It didn't matter, and I knew it didn't.

"I killed them, Officer." Gray mist rose in his voice. "The two women, Mrs. Dyson and—and the Prebble girl, too. I—I stabbed them, and I slashed their precious throats."

O'Heaney glared down at him. "Why'd you do it?" The steno took it all down as fast as she could. So did the guy from the *Star*.

Nichols coughed. "Girls like that never give a—give a short guy a chance. I tried to—to pick them up at my club. They—They just laughed. Not both of them together. Diff—Different times."

Every word was baloney. Nichols was building a rationale for something.

"I—I knew they—didn't want me. I hated—hated them for th—that." Even the whisper was evaporating. "Followed 'em—to their apartments. I got past—past the desk clerks and—went upstairs. Knocked on their doors."

He stopped, gulping a long breath.

The rest of us held ours. "What then?" O'Heaney was still conducting the interrogation. I started to hear a siren wailing a million miles across town.

"Punched them in the—the face the second they—they opened the door." Nichols coughed a couple more times. "Right in the face. Pulled a switchblade. It's in my pocket. Held it—Held it right at—at their throats."

Something wasn't falling into place for me, but I couldn't identify it. You could barely hear Nichols now.

"Stabbed 'em while I—Then slit—slit their throats to make—make sure."

The siren whined closer. But Nichols's eyes became marbles now, and he rolled them up towards me.

Nobody but me heard his last words. "You take care of your own."

FIFTY-TWO

An hour later, after getting my forehead patched and helping O'Heaney piece the "Strawberry Blonde Murders" together at police headquarters in a way that fit what they had—as if Jack hadn't been there—I caught a cab over to the Jazz Club to pick up my car. For a while, I just sat at the wheel by an empty curb.

I hadn't killed a man since the war, and I'd liked Nichols. Meanwhile, a rat gnawed its way into my consciousness: while Nichols's confession solved everything and got Jack Kennedy out of hot water, something I couldn't put a name to was wrong with it.

Why did Nichols kill Betty and Susan? It wasn't about rape. Jack Kennedy provided the only common thread other than the murderer. All of a sudden, I saw it. Nichols hadn't killed Betty. I'd seen him at the Jazz Club until late on Friday night while Betty was murdered.

But somebody killed Betty Dyson within a few hours of Kennedy leaving her. Whoever murdered Betty didn't have to force his way into her apartment. It wasn't Nichols, and she'd never have let Meechum or Reilly in without screaming. Symington and his pet weasel had been wining and dining newspaper publishers far away.

Nichols wanted to take the blame for the first killing as well as the second one. There was no reason to kill Susan other than that Betty had been murdered that way. Nichols wanted Susan's death to look like the first killer's work. Suddenly, the roof of my Nash wouldn't keep the light out of my brain.

*****

I stormed into the Jazz Club and straight to Nichols's office, my .45 under my arm and Snilder's handcuffs still in my coat pocket from two or three days earlier. I needed to look at something. I didn't know what. Something would tell me why Nichols killed Susan.

Nobody waited at the receptionist's desk, but Millie's lamp glowed, and half a glass of something iced stood beside the typewriter. I let myself into Nichols's office.

The flat-top drawer of his glass-topped desk held nothing unusual unless you counted the roll of nickels in a brown paper bank wrapper with "Good luck, Nickels!" scrawled on it. I stared at the silver-framed picture of his delicate wife and their baby daughter, wishing I'd never known they existed.

The door behind me creaked. "Come back for more punishment, gumshoe?" Meechum's eyes were red. I faced him, wrapping my right hand around the roll of nickels.

Meechum stood three inches or so taller than me and toted about thirty pounds more beef on his bones. On the other hand, all the years as a gut puncher had made him slow. He reached inside his black suit jacket toward the bulge of his shoulder holster.

A quick kick toward his groin with my left foot fell short—I knew it would—but Meechum shoved both hands down in front of his fly. I threw all my weight forward as I stomped my foot down, pivoted on it for reach, and punched him hard in the nose with a fistful of nickels. Never hit a man with your empty fist—you'll hurt him, but you'll break some finger bones. The noseful of nickels worked nicely, though. The hulking son of a bitch splattered blood on my white shirt. A lot more of it poured over his mouth. He wadded up his hand to punch me back, so I slugged him in the nose again.

Meechum staggered. I pulled my Army .45 out, cocked it, and shoved the muzzle against his Adam's apple.

"Listen, meathead. I shot your boss, and I killed your pal, Reilly. Want to go next?" Snatching his pistol out of his jacket, I tossed it into a corner and backed away from him. If Meechum wanted to try me, I'd have gladly shot him. But he did just what I thought he'd do.

He muttered, "Shit."

"You're headed for prison, Meechum. Get down on the floor and do a push-up."

Eyes rolling, he sank sullenly onto his knees, dropped forward onto his palms, and lowered his chest onto the carpet.

I put my left foot on his spine and leaned on it. "Awkward,

isn't it? Meechum, if you try straightening your elbows, I'll finish what I started earlier."

He'd started out florid, and by that point, his face became a peeled tomato. "What do you mean?"

"I'll bet you nearly died when you brought the stinking skiff over by the boathouse and saw all those cops and ambulances. You got your bait bucket out of there in a hurry. You should have kept going, Meechum. Now don't move."

I fished one of his horseshoe-crab mitts behind him, snapped Snilder's handcuffs on it, and then matched it with his other one. "Just lie there, Meechum. Pretend I already shot you for wiggling."

*****

The picture I wanted a better look at again hung on the wall in a black wooden frame, along with Duke Ellington, Sassy Sarah Vaughn, and Satchmo, next to Nichols in front of a plane called "Inside Straight." A dozen or so fighter pilots stood posing together on a flat field in the glare of the midday sun. The high noon shadows cast by their noses and the goggles on their foreheads made their faces harder to recognize than if it had been shot indoors with a flash camera by somebody who knew how to take pictures. Even so, Skip Nichols wasn't at all hard to spot, half a head shorter than his comrades.

You could see the story in the way the flyboys stood. Their arms loafed easily on top of each other's shoulders. All of them grinned the way men do in a war when there's time, when nobody's shooting at you, and just being alive together is as great a victory as anything else you've accomplished. They huddled tight together, a P-51 Mustang's four-bladed propeller showing behind them, with the name "Betty" painted on the fuselage. The skinny square-jawed lieutenant colonel in the center of the group, the squadron commander, was Don Dyson.

Now I knew why Skip Nichols killed Susan Prebble and claimed he'd killed Betty.

FIFTY-THREE

"Hey, Vince, I'm afraid it's going to be a long evening." Nichols wouldn't object if I used the black phone on his desk. "I caught Billy Meechum. He's waiting in Skip Nichols's office for a chance to answer some questions. You'll want a couple uniforms and a Black Maria."

I heard a bullfrog grunt. "I just put out an all-points bulletin on the bastard, Junior. We'll run right over."

"Always glad to help, Vince. Meechum and his pistol can probably tie up some loose ends in Nichols's operation for you. Maybe he did some of his own dirty work, too. Besides, once your boys take him out of here, I still plan to drive Johnnie Walker somewhere. I could use a one-sergeant police escort. Two hours tops. I know you're a family man."

*****

Looking at Millie sitting opposite me with her legs crossed beat watching Meechum lie on his stomach with Snilder's handcuffs for bracelets. Still, I kept an eye on both of them.

Her olive-green eyes pleaded, glancing up at my forehead and then back at my gaze. "Honest, mister, I didn't know they did anything wrong. Mr. Nichols told me you passed out drunk and banged your head on the corner of the desk. That's why Reilly and this creep carried you out."

"Shuddup, you dumb—"

I kicked Meechum in the slats. "Go on."

Millie's green-flecked eyes bored into him. "This flabby cube steak thinks his clammy hands are something a girl wants to wear like a black lace brassiere." She grimaced. "He went in and helped take you wherever they took you—the boathouse, I guess." Her jaw relaxed, and she concentrated on wearing out her Juicy Fruit. "It's happened a few times before. Gee, maybe *none* of them were drunks!" Her olive eyes became saucers now, an angel discovering the existence of evil.

Millie wasn't as naïve as she acted. You could see it in the way she arched her back to hoist her lavish breasts, as if she were unaware of the effect—which was, in fact, well worth taking in. She actually wore a black lace brassiere, and fidgeting with the button over it made a nice touch, too, batting her lashes at the same time to suggest I could dream up better uses for her lovely bottom than her sitting on it in a cold, cold jail cell.

"Also, mister, I'm sorry about that line of bull crap the boss had me shovel your way Wednesday." Her repentant expression was cute. "Whenever he mentioned 'Rube,' that cued me to back up whatever he said. Your bald-headed man never came here with a woman. He only saw Nichols."

"I'd figured that. Thanks for confirming it." I leaned over and kissed her beneath her left ear, just below the ends of her short black hair. She smelled a little more like lilacs than a lilac bush does. Kissing her neck seemed a thing worth doing in itself, but it also let me whisper, "It would be very thoughtful if you didn't mention the other gentleman to the police."

"You mean Jack, who's so handsome?"

I nodded. So did she. Smiling, she turned and kissed my mouth hard. I held on for a minute.

"Lipstick," she murmured.

I'd just finished wiping it off when O'Heaney rolled in with a young detective and two mastiffs wearing blue serge.

"How Meechum came by those handcuffs is anybody's guess, Vince. I slapped them on him. He and Reilly burglarized my apartment Wednesday night and roughed me up at gunpoint. I meant to file a complaint. Just now, Meechum came after me with this gun. He also injured my knuckles with his nose." I showed the cops my bruises.

O'Heaney tsked. "Bastard splattered blood on your white shirt, too. That's destruction of private proppity."

I returned his grin. "You're thinking that checking this pistol's ballistics against some of those unsolved shootings could be useful. I'm sure you're right. Millie here tells me she's seen Reilly and

Meechum lug a number of people out of here. She thought they were drunk, but now she wonders. I'd guess if your guys treated her nicely, she'd remember a lot of details. She really wants to be helpful."

Millie smiled with just her eyes while Vince told the second detective to treat her as a cooperative witness. The bulls hoisted Meechum to his feet. He snarled at Millie, rusty hair in his eyes. "Lissen, bitch, keep yer—"

A telephone directory in O'Heaney's hand collided with Meechum's left ear. Vince barked at the uniforms. "Hey, watch what you're doin' with the suspect. That coulda hurt him, y'know." He grinned at me. "Just this week, while I was looking up cases the precincts sat on, I noticed a coupla disappearances with some connection to the Jazz Club. We're gonna treat Millie *very* nicely, Junior."

She batted her eyes innocently at the young detective. "It would help if I wasn't gone long. Somebody's got to open the club tonight."

*****

When I finally shut Nichols's office door and followed Vince out to my car, the group photo in its black-painted frame and the silver-edged Madonna-and-child portrait from the desk nestled in a jacket pocket. So did a half-empty fifth of Johnnie Walker from the glittering bar in Nichols's office.

A paperboy on the corner bawled out, *"Strawberry blonde murderers killed! Extry extry!"* We grabbed a copy of the *Star,* and I drove while Vince read. It came out the way we'd pasted it together a couple hours earlier—Nichols did it all and died in a gunfight along with a bad apple named Reilly. I came off pretty well in what Vince read.

"Yeah, Junior, it's right under the main headline, which yuh gotta like. 'G.O.P. yields in vote fraud probe after all-night Senate session in effort tuh adjourn tomorruh.' They got a Berryman cartoon about two dumb-looking senators with it."

At a light, I glanced over at the picture on the front page of Skip Nichols dying. "Vince, they quoted you at length about the whole thing."

"Oh, yeah, but the story's horse manure, as Truman'd put it if there were ladies around. I warned Captain Magruder we were talking tuh the press before we had the answers."

"You had a confession, though, Vince, and they had the story."

"Yeah. But just before yuh phoned, Junior, the lab report on Nichols came in. Wrong blood type. Magruder says mebbe the lab screwed up the first time around."

"It doesn't matter, Vince. I'll prove that at Andrews Field."

FIFTY-FOUR

O'Heaney absorbed a lot of the Johnnie Walker while the milling sheep of a drowsy afternoon's traffic slowed down our drive all the way out a sun-glazed Pennsylvania Avenue. If I'd had serious plans to abscond with the Scotch, inviting the detective sergeant to ride along with me to Andrews Field would have been a serious mistake. "I'm off duty now, Junior. Officially."

He flashed his badge as we drove right through the front gate at Andrews. I remembered the way to Colonel Dyson's office, gliding past sleek new silver jet fighters baking on a shimmering glass runway.

The scrawny corporal at the desk in the outer room was busy staring at a slick ad for Maidenform brassieres in *Collier's*. He couldn't quite shift gears quickly enough to toss himself between us and the door to Dyson's sanctuary.

A startled Dyson jumped up from working on a chart on top of a tilted drafting table. His one-piece flying suit lay draped over the back of his desk chair, and a plastic helmet gleamed on his desk.

He glared at me. "Get the hell out. Richards, what in the hell did you—?" The colonel mastered himself. "All right, Corporal Richards, just call the MPs." He glanced up at the blood-stained gauze taped to my forehead. "Somebody gave you the poke you had coming. Doesn't appear to have taught you anything."

I handed him our folded copy of the *Star*. "You apparently haven't read the late papers." The headline read

Jazz Club Owner Shot; Dies After Admitting to Strawberry Blonde Murders.

*****

Dyson stared at the headline as if it were a tarantula. He read the first three or four paragraphs carefully, sinking onto a tall wooden stool. *"You killed Skip."* His voice a monotone, he stared in my direction, looking a thousand yards through me. "Didn't you?"

"Yes. I wish I hadn't, but I'd be dead."

He wasn't listening to me. His head moved slowly in all directions, as if somewhere up on the ceiling, there *had* to be half a dozen Focke-Wulfs or Messerschmitts coming in fast. I knew exactly what Dyson was doing because there were still moments when I found myself watching out for gray-green riflemen along Washington's sidewalks.

"Come back down, Colonel." I kept my voice soft. "We need to ask you a few questions about what happened the night Betty was murdered. The night *you* killed her."

O'Heaney's jaw dropped like a stone. Dyson stopped moving, a tightrope walker who hit a glass wall high above the center ring. "You think I murdered my wife?"

A boyish-looking one-star general with command wings and four gaudy rows of ribbons marched into the office just at that point with a captain whose shirtfront was vacant khaki cloth. I'd seen the general at Betty's memorial service. They heard Dyson's question.

The general touched Dyson's arm. "Don, I can toss these two guys off the base if you want me to. Or I can summon a lawyer to run over here if you prefer." He stood a couple inches shorter than me, built like he'd been a halfback once but heavier around the belt buckle now. His squinty gray eyes had probably been able to spot German fighters at a point when they looked like fleas high above the horizon.

Dyson shook his head firmly. "No, thanks, General, but I'd like you to sit in on this conversation. Maybe Captain Benson could just shut the door on his way out."

Captain Benson shut the door on his way out.

They breed generals for civility under pressure. "Major General Paul Brubaker." He offered his hand. "I gather you're D.C. police?"

"I am." O'Heaney shook Brubaker's mitt. "Detective Sergeant Vincent O'Heaney. This guy here's Jack Griffin, a Washington private detective. As yuh heard, we've both been involved in the Betty Dyson murder case. I'm here in an official capacity. We have some unanswered questions."

Brubaker nodded. "Don, the Articles of War put civil crimes under the civilian authorities. If the District of Columbia police ask us to turn you over to them for questioning or arrest, the Air Force will have to do it."

"I can't imagine what you're going on." A sneer like Dyson's wasn't built in a day. "The newspaper says you've got the confession of some dying man that *he* killed my wife and another woman I never met. A man with underworld connections, the paper mentions. I had no reason to kill Mrs. Dyson. All the passion left our marriage a long time ago. This is ridiculous."

"Colonel, maybe you're perfectly happy to let your former wingman go down in flames for this." I handed him the silver-framed photo of Nichols's wife and child. "Maybe it means nothing to you if his daughter grows up thinking her father was a vicious rapist. I don't suppose it matters to you what his delicate widow thinks, either. Skip Nichols gave his life for you, Dyson, and you don't give a damn. Nobody raped Betty either, did they?"

You don't see a lot of snowmen in the Washington area in July, but Dyson froze and turned white, his teeth clenched.

"Nichols murdered Susan, all right, Dyson, but not Betty. He was running the Jazz Club when somebody shattered her face, slit her throat, and stabbed her a dozen times."

"And I spent the whole night out here." Dyson wanted to brazen it out. Sometimes they need to confess—this guy was a cucumber. He laid the photo facedown on his desk.

I waited for the overhead scream of a jet fighter to pass and then spelled out that I knew Nichols had killed Susan Prebble but not Betty Dyson, that Nichols hadn't raped either of them and that, in fact, nobody had been raped at all. I told them how the dying Nichols confessed to everything so I wouldn't figure out what happened to Betty, taking the blame for her death to protect his old commander.

Brubaker waved off the arriving MPs. "A minute ago, Don, you sounded like you didn't know the man. Now I'm hearing he flew wingman with you in the war."

Dyson ignored that. "Why'd Skip say he raped them if nobody did?"

I left Jack Kennedy's name unspoken, as well as my deal with Nichols. "Because it gave everybody a plausible reason for the killings. People commit murders like that all the time—a rapist kills the woman to keep her from saying he assaulted her. A very thorough medical examiner found the residues of sex and jumped to the reasonable but mistaken conclusion of rape. The second crime copied the first, so the police also assumed rape was part of that one."

The last thing Vince O'Heaney wanted was to reopen a closed murder case after the cops had patted themselves heartily on the back in the newspapers for solving it. But he'd never help a wife-killer to go free in a police cover-up. He'd back me.

"Sergeant O'Heaney will ask the general for a list of MPs on duty last Friday afternoon and night at all the gates out here." I held up my index finger. "At least one, Dyson—some enlisted guy who thinks you're an arrogant horse's ass or who won't cover for a man who slit his wife's throat—will admit having seen you leave Andrews Field late that afternoon or early that evening. Someone will recall seeing you return later. Maybe you weren't spotted at the Chesapeake Apartments, who knows? But somebody saw you somewhere in Washington that night. Some sharp-eyed guy pumping gas in a Texaco station or some busybody working late in a People's Drug Store. Somebody watched what you did with your bloody clothes, Dyson, you can count on that."

"The hell they did." He grinned before he could stop himself.

"You told the police you tried calling Betty on Friday and Saturday and again Sunday afternoon before you conned the Chesapeake's manager into finding her body while you hid out here. The neighbors never heard the phone ring all weekend. And all those baloney calls you claim you made to Betty from here *every* weekend. The phone company records won't show them, will they, Dyson? Even though they'd have been long-distance calls from Maryland to Washington, the easiest calls in the world to trace."

O'Heaney butted in. "Anything yuh say, Colonel Dyson, can be taken down and used in a court of law as evidence against yuh." He put his jaw alongside Dyson's. "But we're gonna nail yuh, flyboy, whether yuh talk or not. Why don't you just tell us the whole story? Maybe we can give yuh a break somewhere."

The fighter hero laughed. "A break, my ass. You bastards want to send me to the electric chair for murder, and you won't shed a tear if you do. But I didn't kill my wife, dammit. And nobody can prove I did."

"Betty wasn't your wife, Dyson." I glared at him. "She got a divorce from you on grounds of desertion the day you slit her throat."

FIFTY-FIVE

You could watch Dyson's guts turn to chipped ice. "She wasn't— But how in—how in the hell—?" He slumped into a wooden chair.

"You think I'd make that claim without having read a copy of the decree?" I hadn't, but I knew there was one.

Nobody breathed just then.

Finally, Dyson scratched his left ear, looking resigned. "I suppose I might as well tell you what really happened. I drove back to the apartment to plead with her last Friday night. I wanted to see if there was any chance at all left for us to make our marriage work. A divorce can wreck your career, but it wasn't just that."

He lit up a Lucky Strike and sat still for a moment. After taking a second drag, he stubbed it out.

"I *loved* Betty, you know. And she loved me. People used to call the pair of us the 'House Afire.' There was a *lot* of sex between us. Neither of us screwed around with anybody else. Then Uncle Sam sent me over to England and gave me the fighter plane I named after her."

Then why in the hell, I wondered, did Dyson walk out on a dreamboat like that after the war was over?

"I flew like a goddam falcon, you know. And I was also goddam lucky. Skip Nichols was my wingman for most of the three years I flew fighter missions. That was goddam lucky in itself. Skip saved my bacon—oh—a couple of dozen times. I bailed him out just as often. What made him eternally grateful was the day I mother-henned his shot-up Mustang as we flew down low and headed back over the coast."

"Oh?" I wanted him to keep rolling.

"Yeah, I thought we could nurse him all the way back to

England, but he finally had to ditch in the Channel. A Nazi torpedo boat raced out from the shore to snatch him. I leaned on my throttle and ran straight at the boat—head-on—firing at the Krauts as they shot at me. My plane took a few hits, but the boat blew up in a red-orange ball of flaming fuel. Air Rescue fished Skip out of the drink half an hour later. I won a medal for that. I think it might have been my second Silver Star, but you lose track."

The rest of us in the room kept silent. I pulled the small, black-framed group picture out of my pocket and handed it to him.

He nodded. "These guys were the best. Then the war in Europe ended, and we all got sent home. I expected Betty and me to set the apartment ablaze. Nothing happened."

"Nothing?" O'Heaney had to ask.

"It wasn't that we didn't try. We tried all night." You could hear the Sahara in his throat. "But I—I—well, I just couldn't *do* anything. Understand what I mean? I wanted my wife, and she wanted me, but nothing happened."

The general spoke in a soft voice. "Don, did a war injury—?"

"Paul, my squadron lost dozens of men. My only wound for the whole three years at war was a little cut I got climbing out of my plane one afternoon—I put my right hand where a Kraut bullet had blown a jagged hole near the canopy. Other than that, I sailed through three years of combat completely unscathed."

I put a hand on his shoulder. "Dyson, nobody goes through three years of combat unscathed."

He shook off my grip and glared at me. "Don't give me any of your goddam pity."

Dyson stepped over to the window and stared out at the cotton candy clouds. His reverie didn't last.

"I suppose I found it more and more difficult to take Betty to bed." He looked down at his drafting table. "After two or three weeks, I just stayed out here at Andrews. I couldn't face asking Betty to put up with imp—with impotent sex."

I thought of Jerry and Lucille DiMarco. Dyson's self-pity lit my fuse. "Colonel, your wife would have stuck with you on a march into hell. Did you think sex was all she wanted from you? Betty loved you. Did you even ask for any help?"

Dyson roared at me. *"What, a fucking psychiatrist?* Do you know what that would have done to my career?"

"Less than this." My teeth were grinding. "Tell us about murdering your wife."

The room's evening shadows were all that moved for a minute or two. General Brubaker looked more shocked at Dyson's outburst than at either the murder confession or the sad sex story.

The colonel pulled a half-empty pint bottle of Old Grand-Dad out of a drawer and took a swig. "I wasn't sneaking in, but nobody saw me. I still had my key. When I opened the front door, though, I could hear Betty cooing and moaning, and I heard a guy's voice. There wasn't any question what was going on. She was murmuring, 'Jack, oh, Jack, Jack.' All I could think of was how miserable I'd felt for so long, and here she was happily screwing some joker. How many other guys were there?"

Nobody else said a word.

Dyson rubbed his forehead as if it hurt. "I've *never* lost control like that. I stormed into the kitchen and rifled through the drawers quietly until I found a sharp butcher knife. Then I took a few breaths to steady myself and started out of the kitchen, ready to slaughter both of them. But the guy breezed out the door with his back to me and his knotted necktie in his goddam hand."

He stood up, his right fist clenched. O'Heaney stepped back, but I didn't think Dyson was going to throw a punch. In his mind, he held the knife in his hand again.

"Betty just lay there with her eyes closed. She kept touching herself, biting her lower lip like she used to do with me, moaning, 'Jack, oh, Jack!' She still had on a string of pearls I bought her in Paris. Her dress got all bunched up around her waist. There was one nylon stocking left on. I just *flew* on top of her, crashing down full-length along her body."

Dyson didn't jump, but he raised both arms in illustration, a diver taking flight. "I smashed my left hand down like this to cover her mouth. Her nose just exploded. In the same motion, I guess, I slashed like this across her throat." He showed us a slicing move. "Then I just hacked at her ribs with the knife, stabbing as if—I don't know—as if she had to pay for everything, as if it had all been Betty's fault. She died."

"In twelve seconds."

Dyson stared at me and shrugged, hollow-eyed.

"I suppose so. When it ended, I lay on top of her, I don't know how long, just sobbing and terrified. Then I dropped the knife on the floor and stood up. There was blood all over me, all over the bed, on the walls, the floor. I couldn't even look at—at *her.*"

Dyson sat down again, sat down hard. He picked up a pencil and then set it down, lining it up straight with the edge of the drafting table.

"I locked the front door, stripped off everything I had on, took a fast shower. There were still some clothes of mine in the dresser. I jammed my blood-soaked uniform and stuff in a small suitcase and slipped away around 2 a.m. when the halls and the garage were deserted. Pitched the bag off the Sousa Bridge on my way back here. Fell into bed and slept with a peace I hadn't expected. When nobody called me about it by Sunday, I got nervous and phoned the apartment building office." He sat back down, as if his confession was over.

A jet fighter shrieked its delight as it ripped across the sky over us.

"I got a question." O'Heaney lit a cigarette. "Your pal Skip Nichols claimed he killed both women. We know he didn't. How the hell'd he get involved in this goddam mess?"

Dyson shook his head sorrowfully. "Skip called me Monday morning after he saw the story in the papers, said he was terribly sorry, asked if there was anything he could do for me. I was starting to worry what the police thought. I knew he had some connections with them. He'd done some pretty rough stuff since the war, too. So I asked him to see what was going on."

He picked up the pencil and set it straight again.

"Skip called back and said they suspected a congressman named Jack Kennedy. Jack was the name Betty moaned. But a damn congressman! They'd *never* charge a fucking congressman. And if they didn't, they'd start looking seriously at *my* alibi. As you said, Griffin, there was going to be somebody who'd seen me. When you drove out and questioned me Monday afternoon, I really started sweating."

Vince and I both nodded.

"I drove into Washington Tuesday for Betty's memorial service—a charade I didn't dare avoid. Afterward, I dressed in civvies and met Skip at his club. I told him everything. Everything. I asked him, 'What can I do, Skip?' He looked me in the eye. 'Don, we just need to make sure they charge this congressman. You saved my ass a few times; I'm not gonna let you go to the chair, buddy. You take care of your own. Leave it to me.' On my way out, I ran across you."

I nodded. "All I could think was you were trawling for bimbos."

"I didn't go there to pick up women. What the hell would I do with one? Look, I had no idea Skip would follow Kennedy and kill another woman to make sure Kennedy took the blame, I swear it. When I read about the second murder in the Thursday papers, I threw up all over my office. You can ask Corporal Richards. What happens to me now?"

O'Heaney told Dyson he'd need to come downtown with us.

He nodded. "Mind if I use the latrine?"

The rest of us stepped outside. The thought crossed my mind that Dyson might be looking for a moment alone with a pistol. I never heard a shot. I never heard the toilet flush either. We waited between his car and mine.

Dyson didn't come out.

FIFTY-SIX

After about ten minutes of making small talk about baseball and politics because nobody wanted to discuss what happened to Betty Dyson or what would happen to her husband, O'Heaney looked at General Brubaker. "This guy taking a crap or something? Or is he taking a powder?"

We rushed back inside. A rear window hung wide open, the screen lying outdoors on the grass. The flight suit and helmet had vanished. So had Dyson.

The general snatched up a phone and got the MPs. They called him right back, reporting that Dyson hadn't gone out any of the base's gates. They said he'd hitched a ride on a three-quarter-ton truck headed to the flight line, suiting up as he rode. Brubaker slid into the front of my Nash with me, and O'Heaney hopped in back.

We reached the flight line in a few minutes of zipping past white wooden buildings you could have found on any Army base in the country. On the far side of the field, a shiny silver minnow with straight wings taxied along the runway, picking up speed. A tubby, sweaty mechanic wearing a greasy fatigue cap pointed to the jet fighter and shouted something to the general I couldn't hear above the whine. Brubaker heard it, though, and swore. "That's Don."

The failing evening light showed beneath the flying fish. The thing tossed itself into the darkening sky at a steep angle, climbing with a roar somewhere between a fire hose and a vacuum cleaner in heat. Its mirrored wings waggled, and the fighter became a dot, moving straight away from the tangerine sun.

*****

"You two, this way." We followed Brubaker through a door some white-helmeted MP held, running up spotless stairs to the top of the control tower.

They kept the big room pretty dark, lit mostly by hundreds of dials. A few big screens seemed to show a television program about washing machine tubs spinning slowly. The large-paned windows stayed closed, and you could smell the controllers sweating. Brubaker growled some orders to a potato-nosed lieutenant colonel.

The big, complicated radios in the top of the tower crackled like a rip-snorting bonfire. "I hear you five-by-five, Paul." It was Dyson. "I'm just flying over Annapolis now. The streetlights are coming on." His throat sounded dry. "Everything ahead of me turned dark, Paul. I'm soaring over the open sea. Take care, old buddy."

The baby-faced general tossed me a pleading glance, as if I could do anything. He picked up the desk microphone. "Don, turn your bird around. Come back, Don."

More cellophane. The air felt pretty soupy in the control tower, despite the open door and the earth sloughing off the sun. Two guys who worked there for a living whispered to each other over by the stairs. O'Heaney grabbed a wooden chair and sampled what was left of the Scotch from the Jazz Club. I faced out into the eastward gloom with the young-faced old man wearing stars on his wilted khaki collar. The fighter plane was long gone.

"Don took one of the Shooting Stars, a P-80." The general smiled ever so faintly. "I guess we'll be calling them F-80s pretty soon. In the new Air Force F for 'fighter' will replace P for 'pursuit.' The Shooting Star's our first operational jet. You guys never saw anything like it overhead during the war."

I grunted interest, but I really wondered two other things: what General Brubaker thought Dyson was doing and whether Dyson's pal the general was stalling.

"That baby'll *cruise* at over four hundred miles an hour." Brubaker glanced at a radar screen. "Climbs like a dream. He's reached fifteen thousand already—um, fifteen thousand feet—and he can go three times that high. He—"

"How *far* can he go, General?" I didn't want a sales pitch for his hot-damn little fighter plane. I wanted a clue what was going on.

The general stared at me, his feet firmly on the floor in their spit-shined shoes again. "The P-80's range is a bit over a thousand miles, almost eleven hundred. But I don't see—Oh, you're wondering where he's headed."

"General." One of the tower guys interrupted, a rail-thin captain in a sweat-stained uniform. "Jim Mackenzie and Frank Nordstrom just took off in the chase planes now." I heard the *swoosh* and felt the glass rattle as a pair of quicksilver cigars grabbed the air, one on the other's tail.

The general nodded. "I don't know whether Mackenzie and Nordstrom can overtake him, but I want them to follow on the same course and see if they can even spot him. We can direct them by radar fixes. Visibility's excellent, and the moon's full tonight. He'll look like a dot of fire in the sky to them. Or if they get above him, they may see him against the blue-black of the ocean."

"Visibility's even better above the haze, tower." A pilot broke in on the radio. "We've still got some decent daylight up here."

Brubaker turned back to O'Heaney and me. "Either Don's running for it, or he's not. I think he may just be blowing off steam, trying to work out what he's going to do. He doesn't have a lot of options."

O'Heaney licked the lips of the spent bottle and tossed it into a wastebasket. "I dunno where he thinks he could go that doesn't extradite fugitives charged with homicide. He's wasting our goddam time."

"You're probably right." The general stared at the electronic nebula in front of him. "He's headed due east. Bermuda's easy, but it's British. He could turn south and head to Cuba, Haiti, or the Dominican. I suppose you could get him back from any of them, though I'd remind you he hasn't been convicted of anything yet."

I didn't think that was what Dyson had in mind. "He could double that range of eleven hundred miles you mentioned if he only went one way, right? Twenty-one or twenty-two hundred miles? Can he get across the Atlantic?"

"I doubt he could milk his fuel that far. Even reaching Iceland would be pretty unlikely." Brubaker looked again at the radar. "He's trading fuel for altitude at the moment. That wouldn't do him any good escaping. Again, I think he's just blowing off steam right now."

The lead pilot of the two pursuit planes called in again. "We've got him in sight now. He's climbing fast, *awful* fast, still heading due east. We're out over the Atlantic now. Please advise. Over."

Brubaker picked up the mike again to reply, but Dyson broke his silence just then. “Hey, you two palookas, head home. I don’t want any company where I’m headed.”

“Where’s that, Don?” The general was clearly getting worried.

“There’s something I want to find out.”

FIFTY-SEVEN

"Time to come back, Don." Brubaker worked at sounding casual and chummy.

The crackling of the cellophane seemed to last a long time. "Paul, I've reached forty-seven thousand now, up as high as I've ever flown one of these babies. The coast has fallen way behind me now. *Everything* is behind me." Another burst of cellophane. "Remember Frank Luke?"

Who the hell's Frank Luke? I asked Brubaker, but he didn't answer. "Don, don't," was all he said.

The voice box laughed. "Hey, private eye, I'll give you some fighter pilot history. Frank Luke was a top American ace in the First World War. Brave as hell—he liked bursting German hydrogen balloons. Risky as it got back then. The Krauts stacked up anti-aircraft guns to protect them."

Hydrogen balloons. If you've seen newsreels of the Hindenburg blowing up, you could imagine what Dyson meant. O'Heaney winced. Brubaker's flinty eyes moistened. He mouthed the word "no."

"Well, Frank Luke took off against orders one sunshiny day." Dyson sounded almost chipper. You could hear the decorated flyboy who'd led his squadron to glory. "Did some ferocious flying, busted a balloon or two. Then they hit his plane. No parachutes back then. Landed in enemy territory and jumped out. He fired his .45 at the Krauts 'til they cut him down."

I didn't like where this was headed. The air in the tower was swamp scum by now. Nobody was breathing. We were all sweating our own muddy little creeks. Everybody's sleeves were rolled up.

The speaker crackled. "Anyhow, if Frank Luke had lived, they would have court-martialed him. Instead, he got the Medal of Honor posthumously. Paul, I've climbed to forty-nine thousand now. I'll flip it over in a minute and go into a full-throttle dive."

"Don, DON'T!"

You couldn't hear a sound in the control tower. Then the speaker crackled again. "—want to see what this 'sound barrier' crap is all about. I don't believe there's any 'wall in the sky,' Paul. Just some kind of vibrations that shake the living hell out of a plane."

Brubaker yelled his name again, but Dyson didn't hear him. You can't interrupt on the radio like it's a telephone.

"Maybe this little silver bastard can't take it. Maybe it just needs a top-notch pilot. Here goes."

FIFTY-EIGHT

Not much happened when you saw it on the radar. That creeping dot changed direction and slowed to a halt. I supposed the Shooting Star was roaring straight down, not covering much lateral distance. The little dime-sized glows that represented the two planes chasing Dyson were closing in on him now. "What's going to happen?"

"I don't know for sure." Brubaker's voice sounded somewhere between a trance and a briefing. "The speed of sound is about seven hundred sixty miles an hour at sea level. It will be lower up there—air's thinner. Diving at full throttle, Don can probably go fast enough. *Terrible* impact of vibrations when you approach that kind of speed. The guys who come close blow apart."

I guess the name "Shooting Star" caught my mind. "Will he burn up?"

The general shook his head. "Probably shatter, like a glass hitting bricks." He leaned over the desk mike. *"Don, don't do this.* That's an order. You can get a trial; you can probably beat this." He let up on the mike button.

"—make me laugh. Even if some Clarence Darrow gets me acquitted, my career's ruined, Paul, you know that. I'll never fly a plane like this again after today. *This* is how I want to go out. Christ, Paul, I'm up to five hundred eighty miles an hour now. Nothing below me but the deepest of blues. The light will go soon. G-force is terrific. Five-ninety. Getting some vibrations now."

"Please, Don." Brubaker wasn't using the microphone. Maybe he was hoping he could will Dyson to come back. It's hard to lose a man in wartime, even harder to lose one after.

I was willing for it to end this way.

Shaking hard, you could hear Dyson's teeth were clenched.

"Coming up on six-forty. Altitude thirty-four thousand. Hard to hold her. Thirty-two."

The tower guys stared at the screen, turned to stone. O'Heaney tensed on the edge of his chair.

"I see him," the loudspeaker screamed. It was one of the other jet pilots. "We're at twenty thousand. Here he comes!"

"Thirty-one. Speed six-seven-five. Bucking like a—"

Thunder boomed through the speaker box the way it does when lightning breaks right over your head, followed instantly by silence. The radar screen showed only the two chase planes. We heard more crackling.

Finally, the lead pilot came on again. "It—He—Colonel Dyson just *disintegrated,* General. Flew to pieces. We're following them down now. I think one of the wings ripped off more-or-less intact, or a good-sized chunk of it. I could see it take the moonlight as it twisted and fell."

There was a pause.

"No parachute, sir."

FIFTY-NINE

Breakfast Friday morning in Joe Kennedy's suite was sumptuous. My appetite finally returned after a late night against warm skin that smelled more like lilacs than lilacs did. I downed a Roquefort omelet with smoked salmon and some toasted black olive rolls. The coffee tasted better than whatever they served the Duke of Windsor. Jack fidgeted to my left, picking at his eggs and toast. Moskowitz disposed of a plate of Belgian waffles and sausages.

The Old Man stared me in the eye without glancing once at the crushed plum on my forehead. "So it turned out to be a plot to frame Jack, but it didn't start that way. Then that asshole Snilder and the police superintendent both tried to use it to get what they wanted. Blackmail is a stupid crime, you know. Why anybody ever thinks they'll only have to pay *once* is beyond my comprehension."

He wrapped his teeth around a hunk of currant-glazed fried Smithfield ham that would have choked a wolfhound, then poured himself more tea. "The whole thing makes sense to me now."

Jack stared down at his plate. "If her husband hadn't found me in bed with Betty, she might still be alive. That was my fault."

I rested a hand on his shoulder. "Dyson killed her, Jack, not you. He might have blown up when she insisted on the divorce and done the same thing." Or if I'd won the contest that night, I might have been taking my time in bed with her when Dyson charged in with the knife. I kept my mouth shut.

"So the colonel goes on a homicidal rage." The Old Man spoke while he was chewing. "He barely misses stabbing Jack—that was either dumb luck or providence. Then he murders his wife, drives back out to his airfield, and sweats it out until Sunday afternoon. Nobody's called him by then, so he places his phone call to the apartment manager. Then what?"

The coffee was velvet with caffeine, the very thing I needed. "Then he panics on Monday, Mr. Ambassador. He calls his tough little criminal pal Skip Nichols for help. Nichols's ears in the police department report they're after a hotshot young congressman named Jack Kennedy, who was seen with the murder victim all evening and left the crime scene with his necktie in his hands."

The ambassador's eyebrow arched above his round-rimmed glasses. "But Jack hires a private eye and an ace shyster, and the cops start treading water. Dyson and Nichols get scared the cops will dig deeper. Is that it?"

I layered cream cheese onto another roll. "Yep, that's it. Dyson talks to Nichols again. Maybe he's decided by then that Betty's death was Jack's fault, not his. Nichols orders Jack followed when he takes Susan Prebble out to dinner, so Nichols is waiting when they get back to her place. He slides into the building with them and kills her as soon as Jack leaves."

Moskowitz nodded. "Once he slit her throat, he copied the stab wounds. I'm certain he received the details from Gentleman Jimmy or one of his bought cops."

"No, I don't get it." The Old Man sounded irritated. "You're telling me a man would commit a brutal murder like that just to help out a pal?"

"A killer might, to help a wartime buddy who saved his life, yes. A racketeer who used thugs as a business tool. His secretary claims he may have had other people murdered for getting in his way. A man who had the fix in and was used to breaking the law."

Jack was still fiddling with his fork, eyes cast downward. "The truth is, both Betty and Susan were killed because I slept with them. I'd better learn to keep my fly buttoned." He was scourging himself, but not entirely unfairly.

"Congressman," I said, "we both know Betty Dyson set out to get laid that night. There was never any doubt she could accomplish that if she found a man she liked. And Nichols would have killed Susan Prebble after you left even if all you'd done with her was discuss *Huckleberry Finn* over coffee. *Her* murder was pure frame-up."

"So you went to see Nichols yesterday, Griffin," Moskowitz put in, "just to find a link to the footpads who threatened you. Nichols figured you'd follow the trail from his thug to him."

Jack nodded. "And I drove to the Jazz Club a few minutes later to ask Nichols if he'd seen anybody hanging around Suze's apartment that night. *He* was the guy I needed to ask about. I blundered in as they pulled their guns on you, so they brought me along. I almost took another fateful trip in a small wooden motorboat."

The Old Man wasn't to be put off. "This cop friend of yours will leave the case closed, though, in spite of the blood test results? The way it was in yesterday's papers, with Nichols guilty of everything and Jack in the clear?"

I snorted. "Vince O'Heaney would rather fill out his tax forms with a yellow crayon than reopen a high visibility murder case they've grabbed headlines for. Especially since Dyson's paid the price and can't be brought to trial. Nobody wants to embarrass the new Air Force."

Moskowitz grinned and set down his gold-rimmed cup. "Superintendent Howard is reported to be laying *very* low, thinking up what to tell this new special commission about all the unsolved killings in the District. I happen to know he's asked a lawyer what countries don't extradite murder suspects."

"And all this stuff about Stuart Symington and his aide that Moskowitz told me about." The Old Man kept his eyes on the pecan roll he was buttering. "Was that all horse shit?"

"No, but it simply had nothing to do with Betty's death or Susan's. I watched Symington's aide resign from the service, which pays him back for trying to blackmail Betty into bed. And Symington knows I have the original of the sworn transcript somewhere, so I think he'll be a lot more careful about smearing Forrestal—at least in the short run."

Jack smiled. "Thanks for that. Forrestal's a good man, and he's been a friend to me. No question he's wound up like a clock, but he's no lunatic."

The ambassador put the pecan roll down. "Guess I don't need it." He picked up the *Post* again and reread the headline:

Widowed War Hero
Lost in Jet Crash

"A crap-shooter to the end, wasn't he? If he'd broken this 'sound barrier' thing and lived, he'd have been the new Air Force's first hero, and he'd never have come to trial."

SIXTY

Sunday night, Congress finished up its work and headed home on recess for the rest of the year, loathing Washington in August more than Washington in July. Monday morning's *Post* carried a wrap-up of the end of the congressional session and a rehash of the public version of the Dyson tragedy. It seemed the rape and murder of his wife by a racketeering nightclub owner had shaken the colonel's judgment in a way no German fighter ever had—on a routine nighttime flying mission, Dyson became disoriented and crashed into the ocean. His body hadn't been recovered. To me, he was another casualty of the war.

I sat there reading the story with my feet on my desk while Lana typed a memo to the building manager about a wall socket that wasn't working. Moskowitz'd told me he liked the way I handled things and promised to give me some business. "You'd be surprised how often I need an investigator, and you understand legal issues." The agency was turning around.

I'd picked Lucille up on the way in so she could look at our old spare typewriter and see if she wanted it for writing her memoir. The V.A. expected to send Jerry home that afternoon, and I'd promised to drive. Lucille giggled with anticipation—it'd been over three weeks this time.

I heard the outer door close but kept my nose in the newspaper. "There's a very nice-looking man out here." Lucille stood on the far side of my doorway. "He claims to be a congressman and says he'd like to see you, though he's staring as if he'd rather see *me*." Lana grinned behind her.

"Throw him out on his ear. Remind him—"

Lucille chuckled lyrically. "Jack! I *already* told him I'm married.

I even showed him my engagement and wedding rings."

Kennedy had as much chance of seducing her as he had of riding a duck to victory in the next Kentucky Derby. He laughed when he stepped into my office.

"I'm on my way to meet Dad at Union Station. We've got a compartment on the *Patriot* to Boston. By the way, Dad liked your idea—he bought the Jazz Club from the Nichols woman for more than it's worth and set up a trust fund for the little daughter. Dad understands making a deal."

"It was good of him. Thank him for backing my promise."

Kennedy gestured toward Lucille. "She wasn't here before, was she, Griffin? I know I wasn't too preoccupied to have noticed a girl who looks like that."

"*Mrs.* DiMarco is visiting the agency this morning to give it an illusion of class. I plan to attract a much better grade of clients than we've been getting lately."

Jack was fun to needle, and he enjoyed sparring. "If she doesn't do the trick, you might want to see if my mother is available. I can't stay. I just wanted to give you your check."

I looked at him. "Listen, I've got to admit something. I wasn't sure you weren't the killer 'til I woke up in the boat shed. Sorry."

He nodded. "I wasn't sure either when I read about Susan's death, and I know myself better than you know me. How much money do I owe you?"

"I haven't worked up a bill yet. But my charge will be fifty dollars a day plus expenses." I didn't mention adding ten bucks to my normal rate since his father owned the Eastern seaboard and intermittently got snotty about it. Counting my breakfast meeting on Friday, I'd put in five days. My expenses had been a few telephone calls, six or eight bullets, a gauze pad with some adhesive tape, some dry cleaning, and gas for a couple drives out to Andrews Field and back in my Nash. "Maybe three-fifty, Jack."

"This will cover it, then." He handed me a signed slip of green paper worth two thousand bucks, sporting a Cheshire cat's grin. It fit him pretty well.

"Jack, this is—"

"Well worth it, Griffin. You saved my career and my life as well. If you hadn't gotten us out of that boathouse, I'd be as dead as Kelsey's nuts. I'm really awfully grateful."

I stuffed the check in my shirt pocket. "You're going to stay in politics, then? You seemed a bit bored with it when we met."

"Look." He glanced over at my easy chair as if he wanted to sit down, then winced at the thought of it and stayed on his feet. "I think overall I'm a fairly decent man. I'm reasonably honest, even with beautiful women. I have something to contribute. No speeches, but I want to give something back for all that's been given to me. Life's too chancy to waste it lolling around Palm Beach. In any case, thanks to you, I still have a seat in Congress. I'd like to see what I can do to make myself more useful. That's never been a requirement for me. Or at least it wasn't until the war came. And, of course, the winters are milder here in Washington than up in Boston."

"But the summers—"

"The summers are why God gave us Cape Cod." He glanced at his watch. "I'd better go. If I call you about meeting for lunch some time, will you go?"

"I'd like that." We shook hands pretty hard as I walked him back out to the front office. He smiled at Lana and winked at Lucille, gleaming there in the sunlight as if she were something Cortez stole from the Aztecs.

"Ever think of enjoying a weekend in Europe, Mrs. DiMarco? I'm headed over there next week to visit my sister Kathleen, and I'd love to take you." He had a way of joking when he meant every word.

"My husband visited Europe once." Lucille smiled at him, her big blue eyes moist. "They treated him so badly I don't think he'll go back. I certainly wouldn't go anywhere without him."

Kennedy grinned and shook his head slightly at her deft reply. He probably didn't get turned down very often, and she did it without leaving scar tissue.

After Kennedy left, I closed up the office for the rest of the day. The ladies went with me to the bank, where I counted out two hundred dollars for Lana. "This is your back pay and another fifty for sticking with me, Lana. I've got no agency without you."

Her round red face beamed. "My landlord and my grocer will sing your praises, Mr. Griffin. I've pinched pennies so hard Abe Lincoln squealed. See you in the morning. Nice meeting you, Mrs. DiMarco."

Then I treated Lucille to a lavish lunch at the Hay-Adams. Around two o'clock, we drove over to the V.A. hospital to take Jerry and her new typewriter home to their one-room apartment. That was where I left her—with the husband of her dreams, however long they'd last.

WILLIAM F. CRANDELL

Fighting a dirty war as a rifle platoon leader and then marching for peace afterward gave William F. Crandell a bone-deep understanding of why honor and integrity are life-and-death concerns. Bill came home from Vietnam with a zest for adventure, a skeptic's eye and a hundred-thousand stories. The writing came naturally—he'd been a foreign correspondent for an Ohio newspaper before college, and wrote fiction to stay awake in some jobs he held. Awarded the Maryland State Arts Council's Individual Artist Award for his private detective novel, *Let's Say Jack Kennedy Killed the Girl*, Bill has published short stories, book reviews, scholarly articles, journalism, state and federal reports, political analyses and congressional testimony. An Ohio native, Bill completed his doctorate in American History with a study of McCarthyism and Republican politics. His stories "Miller's Face" and "On Georgian Bay" appear in the Delaware Press Association award-winning horror anthologies, *Halloween Party 2017* and *Solstice* (2018). Published in the *What Sort of Fuckery Is This?* anthology, Bill's short story, "The Last Lootenant Wins His Fuckin' Medal" (a tribute to the men he led in Vietnam) took first place in the NFPW's 2020 National Communications Contest.

Bill and his writer wife, Judith Speizer Crandell, currently reside in Delaware.

HAWKSHAWPRESS.COM

www.ingramcontent.com/pod-product-compliance
Lightning Source LLC
Chambersburg PA
CBHW020304030826
48979CB00027B/2041/J

* 9 7 8 1 7 3 4 0 9 1 8 8 5 *